"One of the great things about this novel is that Bobby keeps learning and growing as the story progresses. He is not a one-sided character, giving the readers the time to grow with him. It is easy to fall in love with the characters within this book. The plot is strong as Boyer seamlessly builds his world and characters. While this book is geared towards young adult readers, fantasy lovers of all ages will enjoy this fast-paced, action-packed book. Bobby Ether has the ability to gain the same popularity as Rick Riordan's Percy Jackson...Get a copy for your shelf today."
– **Starred Review, Pacific Book Review (www.pacificbookreview.com)**

* * *

"This is an evenly paced, action-fueled fantasy read that fans will not be able to get enough of. A strong protagonist, powerful settings and a wonderful and growing mythology make this a stand-out read to be sure. Author R. Scott Boyer's Temple of Eternity *is a must-read book that readers will absolutely love getting ensconced in, so be sure to grab your copy today."*
– **Hollywood Book Review (www.hollywoodbookreviews.com)**

* * *

"Think Indiana Jones, but on a level geared to young adult adventure story readers. Add a dash of cultural intrigue, with warrior descendants of the Mayans determined to take action as souls are claimed by evil forces. Mix in a riddle that evokes the Fountain of Youth, yet seems to negate the legend behind it. What results is a fast-paced adventure designed to keep young readers engaged and guessing throughout... It is a highly recommended pick for teens who like their adventure nonstop and their characters interested in bigger-picture thinking."
– **Midwest Book Review (www.midwestbookreview.com)**

"Boyer expertly evokes the native flavor of Guatemala's jungles, and the warrior descendants of Mayans add a dash of cultural intrigue. The skillful description of Bobby's excursion into the ghost realm makes the whole experience utterly compelling. A heartfelt and satisfying ending suggests there are more adventures to come the teenager's way, making readers anxious for the next installment...This swiftly paced adventure makes for a rollicking good read."

– The Prairie Books Review (www.theprairiesbookreview.com)

* * *

"The story is full of action and adventure...Overall, YA fantasy fans will find Temple of Eternity a page-turning reading experience."

– Blue Ink Review (www.blueinkreview.com)

* * *

"Exotic settings, ancient civilizations, a quest, adventure, danger, magic, a giant, a love triangle, spiritual possessions, good guys, bad guys, secrets, jungle creatures, more danger, even an on-the-fly history lesson or two. What more could any suspense-loving reader want? And want more of? In Temple of Eternity, R. Scott Boyer spins an edge-of-your-seat tale that's sure to produce rapid page turns and even more rapid heartbeats."

– David Patneaude, author of Fast Backward

Temple of Eternity

Bobby Ether Series Book 2

R. Scott Boyer

Main Street Publishing

CHARLESTON, SC

Main Street Publishing
115 S. Main Street
Summerville, SC 29483
www.mainstreetreads.com

This is a work of fiction. Names, characters, places, and incidents are a product of the author's imagination. Locales and public names are sometimes used for atmospheric purposes. Any resemblance to actual people, living or dead, or to businesses, companies, events, institutions, or locales is completely coincidental.

Temple of Eternity / R. Scott Boyer. -- 1st ed.
ISBN: 978-1-6629023-3-8
eISBN: 978-1-6629023-4-5
Library of Congress Control Number: 2020940951

Now and forever,
In loving memory of my big sister,
Michelle Boyer Dykstra

From across the ravaged courtyard of the Jade Academy, the Core agent known as Sandman watched the weathered Navajo and his companions head for the mountain trail leading to the forest below. Sandman ducked into the shadows, remaining there until long after the travelers were gone. Then he turned and jogged back down the trail that led to the garden near the cliffs.

Hidden back amid the rubble, the soldiers under his command stood at attention. "Are we moving out, sir?" asked one of his men. Some of the soldiers rose, checking their weapons and equipment.

"Mission review," said Sandman. "Neutralize the monks if necessary. The students are not to be harmed."

"Rules of engagement, sir?" asked another of his soldiers.

"We're only cleared for non-lethal force. Absolutely no explosives or live fire. Can't risk the noise."

The soldiers saluted as one. "Sir, yes sir."

"Radio silence. I will handle anyone who attempts to engage," commanded Sandman. "Not a peep. I want a bow on this before they even know we're here."

"Sir, yes sir."

Sandman nodded in approval and returned their salute. "Get some rest. We roll out at zero three hundred."

***

Their execution was flawless. In the stillness found only in the dead of night, Sandman and his men crept into the courtyard occupied by the sleeping refugees. The mountain had continued to rumble and shake throughout the night, causing many of the students to have trouble sleeping, especially on the cold hard ground.

Sandman sensed those who were still awake as easily as he would a bonfire ablaze in the dark. With a wisp of anima, he sent each person into a slumber so deep that even being lifted and carried wouldn't rouse them. The children were easy, their minds too poorly trained and undisciplined to shield themselves from his power. Some of the monks were tougher and required several attempts before they succumbed to his hypnotic suggestions.

One monk in particular kept resisting. Sandman picked his way through the mass of sleeping bodies until he located the monk in question.

"You must be their leader," said Sandman. The diminutive monk at his feet twitched, as if he were struggling to break free. He looked like an infant thrashing in a crib, restless with nightmares but unable to wake.

Sandman's soldiers wove through the sleeping crowd. One by one, they picked up the children and carried them down the path to the garden. There, the ropes he and his men had used to scale the cliff were attached to each child to lower them down the mountain.

The process was slow, taking every minute of darkness. *Once the sun comes up, the biological imperative to wake will fight against my control*, thought Sandman as he turned to the nearest soldier and signaled him to quicken the pace.

They lowered the last student shortly before sunrise. Sandman stood in the remaining crowd of sleeping bodies, now nothing but bald, middle-aged men. The baby-faced leader stirred once again, thrashing from side to side.

Sandman sent the tiny monk a deep hypnotic suggestion for at least the tenth time, causing the monk to roll over and resume his slumber in silence. *No nightmares for you. At least, not yet*, thought Sandman. *But don't worry, the nightmare will be real enough when you wake.*

With a final glance around the clearing, Sandman slipped from the circle and headed down the path to the garden. There, he strapped himself to the harness at the edge of the cliff and began his descent.

CHAPTER ONE

B obby Ether sat at the kitchen table and picked at his breakfast. It had been nearly two months since the seventeen-year-old had returned from the Jade Academy, but it still felt strange. From the worn linoleum with its faded sunflowers, to the Formica countertop with its chipped corners, everything was the same but different. Even the carefully cultivated herb garden outside the bay window wasn't quite as he remembered.

Bobby's parents were another story. After fussing over him for weeks after his arrival, his parents had reverted to their pedestrian and annoyingly normal routines. Bobby's father, Nathan, mumbled to himself as he struggled with his tie. His mother, Grace, wore a smile and a brown dress that complimented her skin as she set about making scrambled eggs. Nathan snuck up behind her and stole a piece of toast along with a kiss. Grace crinkled her nose and giggled.

Crushing a piece of hard crust with his thumb, Bobby wiped one hand on his faded jeans and the other on his plain gray t-shirt. His pale blond hair, cut short during his time at the academy, had grown out in the last few months, revealing hints of ginger to match his freckles.

Bobby kicked at the leg of the table with the tip of his checkered Vans. "Since you guys are in such a good mood," he said, "maybe I could go visit today?"

"We've been over this before," said his mother. "I don't think it's a good idea for you to go anywhere right now."

Indeed, they had been over the topic before—many, many times. Following Bobby's return, Chief, Grandpa, and Cassandra had sat down with Bobby's parents and told them the truth about the Jade Academy. They'd explained that the headmistress was Nathan's long-lost sister and Bobby's aunt. Chief also told Bobby's parents about the Core, the secret organization behind the academy that sought to reshape mankind by creating humans with innate metaphysical abilities. He explained how the Core had tested the academy's students in order to find worthy candidates for their perverse experiments.

After the dead silence that followed, Bobby had told his parents how he and Jinx had foiled the headmistress's plans, discovered the Spine of the World, and escaped via the secret passage. Upon exiting the mountain, Bobby and Jinx encountered Chief, whom Bobby believed was an assassin. Bobby would have killed Chief, but Grandpa showed up just in time.

Bobby's escape, as well as everything else that led to the Jade Academy's collapse, could be traced to Grandpa and his vision the day Bobby was born, which predicted Bobby's arrival at the academy. Despite having known about Grandpa's special talents for years, Bobby's parents had a hard time accepting that their son had been at a secret monastery on the other side of the world. Even now, they acted like he had been away at summer camp.

It had proven to be both a blessing and a curse. At first, seeing his parents alive and recovered from the car accident staged by the headmistress was enough to make Bobby giddy. Lately, however, he'd felt confined, as if the space around him had shrunk while he was away.

Grace made herself a plate and sat across the table, her mousy, shoulder-length hair pulled up in a bun to reveal the delicate features of her slender face. Even from behind her reading glasses, Bobby could see the concern in her dark green eyes.

"Is there something you want to talk about?" she asked softly.

Bobby shrugged, unable to convert his thoughts into words.

"You've been acting moody for days," said Nathan. "What's going on?"

Grace set her fork down. Bobby kicked the leg of the table.

"Well?" asked his father.

The doorbell rang. Bobby leaped from his seat. "I'll get it!"

"You will stay right there," said Nathan with a glare that let Bobby know the conversation was not over.

Tall and handsome, Nathan Ether moved with the grace of a natural athlete except for the slight limp in his right leg where three metal rods had been inserted to repair his shattered femur as a result of the car accident. Answering the front door, he was back a moment later with visitors.

"Jinx!" said Bobby, jumping out of his chair to greet his younger cousin. "You're back. What did you think?"

His little cousin had also let his hair grow out since leaving the academy. Once short and spiky, it now formed a bird's nest of russet curls. Jinx's rosy cheeks pushed up into a huge smile.

"It was almost impossible to believe at first," Jinx answered. He glanced at Chief, who had driven him here and whose compound, the Eagle's Nest, he'd been staying at the past month. "The entire place is amazing. I've never seen anything like it." The old Navajo gave Jinx a knowing grin.

"I'm learning so much," said Jinx. He dropped his eyes to the floor. "I just wish the others were around to see it."

"You mean Grandpa and Cassandra?" asked Bobby.

Chief shook his head. "Jeremiah and Cassandra have gone to look for your grandmother."

Bobby grunted. "I know Grandma and Grandpa can't be together because the connection they share allows the Core to track them," he said, "but I thought they had a way to communicate."

"Apparently Melody moved almost a year ago and didn't leave word for Jeremiah in their usual place—something she's never done before," said Chief. "He and Cassandra have been searching for weeks now, trying to figure out where Melody went. A couple of nights ago, they got a lead pointing towards South America. They said they'll contact me when they know more."

The room fell silent as everyone contemplated the news. Bobby had just gotten his grandfather back in his life and now his grandmother was missing.

Chief broke the silence with a delicate cough. "I'm afraid I have some other news," he said softly. "I didn't want to bother you. You boys were so happy being reunited, and after the terrible accident …" Bobby had never seen the old Indian so flustered. "I am so sorry again, Mr. and Mrs. Ether, about the situation at the hospital, and rushing off while you were still recovering. We needed to search for Bobby—"

Jinx stepped in front of Chief and threw up his hands. "Lily and the others are missing! All of the students we left back at the academy… they're gone!"

"Wait—what do you mean they're gone?" said Bobby.

"They were taken by the Core!" blurted Jinx.

Bobby turned to Chief. "Is that true?"

Chief nodded. "We believe so, yes."

For a long moment, no one spoke. Bobby sat at the table, head in his hands, trying to make sense of what he'd just heard. Finally, he lifted his chin. "I knew something was wrong," he said, glaring at Chief. "How could you go all this time and not say something?"

"I wanted you to have some time with your parents before—"

"It's been weeks!" yelled Bobby. He turned to Jinx. "You knew too, didn't you?"

Jinx shrank back. "Don't look at me! It's not like we have phone service at the Eagle's Nest. Besides, Chief said we would tell you as soon as we had a lead."

Bobby returned his steely glare to Chief. "And?"

Chief rubbed his weathered jaw. "Like you said, it's been weeks. I decided it was time you knew."

Bobby folded his arms and glared at the old Navajo. "What the hell, man, not cool!"

Grace threw her son a disapproving look, but Chief met Bobby's gaze. "I did what I thought was best at the time."

"If you come with us," said Jinx, "maybe you can help."

"Come with?" asked Grace. She stood and went to Nathan's side. "What are you talking about?"

Chief leaned against the counter. "The organization behind the Jade Academy may have been corrupt, but their purpose was not," he said. "Bobby still needs to learn how to control his abilities. With the proper training, he could be extremely useful."

"Useful?" asked Nathan Ether. "Are you crazy? My boy just got home. He's not going anywhere."

Bobby opened his mouth to protest but Grace pinned him with a look. Setting a hand on her husband's shoulder, she said, "Maybe we should ask Bobby what he thinks."

Nathan set his palm on top of hers and took a deep breath. "You're right, of course." Turning to his son, he said, "As difficult as it is for us to hear about all of this, I know what you went through at the academy, and what your friends mean to you."

Grace Ether gave her husband a kiss on the cheek. "It's your decision," she said to Bobby. "We will always be here for you."

With those words, Bobby understood what it was that had been different since his return. "This is still my home, and I love you both," he said, "but I've changed. I'm not the same innocent boy who went to school, played basketball, and hung out with my friends. There are things I've seen, things I know exist but haven't had time to fully comprehend. I need to do this—to go with Chief, to learn what he has to teach me, and to help find my friends."

His mother put her arms around her husband, wiped her eyes, and gave Bobby a half smile. And just like that, the decision was made.

CHAPTER TWO

Heading to the Eagle's Nest the next morning was nothing like it had been the first time. Previously, Bobby had been on the run with Cassandra, fleeing from Core agents, with barely enough time to pack a bag. This time his parents helped him pack. His father's face was inscrutable as he pulled clothes from the closest. His mother obsessed over every item.

"Here, take your ski jacket," she said, trying to corral the coat's mounds of fluff into his suitcase. "You never know how cold it's going to get."

"There is an artificial dome over the entire forest," said Bobby. "I really doubt it's going to snow." His father shot him a look that prompted Bobby to add, "But better to have it and not need it, then need it and not have it."

"You know, it's not too late to change your mind," said Grace.

Bobby shook his head. "I need to do this. Besides, what if the people who took my friends come after me? The longer I stay here, the more danger you're in."

A car pulled into the driveway. The front door burst open, and Jinx raced upstairs.

"All set to go?" asked Jinx. Below them, Chief stepped into the foyer.

Bobby nodded as his father helped carry the heavy duffle bags down the stairs. "How're you feeling?" asked Chief. The old Indian wore a tasseled rawhide jacket and loose-fitting blue jeans faded to white at the knees. His raven hair was pulled back into a long braid pinned with a pair of eagle feathers.

"Didn't sleep much," replied Bobby. "Guess I'm a little nervous."

"Don't be," said Chief. "We'll take good care of you."

"And I'll be there," said Jinx, beaming with excitement.

The actual good-byes didn't take long. His mother cried, hugged Bobby tight, and told him to dress in layers. His father shook his hand and looked him deep in the eyes. "I'm proud of you son," he said. "You've done amazing things. I know you're going to do great."

Bobby brushed the dampness from his cheeks. Then it was time to go. Chief carried Bobby's bags to the SUV and loaded them up while Jinx and Bobby climbed into the backseat. Bobby's parents stood on the sidewalk, arms around each other. Bobby rolled down the window and waved good bye as the Escalade pulled away from the curb.

* * *

After driving for two hours into Palm Desert, Chief pulled the Escalade up to a hangar-sized building in the middle of nowhere. The industrial warehouse was three stories of aluminum siding and mirrored windows. Bobby and Jinx hopped out and followed Chief to a steel door that looked like a mouse hole in the side of the monstrous structure.

Bobby's eyes grew wide as they stepped inside. "What are we doing at a nursery?" he asked, taking in the rows of verdant plants and flowers running down the length of the massive interior.

Jinx grinned at his cousin. "Don't tell him," he begged Chief. "I want to see the look on his face!" In answer, Chief turned left, heading for the near wall where a small office sat upon a raised metal platform overlooking the vast expanse of crops. Chief passed the open staircase and ushered them into the service elevator. He pulled the metal scissor gate closed behind them.

Flipping open an access panel, he punched a code on a luminescent keypad far too modern for the rusty box that held it. The floor began to move. Bobby looked toward the second story office before realizing they were heading in the opposite direction. Half of Bobby's torso had already sunk below the ground.

"This is my favorite part," said Jinx, grabbing one of the side rails. Bobby did the same as his head came level with the warehouse floor. For a few seconds, dirty gray concrete slid past the lattice cage. Then a blast of air rushed in, knocking Bobby back as the concrete foundation turned from floor to ceiling.

Bobby's breath caught in his chest. An entire forest lay spread beneath him. He stared, mouth ajar, as they descended the side of a massive redwood with barrel-thick branches spread just far enough to allow for the lift's passage.

Below them, majestic conifers rose up to greet them, their uppermost limbs waving lazily in the mid-afternoon breeze. A cool draft carried the sweet scent of pinecones as they reached the lower canopy. Off in the distance, Bobby spotted a hill with a cluster of familiar buildings on its rise, including a peculiar greenish-brown structure.

"That's the Nexus!" he said turning to Jinx and Chief. "This is the Eagle's Nest. We're coming in from above!"

Jinx couldn't have looked more smug if he'd built the tree-elevator himself. "I knew you'd be surprised."

"The downtown entrance is mainly for visitors," Chief offered as they reached the forest floor. "I find it a bit ostentatious myself. I prefer this entrance as long we're not in a hurry."

Chief unlatched the gate and led the boys onto a bed of moist earth and pine needles. They followed a slender trail through the trees until they came to a rise. Bobby recognized the wildflower-covered slope he'd ascended with Cassandra the first time he'd come here.

They crested the rise, and Bobby got a closer look at the Nexus's polyhedron exterior with its glowing vines and living wood. Bobby headed for the log cabin around back, but Chief stopped him. "We're over here," he said, nodding towards the other end of the plateau.

They crossed to the far edge of the grassy flat and made their way down a short trail to a thick wood doorframe built directly into the hillside. With a flashback, Bobby realized this must have been where Cassandra had gone the night he escaped.

Bobby eyed the entrance warily. "Please tell me it's not a mine. I've had enough tunnels and mineshafts to last me a lifetime." Jinx laughed and dashed into the interior, where he took up a torch and lit a series of braziers.

Bobby followed him into a large circular room adorned with woven tapestries of picturesque landscapes. Across the ceiling, a constellation of spirit animals portrayed the night sky. Bobby gasped. Each creature glowed as brightly as real stars. Meanwhile, a hole in the center of the roof ventilated the smoke from the braziers.

"It's an underground lodge," said Jinx. When he saw the scowl on Bobby's face he added, "Don't worry, even I didn't know what it was before Chief explained it to me."

"It's an adaptation of the dwelling my ancestors lived in," said Chief. "Down here, we are part of the earth, closely connected to its spirit."

"It reminds me of the bear's den," said Bobby, referring to the cave in Tibet where he'd discovered his grandfather's diary.

"It feels like a giant rabbit's burrow at first but, don't worry, you get used to it," said Jinx.

"Why don't you show Bobby to his room?" said Chief. "You can tell him all about the lodge after he's had a chance to settle in."

Jinx turned crimson but recovered quickly, muttering an apology as he showed Bobby to a small room with a large mural depicting a grizzly bear hunting for salmon in a roaring river. Jinx left him and Bobby spent a few minutes storing his clothes and personal items in the oak dresser by the door. Then he laid down on the twin bed in the far corner. As he stared at the ceiling, he realized that the drawings on the ceiling were luminescent, just like the constellations in the main chamber.

When Jinx came to take him to lunch, Bobby asked about the glow. His little cousin gave Bobby a quizzical look. "I don't know what you're talking about," he said. "None of the murals in my room glow."

Chief explained the minor mystery when they met up in the main chamber. "The images on the ceiling are not paintings," he said. "They are composed of the same roots that cover the Nexus. They contain the anima collected from the forest. Such intense spiritual energy can be seen, but only by the extremely gifted, similar to how bees can see ultra-violet auras, but we humans cannot."

"So, most others don't see the glow?" asked Bobby.

"To people without the Gift, the Nexus is just a strange wooden dome covered in vines," said Chief.

"Is that what it's called, 'the Gift?'" asked Bobby.

"The Gift is different things to different people," replied Chief. "To those who look to the planet and feel its power, they see Gaia or Mother Earth. To those who look inside, they see the soul or spirit. But these things are not separate. They are one. The Gift is not the power itself. It is merely the means by which those who have the ability may see it."

***

They spent the rest of the day touring the facility. After getting Bobby familiar with the lodge, they went for a short hike through the forest. The more he saw, the more awestruck he became. A slender brook full of bullfrogs and crawfish meandered along the southern edge of the forest. The subterranean biodome also contained a miniature lake, complete with a ten-foot waterfall that tumbled with sparkling grace into a crystal pool.

When they were done, the three of them returned to the lodge. Chief prepared a simple dinner of steamed rice and vegetables before leaving the boys to their own devices.

Retiring to Bobby's room, the boys chatted well into the night. They talked about the Eagle's Nest, what they would study, and what they would do once they'd mastered their abilities. Neither of them mentioned their missing friends, or the people they'd lost when the academy collapsed. Despite his lively demeanor, something in Jinx's eyes told Bobby his cousin wasn't ready to talk about what had happened. Considering the fate of Jinx's mother and likely his sister as well, Bobby more than understood.

It was late when Jinx finally left. Bobby laid his head on his pillow and gazed at the iridescent patterns on his ceiling. His whole body tingled with a mixture of excitement, nervousness, and awe at the things he had seen and those still to come.

His last thought was of his friends. "We'll find you," he whispered into the dark. Moments later, he was fast asleep.

* * *

After a breakfast of oatmeal and scrambled eggs, Chief announced the boys were to spend the day by themselves.

"What about our friends?" asked Bobby.

"Everything that can be done to locate them is already being done," said Chief.

"What about our training?" Jinx asked.

"Patience. For now, explore the forest," he said. "Your training will happen in due time."

"You sound just like my old teacher, Master Jong."

Chief bowed and thanked him for the compliment, an act that did nothing to improve Bobby's mood. Unable to wring anything else out of the enigmatic Indian, Bobby stuck his hands in his pockets and followed an equally bewildered Jinx out into the sunshine.

"What was that about?" asked Bobby.

"I have no idea," said Jinx. "Usually he tells me to sit in the meadow or down by the stream. Most times I just read a book."

With no place better to go, the boys headed for the lake. It didn't take long before they were splashing in the shallows and doing cannonballs off the top of the waterfall. They sat on the sandy banks and ate a sparse lunch of biscuits and yellow cheese Jinx produced from his backpack.

Before they knew it, the shadows of the trees crept over the water. The boys made their way back to the lodge, where they found Chief meditating on a thick woven rug in the main chamber. As the boys walked in, Chief opened his eyes and stood.

"How did it go?" he asked.

"We had nothing better to do," said Bobby sharply, "so we hung out by the lake."

"And what did you see?" asked Chief.

"What kinda' question is that?" snapped Bobby. "We saw trees and rocks and water and stuff."

"And how did that make you feel?"

Bobby and Jinx stopped to look at one another. Bobby frowned as he tried to figure out what the old man was driving at. "Good, I guess."

"It was fun," said Jinx, "but I think we were both hoping for something more...*tangible* to work on."

"There is nothing more tangible than to be alive and at one with your surroundings," said Chief. "Remember that. To be in the moment and be at peace is the greatest gift of all."

* * *

The next day, Chief sent the boys to the meadow. Bunches of poppies, phlox, and daisies lay scattered throughout the field, infusing the air with the sugary scent of nature's perfume. This time the boys had a better sense of what to accomplish. Unperturbed by ants and other insects, Bobby found a flat rock near the middle of the clearing. Taking a seat, he folded his legs in the traditional lotus position.

Jinx wandered through the clumps of milfoil and milkweed, inspecting the various clovers, daisies, and buttercups. He named each by its genus, phylum, and species before turning his attention to the green, beehive-like box that collected the anima from this section of the forest.

Time slipped by as both boys lost themselves in their respective tasks; Bobby enjoyed the beauty of their surroundings, while Jinx contemplated the science of the strange device. It wasn't until a twig snapped that either boy stirred. Bobby looked up to see a barrel-chested, velvety-antlered buck, accompanied by a tawny doe with big brown eyes and specks of white down her haunches.

Bobby's palms grew sweaty as the deer entered the meadow and froze; their heads cocked to the side. After a moment, the buck lowered its head and began to graze. Bobby let out a breath he hadn't realized he'd been holding.

He sat motionless for several minutes as the beautiful creatures picked their way through the meadow. Then, when he felt confident they were comfortable with his presence, Bobby reached down and plucked a handful of oat-grass. Slowly, he held the grass out in front of him, palm up, fingers spread. The buck ignored him, turned away, and continued grazing, but the doe looked on.

Lowering her nose, the doe took a few tentative steps, sniffing the air as she advanced. From off to Bobby's right, Jinx whispered for him to be careful. Bobby nodded and kept his eyes on the doe, which had closed to within a few feet. Tiptoeing forward, the dappled fawn extended its slender neck and nibbled at the ends of the long grass.

Bobby pulled his hand inward and the deer took a small step, following the food. Slowly, he raised his other hand and extended it towards the creature's neck. The doe stopped chewing but remained still. Bobby gently laid his palm on the animal's soft, warm hide.

The sensation was like nothing he'd ever experienced before. He felt the velvety texture of the doe's fur, the warm pulse of life beneath it, but there was something else as well, something that tapped into his other senses. It reminded him of the time in the mines when he'd found the chunk of jade in the quarry wall.

He felt the animal's thoughts in his mind: friendly and curious about his presence in the meadow. He knew its connection with the stag: siblings, with a bond of strong affection for one another. He experienced the forest through its senses: the musky scent of damp earth, the faint rustling of the wind, the sweet fragrance of the lilac and wild primroses that grew clear on the other side of the glade.

The young doe finished the last of the grass in Bobby's hand, and the moment passed. With a graceful trot she rejoined her big brother. Together, they headed for the trees, their tawny silhouettes speckled in sunlight and shade as they disappeared into the woods.

Jinx came running up to Bobby's side. "That was amazing," he said. "I can't believe she let you pet her. What did it feel like?"

Bobby thought about the question all the way back to the lodge but was unable to formulate an answer. He rubbed his hand as he replayed the moment over and over again in his head.

CHAPTER THREE

O ver a perfectly seasoned dinner of rice pilaf with chickpeas and summer squash, Chief asked the boys about their time in the meadow. As Bobby recounted his experience with the deer, the old Navajo leaned back in his high-backed chair and smiled. "You met my *deer* friend Ehawee and her brother, Huritt," he said with a chuckle. "Ehawee means 'laughing maiden' in the language of my tribe. Huritt means 'handsome.'"

"When I touched her, it felt electric," said Bobby, "like life itself flowed through my hands."

"You touched her spirit; the anima within her," said Chief. "Connecting with a living creature is a special talent. It is the first step in sensing the oneness of all life."

"It felt like I was inside her body," said Bobby.

"In a sense, you were," said Chief. "When you connect with the anima inside another living creature, you share their thoughts and emotions."

"Like the zucchini in the garden back at the academy," Bobby said. "But a monk helped me do that. I did this by myself."

Chief nodded. "Deer and other large animals have large amounts of anima. This makes them easier to commune with than smaller life-forms," he explained. "Of course, you were probably excited, which tends to boost one's abilities, although it also tends to impair focus. The next step is to connect with smaller creatures and those whose energy is more subtle, such as trees and plants. Learn to sense the spirit in all creatures. Only then, can you begin to comprehend the vast nature of the universe."

* * *

For the next several days, Chief accompanied the boys as they visited different spots in the forest, where they meditated and pondered the various flora and fauna. The more he learned, the more Bobby developed an appreciation for the vast ecosystem and its myriad inhabitants. He began to sense a connection with his surroundings and, with it, a growing respect.

Jinx's appreciation for his environment also grew. Unable to form anima bonds with plants or animals without harming them, Jinx set down his textbooks and took to exploring nature rather than reading about it. Chief offered constant counsel, nurturing both boys' burgeoning interest in all things natural.

One afternoon, after almost a week since their studies had begun, Chief looked at Bobby's aura and made a pronouncement. "It's time," he said.

Bobby paused with his hands cupped in a bowl, where a mix of red crested finches, sparrows, and blue jays were feeding on seeds from his palms. Jinx looked down from the lower branches of a nearby elm where he'd been examining one of the bird's nests.

"Time for what?" asked Bobby.

The deep lines of Chief's face creased into a smile. "How would you boys like to see the inside of the Nexus?"

Jinx lost his grip on his branch and nearly fell before clutching at the trunk to regain his balance. The birds around Bobby scattered as he shot to his feet. "No way," he declared. "That would be awesome."

"I think you're ready," said Chief.

The boys ran ahead, racing each other up the hill to the Nexus. They slowed down only after they reached the bizarre structure with its hexagonal panels made of living wood. With no visible door, the boys were forced to wait on Chief. Bobby busied himself inspecting the glowing green vines that covered the surface.

Unable to see the glow, Jinx walked around the building, examining its architecture.

When Chief arrived, he lifted a tangle of vines by the south wall and placed his hand in a sunken indent. With a hiss, the top of a panel swung downward to create a ramp. As he followed Chief inside, Bobby's first impression was of an indoor swimming pool. A narrow catwalk circled the upper deck. But this pool wasn't composed of water, at least not entirely. Ripples flowed too slowly, suggesting some kind of viscous gel. Like the vines outside, the surface glowed pale green, yet there were no lights visible below the surface. On the far side of the catwalk, a retractable metal arm attached to a platform extended out over the middle of the pool.

It wasn't until they'd traversed to the other side that Bobby noticed the monitors and control panels blanketing the far wall. Jinx set to studying the various knobs and dials. Bobby was more interested in the bizarre chair at the end of the metal arm.

Made of a smooth, glossy material that Bobby didn't recognize, it looked like a giant bathtub with a sloping interior. Raised surfaces on either side provided armrests, while an indent at the top contoured for an occupant's head and neck.

"You'll want to change," said Chief, gesturing to a door on his right. "You'll find a wetsuit in there. I find it helps the first time. After that, it's up to you."

"Helps with what?" asked Bobby, but Chief had shifted his attention to the controls and made no reply. Bobby changed as the crane holding the strange tub retracted from the center of the pool. The tub docked alongside the platform. Bobby noticed for the first time a series of tubes connected to the head area.

Chief gave him the go-ahead signal. Bobby climbed into the bobsled contours of the tub and took a seat. "What do I do?" asked Bobby. "You haven't given me any instructions."

"Just relax," said Chief. "I'll talk you through everything when it's time. Jinx, give him the goggles."

Jinx handed Bobby a pair of blacked-out swim goggles. "How am I supposed to see anything in these?" said Bobby.

"Don't worry," said Chief, handing him a mouthpiece attached to a long, narrow tube. "Just put them on and put this in your mouth." As Bobby digested this latest instruction, Chief attached tubes to his forehead using small adhesive patches. He put two more on the back of Bobby's hands and then gave him a pat on the head. "You're all set. Just try to breathe normally."

Jinx hovered over Chief. "What's that do?" he said pointing to the pads on Bobby's face. "They look like biometric sensors. But if he's going where I think he's going, how do they get an accurate reading with all the feedback? And what's that liquid made of? It's some type of organic bioplasma, right? I'm guessing algae based. How does it work? Is the conductivity tactile or kinetic? I once theorized that an algae-based solution mixed with—"

Chief gave Jinx a hard look and he stopped talking.

"Sorry," said Jinx, lowering his voice to a bare whisper. "This is just so exciting!"

"There will be plenty of time for questions," said Chief, turning back to Bobby. "Now is the time to experience. Focus your attention on what, not how, or why. Be absolutely, completely in the moment."

Chief pushed a button on the side of the tub. Slowly, the metallic arm retracted from the platform. Then it began to descend, lowering Bobby towards the pool. He gripped the handholds tight, his arms glued to the armrests.

As he drew closer, the light from the effervescent liquid pierced the blacked-out goggles, forcing Bobby to shut his eyes. His feet touched the surface and a myriad of sensations flooded through him. He became acutely aware of every cell in his body, from his taste buds to the individual hairs on his arms and legs. The liquid rose, squeezing inside the wetsuit to caress his skin. He gasped as every fiber of his being ignited at once.

Then there were the voices; so many voices whispering from all around. He relaxed his grip as he slipped below the surface, trying to focus on what Chief had told him: concentrate on being in the moment. Gradually the cacophony blended together, becoming a melody of sorts. He picked out the high woodwind tweets of birds frolicking in the trees; the sharp percussion of crickets deep in the brush; the big brass tones of the bullfrogs down by the river.

This wasn't like the deer in the meadow where everything was filtered through one creature's perception. This was all of them at once: awareness of every plant, every animal, from the giant sequoias down to the tiniest gnat. He forgot to breathe. Then the melody was there, resonating within him, reminding him of what both Master Jong and Chief had said: that all of creation is one, and that he was a part of it.

His eyes opened wide, no longer bothered by the intense light. Tears of joy mixed with the shimmering fluid all around. There was only the song. Time lost all meaning as Bobby gave himself over to the melody. Mere seconds became a lifetime as he drifted among the thousands of living creatures in the Eagle's Nest, discovering how each individual tune blended together into one.

* * *

Tears of joy and sadness mixed as Bobby broke the surface. The effervescent fluid drained languidly from the tub as he rose into the air to reconnect with the platform.

"I'm sorry to pull you out so soon," said Chief. "Normally we give people more time to get acclimated during their first experience, but we just got news I know you'd want to hear."

"How long was I down there?" asked Bobby, thinking it had been hours, perhaps days.

"Seven minutes," said Chief. Bobby let out an involuntary gasp.

"What was it like?" asked Jinx, standing on his tiptoes to see over the edge of the tub.

"It was like...forever," said Bobby.

Chief stopped bundling the respirator hose and looked up. "Describe it to me." So, Bobby did, telling Chief about the complete self-awareness, the song of oneness, and the sense of timelessness he'd experienced.

"Most people feel only the self-awareness," said Chief. "The oneness, the timelessness you mentioned, that is interesting."

"What is it?" said the boys in unison.

"From what you describe, it sounds like nirvana, a moment of complete perfection. It is said that in that moment, time and space have no meaning. A person is connected to everything, past, present, and future, all at the same time."

"What about you?" asked Bobby. "Have you experienced it?"

"A few times, yes. But that was after years of intense study and prolonged use of the Nexus. Even then, it was never with such short exposure and not on my first use."

Bobby closed his gaping mouth. "So, what's so important you pulled me out?" he asked.

"I just heard from your grandfather and Cassandra. They haven't located your grandmother, but they may have a lead on the missing kids from the Jade Academy."

Jinx gripped Bobby's arm as Chief continued, "Apparently there are rumors about children being taken into the jungle. Your grandfather thinks perhaps the Core has some kind of operation there, like they did at the academy."

"Wait just one second," said Jinx. "What are the odds that while searching for Grandma, Grandpa and Cassandra happened to come across a clue leading them to our friends from the academy?"

Chief turned to his student. "Jinx, you of all people should know by now that there is no such thing as coincidence. It's not only possible; it's highly probable your grandmother heard the same rumors and is down there right now looking for Bobby."

"So where is this place?" Bobby asked.

"Guatemala."

CHAPTER FOUR

T he lone runway at Mundo Maya International Airport in Flores, Guatemala was little more than a dirt strip trimmed to keep the surrounding jungle from reclaiming it. Bobby, Chief, and Jinx hurried from the overwhelming humidity of the tarmac into the only slightly less oppressive heat of the one-building terminal.

Inside customs, faded prints of tropical birds decorated the lime-green walls. Grandpa and Cassandra sat on a row of plastic chairs on the other side of the checkpoint. Grandpa wore native linens, including a short-sleeved charcoal shirt, khaki pants, and a wide-brimmed sombrero. Cassandra favored silk, with a long-sleeved, high-necked blouse and white scarf, all kept miraculously dry despite the jungle's ever-present moisture.

Grandpa greeted his grandsons with huge hugs as they cleared customs and Chief went to gather the bags. Cassandra averted her gaze, staring out the window as if uncomfortable by their displays of affection.

"So where are the kids from the academy?" asked Jinx as they headed to the rented silver Taurus parked in the dirt lot outside.

"All I know are rumors," said Grandpa. "Once we got down here, we started hearing stories about caravans full of children disappearing into the jungle. We tracked down some of the locals who said the kids were all foreigners. No one spoke to them. Apparently, the children were kept away from the public, and were guarded by men in suits."

"Sounds like Core agents," said Bobby. "So, where did they go?"

"The groups headed east, into a part of the forest the locals call La Muerte Verde," said Grandpa.

"It means 'The Green Death' by the way," said Cassandra. "Anyone else think going there might not be a great idea?"

The group fell quiet as Grandpa drove them to the hotel. Chief took a map out of the glovebox and studied it. "So, what's in that part of the jungle?"

"You mean other than death?" asked Cassandra. "Who cares? All anyone ever talks about in this pigsty village is the disappearance of anyone who goes there. That's more than enough for me."

"Actually, there is more," said Grandpa. "I spoke to a villager yesterday who claims there is an ancient Mayan temple in that region. I don't know how much to believe. He said evil spirits haunt the ruins, which is why no one goes there."

Cassandra scoffed. "That same villager wore socks on his hands and had a bottle of mescal big enough to bathe in. Plus, he smelled like rotten avocadoes."

"Still, I sensed no deception, even before I gave him fifty quetzals," said Grandpa. Cassandra harrumphed but made no other reply.

"So, we're headed there, right?" said Bobby. "If our friends are at that temple then we have to go rescue them."

Grandpa shook his head. "Cassandra and I will not be joining you. A foreigner matching your grandmother's description passed through here several weeks ago. I've spoken to a number of people who remember her vividly, but no one seems to recall if she was with anyone or where she went."

"It would seem our paths point in different directions," said Chief. "But perhaps not for long. If your wife did pass through this village, it's possible she headed for the ruins as well."

Grandpa nodded. "Chances are you're right, but I can't go running off into the rainforest until I know for sure."

"Take this," said Chief, handing Grandpa a black satellite phone. "It will get a signal anywhere in the world. I have one as well, so we can stay in contact."

They passed the rest of the car ride in casual conversation until they reached the hotel: a dingy building with stucco walls, cracked and peeling in the hot sun. The tiny bedrooms had no air-conditioning, not even a ceiling fan. Each room held two filthy twin beds. Iron bars crisscrossed the windows.

"I realize it's not a five-star hotel," said Grandpa with a sigh. "Heck, Cassandra threatened to sleep in the bathtub until I went out and bought new sheets and plastic wrap to cover the mattresses."

"The accommodations are fine," said Chief. "If those kids going into the jungle are from the Jade Academy, then the Core is nearby. Better to keep a low profile."

Bobby quickly discovered that "low profile" meant no profile, as he and Jinx were forced to stay indoors while the adults ran errands. Jinx spent his time perusing a stack of books Grandpa had bought about the region. Among them were guides on the local flora and fauna as well as information on the indigenous tribes, all of which differed greatly from anything Jinx had studied at the academy.

Bobby flipped channels on the television, ultimately settling on The Terminator with poorly translated English subtitles and even worse Spanish voice-overs.

Around dinnertime, Chief returned and announced he had secured a guide to take them into the jungle. Grandpa and Cassandra came back shortly after, but left again almost immediately, saying only that they had more leads to follow up on. Chief, Bobby, and Jinx ate from a tamale stand on the corner as heavy rainclouds rolled in. The downpour turned the streets to mud but did nothing to lessen the omnipresent heat.

By the time Bobby drifted off to sleep around midnight, it was to thoughts of rescuing his friends mixed with the image of Arnold Schwarzenegger declaring, "Volveré!" in the false baritone of a Spanish teenager.

* * *

It was drizzling the next morning when Bobby and Jinx met their guide, Javier. The short, middle-aged local had a flat nose, broad forehead, and even broader smile that bulged to one side from the tobacco leaves he constantly stuffed into his mouth.

Changing into hiking boots and rain gear, the boys loaded their luggage onto Javier's old Wrangler. As they drove, Jinx peppered their guide with questions about the jungle and what to expect. Javier answered in broken English while spitting gobs of tobacco out the window. This lasted several hours until Jinx started asking about the exact genus and phylum of specific species, at which point Chief suggested a game of animal, vegetable, or mineral. Bobby played along until Jinx won the fifth game in a row, at which point they settled for staring out the window at the kaleidoscope of trees and plants.

The truck shook as they transitioned from paved road to gravel. It grew worse when the gravel gave way to rutted dirt. When Javier finally stopped the truck, the vegetation on either side of the road was so thick they could barely get the doors open.

"No more road," explained Javier. "Walk from here, comprende?"

Chief nodded and began unloading their gear, all of which had been transferred into backpacks the night before. "Neither one of you is fully trained," he reminded the boys. "Stick close and do exactly as I say."

With solemn nods, the boys strapped on their backpacks and followed him into the jungle. Their guide led the way at a deliberate pace, swinging his machete back and forth to clear a narrow path. In moments, the truck disappeared behind them as they were swallowed up by the wilds.

* * *

In the steamy, light-starved depths of the rainforest, Bobby caught only glints of Javier's machete as he hacked his way through the brush. In the upper canopy, howler monkeys screeched, and tropical birds cried. Jinx and Chief followed close behind their cheery guide, conversing in Spanish. Unable to follow the conversation, Bobby focused on avoiding the omnipresent mud puddles that carpeted the ground.

For a while, time lost meaning as they probed deeper into the dense jungle. Then Javier pulled the group to an abrupt halt. The forest grew silent as he bent to examine something at his feet. Bobby came forward to discover their guide staring at two thick branches lying diagonal across one another to form an "X" across the path. The tips of each branch had been painted red, with black stripes in the middle where they crossed.

Javier spat into the bushes. "We go," said the guide, gesturing back the way they had come. "Very bad," he said. "We go now."

For several minutes, Bobby waited as Javier and Chief spoke in heated tones. Finally, Jinx translated. "Javier says we have reached La Muerte Verde. These sticks are a warning: a sign left by the jungle people that we must not go any farther."

"Chief says we must keep going, no matter the warning," he continued, "but Javier refuses. He says to keep going is to die."

Javier spat his entire wad of tobacco at Chief's feet. "I go," he declared emphatically, and brushed past Bobby. "Vaya con Dios," he said over his shoulder. The previously affable guide ducked between a cluster of philodendrons and a giant fern. In two strides, he disappeared into the brush, leaving Bobby, Chief, and Jinx utterly alone in the dense and suddenly ominous jungle.

CHAPTER FIVE

B y the time they came across the third pair of sticks, Chief didn't even bother to slow down. Bobby stepped over them with a worrisome groan but kept pace with Jinx, who cast nervous glances at every shadow. It wasn't until they reached a clearing where an ancient elm had fallen that Chief stopped. Gesturing the boys to gather close, he walked over to the tree's moss-covered corpse and took a seat.

"What is it?" asked Jinx. "Why are we stopping?"

"Can't you feel them?" asked Chief, looking at Bobby.

"I sense…something," said Bobby. "There is a presence around us, but I can't tell where it's coming from."

"That is because they are all around us," said Chief, setting his backpack by his feet. "Come. Sit on this log and do not make any sudden moves."

The boys did as instructed, dislodging chunks of spongy, rotten bark as they climbed up out of the mud onto the massive log. Movement in the nearby bushes drew their attention.

The first native to appear wore a loincloth and a stack of bone necklaces that didn't make a sound as he slid from behind a tree into the clearing. An old man with white hair, he carried a thick staff etched with plants and animals along its weathered length.

Moments later, a dozen other natives materialized out of the shadows. Some wore vests made of fur and animal hide. Several carried long wooden spears. Others carried bows with quivers full of brightly feathered arrows strapped to their backs. One wore a necklace of jaguar claws. Bobby lifted a hand to plug his nose. All of them were covered in some kind of brown paint that stank like dung.

Chief laid a reassuring hand on Jinx as the youth tried to scramble down from the log. "Stay calm," said Chief softly. "We don't want to upset them." Chief lowered himself onto both knees. "I don't recognize this tribe," he whispered to Jinx over his shoulder. "Any chance you know who they are?"

Jinx wheezed and shook his head. "The Ch'ol tribes of the Chiapas region carry similarly crude weapons, but their habitat is hundreds of miles north of here in Mexico. The Ch'orti live much closer to this region, but they don't use body paint, and they trade with the outside world. They would be carrying steel knives and guns, not bows and spears." As Jinx gasped for air, his pitch took on an almost frantic tone. "How are we supposed to know how to communicate with them if we don't know who they are?"

Chief's backpack buzzed with an incoming call. A scary-looking native with a jagged scar on his right cheek raised his spear and thrust it into the pack. With a loud crunch, the buzzing ceased.

"They smashed the sat phone!" said Bobby. Jinx's face turned purple.

"Remain calm," said Chief, without taking his eyes off the natives. He stood up, hands raised over his head. Several of the men around him shook their spears and stepped closer.

Jinx grasped at his throat. Chief reached for his backpack and started to open it. One of the tribesmen pulled back his bow and let loose an arrow that sank into the mud between Chief's legs.

Chief dropped his backpack and stepped away. The natives started yelling amongst themselves. Bobby didn't understand most of it but caught a few names. The leader was Itzamna. The warrior with the jaguar claws was Votan. The scarred native named Tohil pointed his spear at Chief. The hunters behind him kept their bows trained on all of them.

For a moment, no one moved as Jinx faded from purple to white. His cheeks puffed and his chest heaved as he tried in vain to draw air. Chief moved toward him. Tohil pulled his spear back, ready to strike, but Itzamna barked an order and the hunter relaxed his arm.

Chief laid his hands gently on Jinx's chest and closed his eyes. Bobby felt a tingle in the air, accompanied by pale green light as Chief chanted a wordless melody.

A ripple of murmurs swept through the natives. A whooshing noise erupted as air flooded Jinx's lungs. Bobby held his cousin upright as his Jinx drew in ragged breaths, his color growing visibly better with each gulp.

Long moments passed with Bobby intently watching his cousin's face. Finally, Jinx raised his chin and waved Bobby away. "I'm alright," he said as Chief took a step back to give him some room. Bobby looked up to discover that all of the natives had laid down their weapons and fallen to the ground.

* * *

Bobby, Jinx, and Chief stared in wonder. Itzamna remained still, clearly unfazed by whatever had riled the others. Leaning heavily on the staff, he walked up to Chief and brought his palms together in a cupping gesture. The other natives rose, reclaimed their weapons, and gathered around.

"What's going on?" asked Bobby, staring at the bizarre scene.

Chief held up his hand, asking for patience. "I believe this is their shaman," he said, gesturing to the old man. "He must have felt the healing I performed on Jinx."

Itzamna brought his arms up and extended them towards Jinx, who started to pull away. Chief stopped him. "I don't think he intends you harm."

The shaman laid a hand on Jinx's chest and closed his eyes. After a moment he stepped back and said something to the other natives. A ripple of murmurs went through the crowd. Itzamna went next to Bobby. A tingle spread across Bobby's chest as the shaman placed a hand over his heart. Finally, Itzamna stepped over to Chief. The old Indian cupped his hands, mimicking the shaman's gesture from a moment ago then opened his arms, inviting the shaman to approach.

Bobby held his breath as Itzamna placed a hand on Chief's shoulder. After a brief moment, Chief extended a hand and clasped the shaman's forearm. The two men stood motionless for a long time. None of the other natives so much as twitched. Bobby glanced at Jinx, but his cousin just shrugged.

Finally, the two men opened their eyes and stepped apart, breaking the bond. Ducking his head, Chief whispered to the boys, "Don't worry. They were going to kill us but not anymore. Now, they're just going to take us to their village, deep in the jungle."

* * *

Bobby paced back and forth outside the thatch hut, with its walls wrapped in animal hides and roof covered with palm fronds. "How exactly is this better than being lost in the jungle?" he asked Jinx.

The question hung in the air unanswered. After trekking through the dense foliage for several hours, the hunting party had arrived at a small mud-and-stick village. Chief had immediately disappeared into the hut with the shaman. Now the boys sat outside the lean-to, with only their fears and the cold stares of the natives to keep them company.

Tohil, the warrior with the deep scar on his cheek, leaned against a tree a short distance away, his mahogany eyes fixed on the boys the entire time. Votan stood nearby. Meanwhile, women and children from the village gave the boys furtive glances as they hurried about their business. Bobby didn't know how long Chief and the shaman had been inside, only that they'd arrived just before dusk, and a waxy moon had passed overhead long ago.

Bobby hung his head between his knees and rubbed his aching legs. The flap to the hut swung open and Chief emerged, followed closely by Itzamna. Chief shook Jinx. The younger boy had fallen asleep propped against a stump, drooling on his sleeve and snoring softly. Overhead, the sky bloomed pale orange with the arrival of dawn.

"I have much to tell you both," said Chief. "But first, we need some rest."

Bobby yawned and rubbed at his eyes as a young woman with hair down to her waist came forward. She took him to an empty hut, gesturing to the cot inside. No sooner than his head hit the pallet did he fall sound asleep.

CHAPTER SIX

It was dark again when Bobby rose. Drinking from a bowl of water next to the bed, he rummaged through his pack and changed into jeans and a gray microfiber t-shirt. Emerging from the hut, he located Chief, Jinx, and Itzamna sitting by the fire pit in the middle of the village.

The shaman wore the same attire as the day before. His staff leaned against the tree behind him. Chief wore army fatigues with combat boots, while Jinx wore a gray hoodie, fanny pack, and black cargo pants with bulging pockets. The three of them were eating, with an empty spot between Chief and Jinx. Itzamna handed Bobby a wooden bowl and gestured for him to sit.

"How did you sleep?" asked Chief.

"Well enough, I guess," said Bobby, inspecting the bowl to discover a pungent, green soup with brown lumps. His mouth watered. "What's in it?" he asked, stirring the broth with a heavy wooden spoon.

"No idea," said Jinx, "but it's delicious."

Bobby dove in with gusto, tasting some kind of tangy meat, along with a fibrous root that reminded him of asparagus. The broth was creamy with a hint of spice. Only after he had drained the bowl along with half of another did he lean back and sigh with contentment.

"I now understand the reason they call this place La Muerte Verde," said Chief. Bobby frowned into his bowl. "Don't worry," said Chief. "The food isn't poisoned. We are honored guests here."

"Yesterday you said they were going to kill us. Not that I'm complaining, but how can you know for sure they aren't still going to poke us with spears?"

"We communicated telepathically," said Chief. "I saw images in his mind of these people and what they want."

Jinx looked ready to jump out of his seat at this revelation. "We've discovered a new, indigenous tribe," he said in a rush. "And they're telepathic! This is amazing. Someone should be documenting everything. Where did I put my camera?"

Chief coughed. It was only then that Bobby noticed the ring of men and women gathering around them. None of them spoke a word. They stared with wide, curious eyes. Bobby spotted young children and elderly among the circle.

"These people protect the jungle," said Chief. "At the heart of this forest is the ancient temple we were told about. The natives believe it's haunted. Itzamna showed me an image shrouded in darkness. The air around it glows at night without the presence of fire. The earth trembles and the sky roars without clouds or thunder.

"The temple was once sacred to their people. Now they see the shadows of the Spirit Men at night and hear the horrible wails of their ancestors, who cannot find peace because the Spirit Men have come and disturbed their rest."

"What are these Spirit Men?" asked Jinx, scribbling madly on a small notepad he'd extracted from his backpack.

"The Spirit Men appear to be people like us, people with the ability to connect with and manipulate anima. Itzamna showed me images of armed men passing through the jungle. In one of those images, I saw children who I believe to be from the academy. It is likely your friends were among them."

Several of the natives leapt back as Bobby sprang to his feet. "So why are we sitting here talking? Let's go rescue them!"

Chief took Bobby's arm, pulling him back to the ground. "If the Spirit Men are members of the Core, then we must use extreme caution."

"Why do the natives bother them in the first place?" said Bobby. "Are they cannibals or something? Why don't they just let these Spirit Men pass?"

Chief's face turned grim, the contours of his face like deep valleys. "Itzamna and the other members of this village believe the Spirit Men have corrupted the temple, turning it into an evil place where the hearts and souls of any who go there are twisted and tortured for eternity.

"So that's why this place is called La Muerte Verde? Because the haunted temple takes people?"

Chief shook his head. "I'm afraid it's not that simple. Itzamna and his people believe they have a sacred mission. In order to prevent outsiders from becoming damned, he and his men kill them rather than allow them access to the temple. They believe they are doing these outsiders a great service by saving their souls from eternal damnation."

The pen slipped from Jinx's hand and fell into the dirt. "You mean the mysterious disappearances are because of these natives?"

"There's more," said Chief. "Apparently they have a legend about a pair of champions from a faraway land. Legend says the champions will banish the Spirit Men and rescue the souls trapped within."

Jinx looked confused, but Bobby understood when the shaman walked up to him and extended his hands.

"He thinks we're the champions," said Bobby.

Chief nodded. "He wishes permission to speak your future, so that all may hear what he believes to be true."

"What does that mean 'speak my future'? What do I have to do?"

"He only needs to touch you. I will join as well in order to translate."

"What about Jinx? Does the shaman want to speak his future too?"

"Itzamna says he cannot speak Jinx's future, only yours. Besides, one will suffice."

Bobby searched Jinx's face for advice. His little cousin's eyes sparkled with excitement as he flipped to a new page in his note pad. "Are you kidding me? I can't wait to write about this!"

Bobby gave a tentative nod. "Then I guess it's settled. Let's do it."

* * *

They sat in a tight triangle, knees nearly touching, hands resting on thighs. A stick of incense sat in the middle, sending up tight curls of gray smoke.

Bobby couldn't be sure but thought he caught the pungent scent of the anima-amplifying transitivo paradoxa mushroom. *No forgetting that smell*, he thought.

Itzamna sat on his left, Chief on his right. Villagers gathered in a loose circle to observe the ceremony. Most were women and children, but Bobby spotted several members of the hunting party. Tohil, the warrior with the scar, leaned casually on his spear, his painted face an unreadable mask.

"Take my hand," said Chief. "Take Itzamna's in your other hand and try to relax." Bobby rolled his shoulders a few times, then took a deep breath in through his nose and out through his mouth.

"Close your eyes, and let your mind go blank."

Bobby sat there, his thoughts drifting aimlessly. Itzamna squeezed his left hand firmly and began to speak. After a moment, Chief translated through the link.

"The arrival of the Spirit Men has disturbed the ancient Mayans who once lived in this sacred place. Our prophecies speak of a great warrior, a Holcan, who will free the souls of our ancestors and put them to rest."

Dropping Chief's hand, Itzamna took Bobby's head between his palms and gazed deep into his eyes. As if reading Bobby's soul, the old shaman recited a phrase that took Chief a moment to translate.

"He says you have the Gift: the power to see into the spirit world."

Itzamna reached into his medicine bag and pulled out a figurine of a bizarre skeletal creature perched on top of a man with a large tableau necklace and bone headdress.

"Itzamna told me about this last night," said Chief. "It's a talisman of the Mayan god, Hunhau. He believes it will allow you to cross the veil between the living and the dead. At first, you'll need direct contact with the idol but it should become easier over time."

"Wait—what?" said Bobby. "I don't wanna talk to a bunch of restless spirits."

Jinx rushed to his side to examine the idol. "You mean Bobby will be able to commune with the dead? I've read about this sort of thing before but—"

"According to Itzamna's visions, there is no choice," said Chief. "The spirits speak to the Holcan. The Holcan will face the trials, and then the Holcan will free the spirits."

Bobby groaned. "Now there's trials, too? I hate trials."

Chief reached out and clasped the shaman's arm. Both men closed their eyes and swayed as if in a trance. Ethereal voices whispered in the wind. Itzamna's mouth began to move but it was Chief who spoke.

"Three trials will be thrust upon the Holcan. First, he will cross a river of teeth without moving. Second, the Holcan will walk across the sky without wings. Finally, the Holcan will live for eternity without aging a day. Once these three prophecies have been fulfilled, the Holcan will free the spirits of our ancestors and bring peace to the land."

The whispers continued for a few more moments and then died away, leaving behind a deathly silence. Itzamna released Bobby's hand and slowly stood up. The old shaman, with his weathered skin like mottled snakeskin, walked to his hut. Pausing in the doorway, he looked back. His dark brown eyes glinted with unreadable depth. Then he closed the door.

"He believes your future is a heavy one," said Chief, "and from what I saw of his visions, there is no certainty you will pass any of the trials."

Bobby stared at the strange idol in his hands. It felt incredibly heavy, like a thousand pounds of responsibility and duty weighing him down. Jinx came over and squeezed Bobby's shoulder. "Don't worry, buddy. If anyone can do it, it's you."

* * *

They waited until daybreak the next day to depart. Through hand gestures and drawing in the dirt, Bobby and Jinx communicated with the natives, asking questions and learning about their culture. Jinx was still furiously drawing pictograms with a pointy stick when Chief ordered him to grab his backpack and head out.

Itzamna and six hunters provided escort. As Chief explained, he'd been able to telepathically convince the shaman that they needed to visit the temple, but the tribal leader refused to let them go alone. Instead, Itzamna and his men would act as guides, leading them through the nearly impregnable underbrush. Detouring around bogs and sinkholes, they stopped constantly to avoid wild boars, poisonous frogs, and a vast array of other deadly denizens.

When Itzamna finally ordered them to halt, Bobby had no idea why. The jungle looked the same as it had for the past several hours, a verdant blanket of dense vegetation that swallowed all visibility beyond a few feet in any direction. It wasn't until the shaman pointed with his staff that Bobby spotted the reason.

Spanning the gap between two ficus trees was a tall metal fence topped with barbed wire. Almost imperceptible in the dim light, he might not have noticed it at all except for the dead monkey lying below. The creature's fur had been singed as if someone had set it on fire, the flesh boiled and black.

"Itzamna showed me this vision," said Chief. "I wasn't sure what I was looking at. All I saw were bursts of light in the jungle and creatures falling to the ground. It makes sense now; the natives have no concept of electricity."

"You mean that fence is electric?" said Bobby. "Why would someone go to so much trouble all the way out here?"

"The natives believe it is a net cast by the evil spirits to trap souls. They know only that it lights up whenever something touches it and that death immediately follows, like with that monkey."

"We've gotta get through it," said Bobby. "We can't see the temple from here."

Walking up to the shaman, Jinx extended a hand towards the staff. Itzamna cocked his head to one side and glanced at Chief before relinquishing his talisman of authority. Metal had been molded over the base of the staff, probably from a tin can or other piece of junk dropped by a traveler unlucky enough to wander into the Muerte Verde. Gripping the staff with both hands, Jinx extended the tip and grazed the fence. Sparks flew from the glossy steel wires, casting the dead primate in a ghastly sallow aura.

All the natives, including Itzamna jumped back, murmuring and clasping their hands together. Several fell to the ground, touching their foreheads to the jungle floor.

"There's no way we're gonna climb over," said Jinx. "With as much power as that current is drawing, the slightest contact could fry your skin."

Tapping Itzamna on the shoulder, Chief pointed at the fence and said something unintelligible. All of the natives except Itzamna looked surprised, gesturing back and forth between Chief and the fence.

"What just happened?" asked Jinx.

"I picked up a few words when I shared thoughts with Itzamna," said Chief. "I just told them I want us to go through the fence. I'm pretty sure they think I'm crazy."

Chief repeated his request. Several natives shook their weapons and pointed back the way they'd come. "They don't want to be here anymore and think we should leave," interpreted Chief.

Bobby folded his arms. "My friends are in there. We need to find a way through."

After a brief discussion with Votan and Tohil, Itzamna turned to Chief and beckoned. "He wants us to follow," said Jinx. "Maybe they know a way around the fence." Several minutes later, they stood before a massive fallen tree so ancient that other, younger trees grew from the mossy pulp of its rotting carcass.

At first Bobby didn't see why they'd been brought here. The fence straddling the fallen giant had been pinned down all along its massive girth, providing no opening through which to pass. Then one of natives stepped over to the trunk and lifted up a thick section of moss-covered bark. Within, the tree's core had rotted away, leaving a hollow running down its length. The space was too narrow for any of the adults, but Bobby felt confident that he and Jinx could squeeze through.

"Looks like it's just us," said Bobby, clasping Jinx on the shoulder.

Chief scowled. "I don't like you two going in there by yourselves."

"It doesn't look like we have a choice," said Bobby. "We need to know what's in there. We'll have a quick look around and be back, lickety-split."

Chief paced back and forth. "Under no circumstances can you allow anyone to see you or know you're there. If you see your friends, come back here and report immediately."

Bobby was already stripping off his backpack. As he set the pack down, Chief set a hand on his shoulder. "Please be careful. I saw things in Itzamna's vision that I can't fully explain," said the old Navajo. "There are powerful forces inside the temple."

Bobby pulled out the idol of the jaguar god, Hunhau, and stared at the bizarre obsidian and quartz sculpture before tucking it into his pocket. "I will," he said with a solemn nod.

Beside them, Jinx shed his backpack and donned a plastic rain slicker to cover his clothes. Bobby pulled up the hood on his poncho and turned to his cousin. "You ready to get filthy?"

CHAPTER SEVEN

The inside of the log smelled of mildew and decay. Everywhere he placed his hands, bugs skittered out from beneath his palms. He prayed none of the creepy crawlies were poisonous. He already had half a dozen bites on the back of his hands.

Squirming on his belly, Bobby inched his way through the damp, rotten core. Behind him, Jinx sneezed constantly, his breathing labored and raspy as he scratched and scraped his way along. Using the penlight he'd obtained at the academy, Bobby scanned the hollow.

The narrow space ended a few feet ahead. Bobby pressed his hands into the wood, probing for an opening. It took several attempts before he located a section soft enough to dig into the rotted wood with his bare hands. He tore at the opening until it was large enough, and then wedged himself into the hole. Arms first, he pushed his head through and wriggled out.

Taking a moment to brush himself off, Bobby froze as he turned to help Jinx. A black jaguar stood on the branch of a banyan tree not twenty feet away. Its golden eyes glowed in the pale half-light. The majestic creature extended its front paws and lowered its head. Bobby gasped as he recognized the same action performed by the mother bear back at the academy.

"What is it?" asked Jinx, as he squeezed his way out of the hole. Bobby took a moment to help his cousin up. When he looked back, the jaguar was gone. He caught a fleeting glance of movement high overhead. A moment later, it emerged on a limb at the very top of the canopy, so high it rose above the electric fence.

"There, look there," said Bobby, pointing at the magnificent creature.

With a mighty leap, the panther sprang from the banyan tree, over the top of the fence, and alighted nimbly on a slender branch on the other side of the divide.

"Wow, a melanistic Panthera onca," said Jinx. "Did you know that 'panther' can actually refer to a leopard, jaguar, or even a mountain lion? Leopards live mainly in Asia and Africa. Jaguars live here in Central and South America and can grow to weigh twice that of a leopard."

Bobby watched the panther retreat into the shadows. "That's a jaguar, and a smart one," Jinx continued. "Looks like it found its own way past the fence. Too bad Chief and the others can't climb trees like that."

Bobby just nodded and stared up into the canopy, hoping for another glimpse. Jinx tugged on his sleeve. "Come on, we should get going."

"Yeah, right," said Bobby, turning back to his cousin.

The electric fence ran behind them, only ten feet away yet barely visible through the dense foliage. The hollow log lay similarly hidden beneath a mound of ferns, rhododendron, and bromeliads. Half buried beneath the ground, only the tree's massive upturned roots gave witness to what lay below the surface.

Lamenting the absence of their gear, Bobby struck out toward the temple, making sure Jinx stayed close behind. Light appeared up ahead as the vegetation began to thin. When they broke through the tree line, both boys stopped and stared.

The ancient Mayan ruins were not a single structure but an entire city. In a hole the size of a crater, crumbling stone structures draped in creeper vines covered four levels of descending plateaus. This was where the citizens had lived, planted their crops, and raised their families.

At the center, an ancient step pyramid squatted like a massive grey toad. Flat on top, with broad stairs running up each side, there could be no doubt this enormous ziggurat was the temple to which the natives had referred. Bobby thought of the log he and Jinx had crawled through, and how most of it lay submerged below the surface. Something told him there was far more to the temple than what they saw.

"That must be what powers the fence," said Jinx, pointing to a large black generator in the middle of an overgrown field.

"That's a lot of juice," said Bobby, spotting at least half a dozen other generators scattered across the terraces.

"One thing's for sure, they didn't bring those in through the jungle," said Jinx. "There's no road." Indeed, the only visible gate was barely wide enough for two people to walk through side by side.

"They must have flown them in by helicopter. The expense would be astronomical, not to mention the bribes to keep it all secret."

As he stood there, imagining the immense scope of the Core's operation, Bobby heard whispering, just as he had during Itzamna's prophecy. As faint as rustling leaves, the voices called to him. He thought they were saying something about the temple but couldn't make out most of the words.

Then, one voice rose above the others, so clear and distinct that Bobby looked around to see who had spoken. "Please, help me," it said. Bobby swiveled his head, trying to locate the source.

He took off walking, heading straight for the tree line. Jinx raced to his side and grabbed Bobby's arm, trying to pull him back. "What are you doing?" asked Jinx. "We have to stay hidden!"

Bobby shrugged off his cousin and continued walking as he followed the voice in his head. Reaching a row of stone ruins, he climbed and weaved his way through the structures. He came to a stop inside a crumbled building with three walls and no roof.

Bobby padded slowly through the empty space. "The voice is coming from somewhere inside this room."

"Voice? What voice?" asked Jinx.

Thrusting a hand into his pocket, Bobby grasped the Hunhau idol. He closed his eyes and turned in a circle. His eyes popped open and he moved to a pile of boulders in the far corner. "Here, help me search," he said. Dropping to his knees, he began digging through the rubble.

"What are you doing?" asked Jinx. "We don't have time for this! We need to rescue our—" He broke off midsentence as Bobby lifted a large flat rock to reveal a human skeleton. The skull poked out of the dirt, with the arms and torso only partially visible above the earth.

The skeleton appeared ancient, likely dating back centuries to the age of the Mayan empire. Jinx rocked back on his heels, staring at the skull. "How did you know?"

Bobby didn't answer. As if in a trance, he pulled out the idol of Hunhau. He set his other hand on the forehead of the skull. The idol began to glow as memories from the dead Mayan flooded through him.

"I am here," said Bobby. "Tell me your story."

***

His name was Maximon. He grew up in a village far from the temple at a time designated 1518 by the conquistadors who would invade his land. His mother died in childbirth. His father raised him alone, teaching Maximon how to fish and navigate the currents of the ubiquitous rivers.

The only girl in the village near his age was three years younger than Maximon. Her name was Lingya, and she was the raven-haired daughter of the medicine woman. She was long limbed with mysterious eyes and a smile like the midday sun.

Lingya would often come to Maximon's father on behalf of her mother, seeking reeds and plants gathered from the fast-flowing currents of the rivers. Maximon found himself unable to speak whenever Lingya was close. If he spotted her looking at him, he would duck his head and make an excuse to return to his chores.

When Maximon was ten, his father died in an alligator attack. Maximon went to live with his uncle, Nohchil, who was the village leader. Nohchil already had a son named Ek Chuaj, leaving little room in his heart for the young orphan.

Two years older, and larger than Maximon, Ek Chuaj was in line to become chief, with Lingya promised as his wife since birth. Ek Chuaj was boorish and rude, showing distain for other children and adults alike. When he was twelve, he knocked over a blind elder and laughed as the old man crawled around on his knees, searching for his cane.

Ek Chuaj took particular delight in tormenting Maximon, calling him orphan boy and claiming that no one loved him. Making any excuse to dodge his brutish cousin, Maximon fled to the water, fishing and playing on the banks of the river with only the lullaby of the rushing current to keep him company.

Despite his self-imposed solitude, everything changed when Maximon turned sixteen. Considered a man, Maximon moved out of Nohchil's lodge and reclaimed his parents' hut near the water. Soon after, Lingya started finding excuses to stop by, asking if he could help her locate rare water plants she couldn't find on her own. At first, he resisted, claiming he was too busy, but Nohchil ordered him to help; aiding the medicine woman and her daughter was the responsibility of all the members of the tribe.

The two took fishing trips together. Maximon discovered that Lingya was more than just a rare beauty. She was funny and playful, clever and creative, with a mind that opened his to the wonders of the jungle beyond its aquatic terrain.

In time, Maximon began to seek out Lingya as well. They explored the forest together, where he helped her forage and gather supplies. It wasn't long after that he realized he'd fallen in love with the one girl he could never have.

All the while, Ek Chuaj hovered nearby, growing more jealous and cruel towards Maximon with each passing moment. One day, Maximon went to the dock to find a hole punched in his canoe, sinking it deep in the mud. Another time, he pulled up his fishing lines to discover a giant hole cut in the middle.

The times when Ek Chuaj caught Maximon with Lingya were the worst. Much taller and bigger, Ek Chuaj would waylay Maximon, kicking and punching him until he lay on the ground, crying. Lingya would beg Ek Chuaj to leave him be, a request Ek Chuaj would only grant after Lingya allowed him to grope her breasts, grab her rear, or perform other obscene acts.

Desperate to spare Lingya's pain more than his own, Maximon sought out Lingya's company less and less, returning to the rivers, where his lonely tears were swept away by the endless currents.

For a while, everything returned to normal. Maximon didn't see Lingya much, and Ek Chuaj left them both alone. Then came the fateful night when everything changed.

Maximon was out late, hunting for catfish, his canoe tucked among the reeds as he trolled the slow, summer current. When he heard screams, he knew it was Lingya.

Her voice came from upstream, cutting through the roar of the river like a piranha, biting into his soul with her gut-wrenching cries. At first, he thought she'd been attacked by a predator, perhaps an alligator or a jaguar. But as he paddled toward her, he heard a second voice.

"I am done waiting!" Maximon recognized the angry tone of Ek Chuaj, like the hiss of a forest viper. "I will have what is mine!"

Maximon steered his boat around a bend, and the two teens came into sight. Lingya lay on the banks of the river, drenched in mud. A water vase lay beside her, discarded as she struggled with Ek Chuaj. The brutish teen sat atop of her, pinning her arms beneath his knees. With his hands, he tore at her clothes and pulled up her dress to expose her thighs. Lingya thrashed and screamed at him to stop, but Ek Chuaj just laughed.

"Leave her alone!" yelled Maximon, but the river carried his voice away as surely as it carried flotsam downstream. He paddled towards the shore with all his might, rowing upstream until he thought his arms would fall off from the effort.

The gap between them narrowed with agonizing slowness as Ek Chuaj had his way with Lingya. She fought like a gazelle in the jaws of an alligator, but it was no use.

With enough momentum to carry him to shore, Maximon tucked the paddle under his arm and leapt from the canoe. With Ek Chuaj preoccupied with his conquest, Maximon pulled the paddle back and swung at his cousin's head. Ek Chuaj turned at the last moment, catching the blow on his right temple. With barely a groan, the chieftain's son slumped onto the muddy shore of the river and lay still.

Lingya pushed Ek Chuaj off of her and scrambled to her feet. Her clothes had been reduced to rags, revealing bruises and blood where Ek Chuaj had clawed at her in his eagerness to have his way. Her wild eyes went from Maximon to Ek Chuaj, to the bloody oar still in Maximon's hand.

"What have you done?" said Lingya, returning her gaze to the limp body of her assailant. Almost involuntarily, Maximon dropped the paddle. Kneeling beside Ek Chuaj, he checked for a pulse.

"He's still alive," said Maximon.

"What about us?" asked Lingya. "Surely, he will kill us when he wakes." Lingya hugged her sides and trembled. "What are we going to do?"

"We could drag him into the water," suggested Maximon. "Everyone would think the alligators got him."

"And what about me?" said Lingya, gesturing to the bruises and cuts all over her body. "How do we explain this?"

Maximon grabbed his head in search of answers. "I couldn't just do nothing."

As if a celestial calm had eclipsed her panic, Lingya put out her arms and came to him. Taking Maximon's hands from his head, she lowered them until they stood a foot apart, arms clasped between them. "We need to flee," she said. "No matter what we do, they will know what happened. We need to flee the village and never come back."

Even disheveled and covered with mud, she was beautiful. Maximon gazed into her large green eyes. "I will go with you anywhere."

Grabbing Ek Chuaj by his feet, they dragged him near the village where one of the others would find him at daybreak. Then, while everyone else slept, they went to their respective homes to gather what supplies they could. With only a few possessions and no one to bid farewell, Maximon was in and out in less than two minutes. He found Lingya waiting for him, her own belongings bundled into a small satchel on her back.

Hand in hand, they left the village. Lingya looked back over her shoulder frequently, no doubt thinking about her parents and the life she was leaving behind. Maximon never looked back. His eyes remained straight ahead as he took Lingya's hand and led her firmly towards their future.

***

Jinx shook Bobby so hard his head snapped back, breaking his contact with the skeleton on the ground. "Wake up, Bobby," said Jinx. "We've got trouble!"

Bobby rubbed his eyes and shook his head. Being awakened so abruptly felt like being doused with a bucket of ice water. "What is it? What's going on?"

"I heard voices," said Jinx gesturing towards the grassy plain that descended to the pyramid. Creeping to the corner of the wall, Bobby spied a group of kids accompanied by several armed guards just beyond the ruins. The guards didn't appear to be searching, but rather, were keeping a close eye on the children.

Bobby made to retreat into the shadows, but a hand shot out and snatched him by the wrist. A soldier in black fatigues and a machine gun strapped to his hip pulled Bobby from his concealment. "What are you two doing back there?"

CHAPTER EIGHT

Bobby's brain spun wildly. He didn't recognize the soldier, or any of the kids, but the man leading the group wore a navy-blue suit, dark tie, wingtips, and a constipated expression. Thinking back to Simpkins' attire during their fieldtrip at the Jade Academy, Bobby wondered if any of the Core's agents dressed for the occasion, or if they all had a penchant for looking as ridiculous as possible.

"What are you two doing over here?" the soldier repeated. "You had exactly two minutes to go to the bathroom. Time's up, now get back over there with the others."

The man flipped the safety on his M-4 assault rifle, waiting for them to comply. Jinx stared at Bobby, his eyes pleading for guidance. Recognizing the hopelessness of their situation, Bobby gestured to his cousin. "Come on. Let's get back over there with the rest of our group."

Bobby took Jinx's hand and drudged towards the other kids, none of whom seemed to notice the sudden additions to their ranks. A mixed group of over a dozen girls and boys, the other children kept their heads down, their eyes at their feet, evidently afraid to make eye contact.

"I swear, if it were up to me, I'd let the whole lot of you run off into the woods. Nasty shock that would be," said the agent in the navy-blue suit. "Maybe then you'd learn to follow instructions."

"We've got to slip away and report back to Chief," Jinx whispered.

"I know," said Bobby, "but that guy has a gun. Besides, I'm not sure I can find the log again. It's dense in those bushes."

"Let's go," said the agent. "Head back to the temple. Yard time is over for today."

The boys had no choice but to fall in with the other kids as they crossed to the steps and descended to the lower courtyard. Up ahead, the pyramid loomed larger and larger until it felt as if it would swallow them whole.

Bobby didn't see the entrance until they were nearly on top of it. The gap between unadorned blocks near the far-left corner was so inconspicuous as to be nearly invisible. *Most likely a service entrance for the clergy and staff,* Bobby told himself.

Neither he nor Jinx had time to think about the temple's original use as the limestone passage doglegged to the right, dumping them into a much larger and broader corridor. With both the agent and armed guards leading the group from the front, Bobby grabbed Jinx's shirtsleeve to slow him down. With luck they could linger towards the back and slip away, making their way up the terraces and into the jungle before anyone noticed they were gone.

Then he spotted the soldiers standing on either side of the doorway behind them. With a sigh of disappointment, he let go of Jinx's arm and trudged after the rest of the group. They might not have noticed two extra kids coming in, but they would most certainly notice them trying to leave.

* * *

The central chamber of the ancient Mayan pyramid was so vast that Bobby could barely see across to the far side. All throughout, thick pillars supported a high-vaulted ceiling, while elaborate red, white, and green murals decorated plaster-covered limestone walls. It wasn't the pillars or walls that captivated Bobby's attention, it was what lay within: kids, hundreds upon hundreds of kids.

Bobby smiled wide and hugged Jinx. "We did it! We found the kids from the Jade Academy." He gazed out over the crowd, recognizing the face of a young boy over here, an older girl over there. On cots and rugs, sleeping bags and blankets, children filled the entire chamber.

It reminded Bobby of the homeless shelter where he and his mother had helped feed the needy and, in a way, he supposed that's exactly what this was. Here were all the refugees from the academy with no place to go, no one who knew they were here, or even that they were missing, except him and Jinx.

One of the guards stationed inside the door noticed the two of them staring out over the mass of bodies. "Go on," the man said. "Get back to your places. You know the rules, no standing around in the doorways."

Gripping Jinx's hand tight, Bobby waded into the sea of children. Some sat in groups of three or four, chatting or playing with one another. Kids sat on cots or lay on rugs by themselves. Most stared wordlessly as Bobby and Jinx passed by.

Despite the chamber's size, the entire space was packed. When no other path lay open, the boys picked their way through makeshift camps stuffed with kids in sleeping bags or wrapped in blankets. They passed a young girl in a pink polka dot dress. Curled in a ball, she clutched a battered doll that looked startlingly like her. The girl watched them through aqua eyes brimming with tears.

"I recognize her," said Jinx, "Her name is Anastasia; eight years old, from St. Petersburg. She was brought to the academy a few days before it collapsed. Probably didn't even have time to make friends yet."

Bobby knelt beside the girl, brushing back a dirty blonde pigtail to stroke her forehead. "It's okay," he said. "Everything is going to be okay." The girl made no reply, turned her face deeper into the pillow, and began to wail in earnest. Bobby straightened up, afraid the guards might have taken notice. Sullen faces near the door showed not the slightest bit of interest. Bobby and Jinx hurried on.

They searched for what felt like hours, picking their way across half the chamber before shouts broke out from off to their left. Bobby barely had time to turn before Lily threw herself into his arms. Long copper hair flew in his face as she squealed and hugged him close. "Goodness gracious! Where have you two been?" she cried. Her voice carried a touch of reproach, but her bright eyes shined with delight.

Per usual, Trevor and Jacob followed close behind. Much taller and more athletic, Trevor reached them first, with the short, stocky Jacob hustling to catch up.

"'Sup bro. Good to see you." Trevor slapped hands with Bobby and wiped a tangle of twisted braids off his forehead. The ebony teen wore board shorts and a pastel Hawaiian shirt that made him look like a tacky American tourist.

"Jinx!" Jacob scooped up his friend and spun him around. "I missed you, Nerd Boy." The fiery redhead had on dark jeans and a bright orange shirt with a picture of a hamburger on it that said "Eat Me."

"Yo, where you been?" asked Trevor. "We looked everywhere. Thought you were buried in the mines or something."

Thick emotion choked Bobby's throat. It wasn't until Lily gave him a playful punch on the arm that he broke into laughter. "For heaven's sake, Bobby, don't ever disappear like that again." she chided. "The same goes for you, Jinxy." She wore a green print dress with white flowers and a matching ribbon in her hair. Always with a sunny disposition, she looked beautiful despite the circumstances.

"So, where the hell have you been all this time?" said Jacob.

As Bobby and Jinx told the story of what had happened since they were separated in the archives below the Jade Academy, Lily led the way to a small space up against the back wall where Lily, Trevor, and Jacob had set up camp. A canvas tent sat beside a flannel bedroll, providing some modicum of privacy in the otherwise wide-open hall.

The three were dumbstruck as Bobby told them about the secret lab he and Jinx found in the jade mines. They were even more amazed when Jinx regaled them with the story of how he and Bobby had located the Spine of the World, narrowly escaping right before the tunnel's collapse.

"The Eagle's Nest sounds sick," said Trevor. "I'd love to check it out."

"I'd love to show it to you," said Bobby, "but right now we're stuck here same as you guys. I'm sure we can find the hollow log again if we manage to escape. So far I haven't seen any way of getting past the guards."

"Believe me, we've tried," said Jacob. "Lily pretended to faint while I slipped past the guards into the hallway. Fecking hell, I didn't get more than a few yards before four other guards hauled me back. Jerks took both of our blankets and food for two days after that."

"Any idea what they want?" said Jinx. "I mean, why bring everyone to an ancient temple in the middle of nowhere? Anyplace is more convenient than this place."

"Goodness knows they want to keep our existence a secret," said Lily. "Even when we were put on planes and buses to be brought here, they kept us isolated. I assumed they were worried about kids trying to escape."

"That still doesn't explain why here," said Jinx. "There are plenty of isolated places that don't involve treks into the middle of the world's largest jungle."

"Isn't it obvious?" asked Jacob. "The bastards are looking for something."

Jinx arched an eyebrow in surprise. "What do you mean?"

"From what we can tell, this was a Core base of operations before we arrived. They've got all sorts of machines on the lower levels."

"How do you know that?" asked Jinx.

"Cuz you can hear the damn generators," cursed Jacob, "like sucking mosquitos buzzing in the middle of the night."

"That's not all," said Trevor. "Older students have been taken away and haven't returned. Word is that they're being used somehow."

"Speaking of older students," said Jinx. "Has anyone seen my sister?" He dropped his gaze. Last time he'd seen Ashley, she and her goons had attacked them in the archives.

Jacob and Lily averted their eyes.

"What is it? Is something wrong?" asked Jinx.

It was Trevor who finally answered. "Man, you gotta understand. Things have been crazy ever since the academy's collapsed. A lot of peeps are still missing. We haven't had time to—"

Jinx glared at his friends. "I know you guys don't like her. Hell, I don't like her most of the time, but she's my sister."

"Honest to goodness, it's not that," said Lily. "It's just that she—"

A squad of soldiers interrupted whatever Lily had been about to say. A huge, bald man with a flat nose and forearms the size of Bobby's thighs planted a meat hook on Bobby's shoulder.

"You five, come with us," said the burly guard.

Lily lowered her head and whispered, "That's Sandman, captain of the guards. I've heard stories of what he does to kids who don't behave."

The kids were denied further discussion as the soldiers marched them from the refugee hall to a long corridor on the far end. From there, they went up a series of shadowy stairs and dim corridors to a wide doorway with a jagged archway that reminded Bobby of a gaping maw. The narrow room beyond had a ceiling that tapered towards the back, giving the impression of having stepped into a beast's mouth.

In the middle, where the throat would have been, a polished steel table gleamed like a quicksilver tongue. Dressed all in white, Willy the Creep sat on the right with an albino monkey perched on his shoulder. The bizarre primate hissed and bared her teeth as Bobby and his friends entered the room. Bobby barely noticed, his attention focused entirely on the person at the middle of the table.

Ashley sat in the deepest, darkest part of the beast's throat. Her hands were folded in front of her, and a smug grin was plastered across her face.

CHAPTER NINE

Ashley stretched her arms out wide and stood. Her icy smile filled the air with a haughty chill. "Look what we have here. They told me they'd checked everyone, but I knew you had to be here somewhere. We all knew none of you had the brains to escape or the decency to die back at the academy."

She spoke to all of them, but her eyes were locked on Bobby, who stifled a reply. "That is except for you, little brother," she said, shifting her glare to Jinx. "Of course, I'm glad to see you're safe. The Tex-Mex twins weren't so lucky." Her gaze shifted to the rest of the group. "Still hanging out with these losers, I see. Not even injured a little bit? How unfortunate." Trevor shrugged but Lily stiffened as Jacob balled his hands into fists.

Jinx stared back at his older sister. "What's going on here? Why does it look like you're in charge?"

"Someone had to step in and organize these brats," said Ashley. "No one has seen mother dearest since the academy's collapse. I assume you two had something to do with that."

An awkward silence filled the room as Bobby and Jinx struggled for a suitable reply. Bobby lifted his gaze to meet his cousin's cold stare. "I'm sorry, Ashley, but your mother didn't make it. She tried to compel Jinx to obey her and brought the entire mountain down on herself."

Anger flared in Ashley's eyes. She placed her hands on the table and appeared ready to scream. Then her shoulders relaxed as if a terrible weight had been lifted. The captain of the Core guards, Sandman, coughed loudly and stepped forward. "What are your instructions, sir?" he asked Ashley. "Are these cadets to be tested?"

Jacob snickered. "We're not part of your creepy little army, you sucking psychopath."

Sandman crossed the distance in two strides, grabbed Jacob by the collar, and hoisted him off the ground. Jacob tugged at his captor's arms, but Sandman's massive biceps didn't budge. With measured precision, he lifted Jacob until their eyes were level. "As long as you're under my command, you are what I say you are. Got it?"

"That's enough," snapped Ashley. "We don't have time for this." She stared off into the distance at some message only she could see.

Sandman dropped Jacob and stepped back. "Sir, yes sir." The room fell silent, waiting for Ashley's command.

"The Creep thinks you should send them all," said Willy. The ghostly monkey on his shoulder leapt onto the table and began screeching. "Yes, Mercy likes that," crooned Willy. His bizarre pet howled and pounded her fists on the table. "Mercy wants them all to be tested."

Bobby whispered to friends. "Since when did Willy start referring to himself in the third person?"

Lily sighed. "Poor soul, Siphon's death really unhinged him."

"Freak was always one dancing monkey short of a circus," quipped Jacob.

Trevor chuckled. "Seriously, not anymore."

Ashley's eyes snapped into focus as if seeing them for the first time. "Just those two," she said gesturing to Trevor and Bobby. "Testing my brother is beyond pointless. The others are nearly as inept. Throw them back with the rest." She paused, eyeing her brother. "Unless you've had a change of heart? You could be a valuable asset to our work here."

Jinx turned pale. "No one's going anywhere,'" said Jacob. "I don't know what you jerk wads did to be sitting here while the rest of us are being held prisoners down below, but we're not having it."

Trevor put his back against Jacob's. Together, they turned to the guards.

Ashley watched them coolly, a smirk tickling the corner of her mouth. She raised her hands and Bobby felt the air hum with power unlike anything he'd felt since the headmistress's meltdown back in the mines.

"You're not the only ones who have learned a thing or two since we last met," said Ashley, the cocky grin now on full display. "The Core has taught me more in the past few months than I learned in years at the academy."

Heat stung Bobby's eyes as he stepped next to his friends. Together they formed a wall, ready to face whatever Ashley had in store for them.

"Halt!" commanded Sandman. The captain of the guard stepped between them, blocking the two parties with his bullish mass. Over his shoulder, he said, "I have strict instructions from the Scarlet Seer that the cadets are not to be harmed without authorization."

Ashley glowered at him and lowered her hand. The intense heat dissipated almost as quickly as it had risen. "Fine, then you deal with it."

Sandman turned towards Bobby and his friends. "Roger that." He lifted his arms and a new, very different heat arose. This one started inside Bobby's head, its fuzzy warmth making it difficult to think. His eyelids grew heavy as he staggered on his feet. Beside him, Jinx slumped to the floor and began to snore. A moment later, Lily lay down and closed her eyes, followed soon after by Jacob and Trevor.

Bobby lasted only a few seconds longer. Unable to keep his legs stiff, he dropped to the ground next to his friends. His eyelids drooped. The last thing he saw was Mercy climbing on top of Trevor's prone form, pounding her chest, and howling with all her might.

* * *

Chief Benson Eagleheart was not a man who worried easily. Among the lessons he'd learned during his six decades on the earth was that needless worry drained one's energy, energy that was better directed toward other endeavors.

Yet Chief could not help but worry under the circumstances. Bobby and Jinx had been gone well past the rendezvous deadline.

There could be no doubt something unexpected had occurred on the other side of the electric fence.

He cursed himself for allowing the situation to occur in the first place. He should have been better prepared. Upon discovering the temple and its defensive perimeter, he should have taken the boys back to town, called for one of his lieutenants to bring a team, and waited. He'd wanted more information, and his gut had told him the boys could handle the situation. Their time spent at the Eagle's Nest revealed a remarkable capacity not only to succeed but to excel at whatever task they were given. If there was any lesson he knew better than the need to conquer fear, it was to always trust his gut.

The natives didn't seem to know either of these lessons. The moment Bobby and Jinx disappeared into the hollow log, Itzamna and his band of hunters paced nonstop, combed the nearby jungle, and climbed trees in an effort to see what transpired on the other side.

Chief remained seated near the log, eyes closed in a semi-meditative trance. Something affected his ability to sense beyond the fence. Perhaps it was the ambient electricity. Perhaps it was something more occult. Either way, he didn't need a sixth sense to tell him to act before things got out of hand.

Shaking his head, Chief rose and went to find Itzamna. Extending his hands outstretched, palms open, Chief communed with the village leader, projecting a mental image of the village into the shaman's mind. Itzamna nodded his understanding and turned to the nearest hunter. Within moments, the warriors had assembled. Itzamna gave the instruction, and they departed, heading back to the village.

* * *

The fog lifted slowly. Unable to move his arms or legs, Bobby thought perhaps he'd been paralyzed. Only after several failed attempts to rise did he realized he was strapped to a table. Images of stainless-steel scalpels and masked men in surgical gowns came unbidden to mind.

Thankfully, he felt the receding effects of Sandman's sleep mojo, but not the dull ache or numbness indicative of an operation. Before he had a chance to investigate further, a door behind him slid open and two people walked in.

Pretending to be asleep, Bobby cracked his eyes open just enough to spy on whoever had entered the room. The two men passed a gurney and came to stand at a row of cabinets near Bobby's feet. Bobby stifled a scream. Even with their backs to him, he instantly recognized the two men.

Simpkins was gaunt and sallow. His pinstriped suit hung like an oversized football jersey on his skeletal frame. Hayward looked like he barely fit into his, with rolls of fat protruding from atop his wide collar.

Both men wore the same retro seventies suits as the last time he'd seen them: wide-lapelled blazers with narrow ties, bell-bottomed pants, and black wingtips. The two men were busy talking. Neither man turned as they set about organizing an array of medical devices taken from the cabinet.

"I still say she should let me do it," said Hayward. "We both know I'd do a better job than that simpleton in there."

"You'd enjoy it too much," replied Simpkins. "Besides, you're not immune if one of them should pass the test. You don't want the ordeal of being birthed again so soon, do you? I know I don't."

These last words rattled around inside Bobby's head. *Birthed again? What the hell did that mean?*

"Don't make me laugh," said Hayward. "None of these punks have the juice to hurt me. Without full training they're just pigs to the slaughter. Not that I care, mind you, but if you'd just let me push them a bit—"

"Enough," said Simpkins, not angrily. "The Scarlet Seer commands and so we obey. Or have you already forgotten what happened the last time you decided to take matters into your own hands?"

"I remember. And I remember the brat who caused it."

Walking to a nearby medical fridge, Simpkins extracted a sickly green-colored vial from a long row of similar ampoules. Affixing the tube to a long syringe, he turned to Bobby.

* * *

A moment of absolute silence permeated the room. Bobby lay on his back, with his arms strapped to his sides. His eyes were wide, staring at the two former agents from the Jade Academy.

"Well, what do we have here?" said Hayward with a grin just as gap-toothed and laden with malice as ever. In fact, everything about the obese sadist looked exactly the same, from the triple chins to the thin wisps of hair on his shiny bulbous head.

Simpkins, on the other hand, looked far different. His previously sallow cheeks had sunk even further, drawing his face so tight that he looked like a living skull covered in paper mâché. His greasy black hair seemed to have crawled up his forehead a good inch, pulling the remaining flesh along with it. His eyes remained the same however: dead pools devoid of all emotion except for the lucid insanity Bobby had witnessed so vividly the last time they were alone.

"Where did you come from?" said Simpkins with something akin to surprise. "I triple checked the roster when we vacated the academy."

"I know I would have remembered," said Hayward.

"I guess you two really are as stupid as you are ugly," said Bobby.

Simpkins pressed the plunger on the syringe until green goo oozed out the tip. "And yet you're the one strapped to the table."

Hayward rubbed his hands together. "Let's handle this one ourselves. We owe him. I owe him. We can tell the others there was an accident; that he responded violently to the treatment and we were unable to save him."

"And risk the mistress finding out?"

Hayward gave an involuntary shudder. "You're right. Even I'm not that crazy."

"There's something about that woman," said Simpkins.

"A right peach, that one," agreed Hayward. "She burrowed into my brain 'til I was bleeding out my ears."

"Obviously, how she got her name," explained Simpkins.

Bobby suppressed an involuntary shudder. "She sounds almost as delightful as you two."

Hayward's lips curled up into a snarl. "I hope you get a chance to speak to the Seer with that tongue. She'll have blood pouring out your teeth."

Simpkins harrumphed. "Unfortunately, you'll have to survive the test first. Something I doubt you'll manage."

Bobby had no reply as Hayward grabbed his hair and yanked his head back. He felt a sharp sting as Simpkins plunged the syringe deep into his neck, then a warm sensation as the contents flooded his bloodstream. Setting aside the syringe, Simpkins held him while Hayward undid his restraints. Bobby tried to break free, but Simpkins's grip was like iron. Hayward grasped his other arm and together the two agents hoisted Bobby onto his feet.

Dragging him across the room, Simpkins opened a door and kicked it open. Then, before Bobby had a chance to react, the two agents shoved him through and slammed the door behind him.

CHAPTER TEN

L ike stepping off a cliff, the floor disappeared as Bobby went through the door. He fell hard, landing ten feet below on a straw pallet. Scrambling to his feet, he surveyed his surroundings. He stood in a circular stone room that resembled the bottom of a well, bare except for the straw on the floor. The only way in or out was a large iron gate on the far side.

For over a minute he stood there, alone in the ring. Then from behind the gate he heard Hayward shouting, followed by a high-pitched screech. At first, he thought the screech was the gate's metal crank as it began to ratchet up. Then the sound changed, becoming the wail of someone in terrible pain.

From the shadows of the gate, a figure emerged. Bobby's breath caught in his lungs. It was the biggest man he'd ever seen. Nearly seven feet tall, he had to duck under the gate even as he turned sideways to fit through.

The giant straightened. Dozens of red burns, black scars, and yellow-purple bruises covered a massive frame. On his face, the giant wore a brown leather mask with air holes poked in the mouth and nose. Only his eyes and the top of his head were exposed. Splotches of straw-colored hair stuck out the top, as if someone had randomly torn out clumps with their fists.

The giant took a step toward him and Bobby retreated until his back hit the wall. He didn't know the first thing about hand-to-hand combat. Come to think of it, no one at the Jade Academy had even tried to teach him. And yet many of them had already been tested. That got him thinking.

His ruminations were short lived. With a wild yell, the giant threw out his arms and rushed at him. Bobby stumbled backwards, tripping on the edge of the straw pallet that had broken his fall moments before. The giant missed him by inches. Plowing through the empty air, he slammed into the wall.

"He's in rare form today," observed Simpkins from behind the gate.

"Like a rodeo bull with his balls on a leash!" laughed Hayward. "Guess I got him a little riled up," he shouted to Bobby. "Sorry about that!"

The giant rushed at him again. This time Bobby was ready. Diving to the side, he rolled out of the way. They circled each other. The giant feigned, looking for an opening. Thankfully, he was nearly as slow as he was big. Bobby sidestepped easily. The giant lunged again, but Bobby slipped out of reach.

The giant tried several more times, but Bobby moved too quickly. Frustrated, the giant threw back his head and roared, "SLAAAAAAB!"

Bobby ducked out of the way as the giant tried to grab him again. Where had he heard that name before? He was still circling the room, maintaining as much distance as possible when it hit him: the kid from the Jade Academy, the one who had injured Hayward and caused the damage in the forest. The one with the Omega gene…

Just like that, Bobby understood the purpose of the test. He also knew he had no chance of winning. He had no powers, no abilities, nothing that could stop Slab or even slow him down. Slab's special ability was his complete immunity to other people's powers.

That left Bobby in a predicament.

"Jimmy? Jimmy Thompson, right?" Bobby watched the giant pause as he spoke his name. "I know who you are. Your name's not Slab, it's Jimmy. You were a student at the Jade Academy, just like me."

The giant straightened up from his poised crouch, studying him with curious eyes. Bobby kept talking, repeating his name. Slowly the giant's hands unclenched, his arms dangling limply at his sides.

"You were a good kid, quiet, thoughtful. You don't have to do this."

As he spoke, Bobby pictured the connection he made with the deer in the meadow back at the Eagle's Nest. Reaching out with his thoughts, he tried to gently brush Jimmy's mind. Instead he felt… nothing. Slab stood there, head cocked to one side. Bobby tried again, desperate to feel something, anything at all. He might as well have been trying to connect with the empty air.

From behind the gate, Hayward yelled into the arena. "What are you doing, you stupid ox? Do as you're told, or I'll punish you so hard you'll be pissing blood for weeks."

Pale eyes that had been distant and plaintive snapped into focus. Slab clenched his fists and roared, then dove at Bobby with renewed fervor.

Bobby dove out of the way in time, suffering a stab of despair as Slab hurled past him only to wheel back around a split second later. His gambit had failed. This left Bobby only one option. The next time Slab rushed at him, Bobby made no attempt to move. Instead, he simply raised his arms and waited.

* * *

The atmosphere at the village turned cloudy when the hunting party returned. Word spread faster than floodwater that the boys were missing. Villagers murmured and gathered around Chief. Women and children brought baskets full of food, talismans of bone, and carved figurines.

It didn't take communing with Itzamna to know the natives believed Bobby and Jinx to be gone for good, lost to the Spirit Men of the temple. The gifts were their way of offering condolences. Of course, there was very little chance Bobby and Jinx were actually dead. Most likely they'd simply been taken captive.

Chief thought about trying to explain this but decided against it. He'd tried to describe electricity and technology to Itzamna, but the concepts were too foreign. All he got in return were confused images of lightning storms and angry gods.

What Chief needed wasn't so much their understanding as their patience. If they stayed away from the temple, he could handle the situation—call in a team and properly investigate. However, if Itzamna or one of the others decided to attack the temple, there was no telling what might happen.

Checking the time on his tactical wristwatch, Chief retreated to the small hut he'd been given by Itzamna for personal use. Assuming the lotus position, he took a moment to center himself, and then wrapped his chi around him like a cocoon. Once satisfied that he was properly shielded, he sent a tight beam of anima down to wrap around the core of the earth. Then he waited.

If any of his people were at the Eagle's Nest, he would sense their presence and communicate telepathically. He lingered for twenty minutes, but no other presence appeared. That meant that not only were Jeremiah and Cassandra still out searching for Melody, but his own operatives were similarly engaged.

Withdrawing from his meditative state, Chief left the hut and went to find Itzamna. He didn't want to do what came next but had no choice. Sharing his thoughts with the shaman, Chief showed images of himself returning to the city where he would have access to communications, including a backup satellite phone.

As expected, the shaman returned confused images of a village, larger and shrouded in fog, a clear indication he failed to grasp the concept of a city or civilization.

Disappointed but not surprised, Chief switched to the shaman's spoken language, a mix of ancient Mayan and the more recent Ch'orti dialect, but again failed to properly convey his intention. Out of options, he settled for addressing all the warriors, asking them to remain calm and wait, stating repeatedly the temple was bad and they needed to stay away and not go near it under any circumstances until he returned.

As he gathered his pack and prepared to strike out into El Muerte Verde, Chief had an uneasy feeling. Bad things were coming. The best he could hope for was a quick journey so he could reach the outside world and call for backup.

* * *

The impact wasn't as bad as Bobby expected. With his monstrous mitts, Slab caught Bobby by the front of his shirt and hoisted him off his feet. It hurt when the giant wrapped his arms around Bobby and squeezed, but the pressure was bearable, at least for the moment.

Arms pinned up over his shoulders, Bobby placed his hands on Slab's head, searching for exposed skin. The eye slits were too small. The thick leather mask covered everything else: mouth, nose, even his ears. Bobby slid one hand up to the top of Slab's head, the other to his thick, bulging neck.

Nothing.

Even with physical contact Bobby couldn't sense a damn thing: no energy, no emotion, not even the basic spark of life. It was as if the giant were dead inside…except for the eyes. Bobby stared into Slab's pale eyes, the color of a perfect, cloudless sky. *So innocent and pure,* he thought. Yet raw emotion—anger and pain, hate and fury—lurked behind that childlike gaze.

Slab tightened his grip. Bobby screamed in protest as the air fled his lungs.

"Fight!" demanded Slab. Bobby kept his palms flat, refusing to dig his nails into Slab's flesh or yank on his hair. He just stared into the giant's eyes.

Slab bounced Bobby on his chest and squeezed tighter. "Fight me!"

Bobby blinked back tears as his ribs threatened to crack. Unable to breathe, his vision blurred. His body ached from lack of oxygen… everything except for his hands. Where his fingers rested on Slab's head and neck, Bobby felt better, almost as if the giant's skin somehow absorbed the pain.

Bobby probed deeper with his hands, not digging or scratching, but pushing into the giant's head and neck. Slab's grip relaxed enough for Bobby to draw a ragged breath. Clearly this was a tactic the giant was not expecting.

Pinching his fingers, Bobby felt a gossamer film coating Slab's skin. This was what shielded Jimmy from other people's anima, a thin veneer that clung to the surface of his skin, protecting him from all attempts to invade his senses.

Bringing both hands up to Slab's head, Bobby began to rub at a spot in the middle of Slab's forehead, just above the mask. The giant held tight but ceased trying to crack his ribs. Instead, he held Bobby's gaze as Bobby rubbed and rubbed at his forehead.

"You go now?" asked Slab, a plaintive cry in those baby blue eyes.

"No more pain," said Bobby softly. Then he cocked his head back and head-butted Slab as hard as he could, right on the forehead.

Instantly, Slab relaxed his grip. Bobby slipped from his arms, slumping to the ground to cradle his throbbing ribs. He stared at his hands. They looked bigger and thicker than he remembered, almost as if they belonged to someone else.

He was inside Slab's mind, experiencing his thoughts and memories from a day in the woods back at the academy. There had been a rabbit in those hands. He'd caught a hare in the woods and had been holding it. *"Can I keep it?"*

He heard himself say the words aloud, but they weren't his words. Someone took the rabbit from him. He watched as cruel hands lifted the delicate creature with its soft brown fur and floppy ears in front of his face. Then the cruel hands twisted the poor creature until its head touched its short fluffy tail.

Bobby screamed. He screamed and screamed, but it was not his scream. There was a bright light, a blinding haze of anger and pain. The cruel hands that had twisted the hare lay on the ground, unmoving. Others also lay unmoving, and so he did as well.

Bobby lay down in the fighting pit next to Slab. He lay there until people came and lifted him up. They carried him from the ring and lay him down on a table. They strapped him down so he couldn't move, just like they had done to Slab long ago.

They asked him questions, just like back then. "How did you do that? Do you feel different? Can you do it again?" He made no reply. They poked him with needles. He didn't flinch. Then the man with the cruel hands came in. It was Hayward, the man who had twisted the beautiful creature and made it be still.

Bobby smiled. Back then, Slab had made Hayward be still as well. Except Hayward had returned and hurt him. They cut Slab and burned him and did all sorts of things to try to make him explain the bright light. He resisted until the pain became too great to bear. The bright light came, and he made the hands pay.

They paid him back. More cuts and bruises and burns all over his body. Always the cruel hands hurting him. The scars all over his body weren't from fighting in the pit. They were from Hayward, the cruel man who'd tortured him.

Bobby screamed again. This time the pain was definitely his own.

CHAPTER ELEVEN

The sleeping bag outside Lily's tent belonged to Trevor, but Jinx used it now that his friend was gone. The main chamber was quiet. Jacob was off somewhere with Mikey Blanchert scheming up a new escape plan. Lily was inside the tent supposedly napping, but Jinx could hear the sobs. Bobby and Trevor being taken had hit her hard.

That left Jinx. He sat alone on the navy-blue bedroll and picked at a loose thread in the sleeping bag's gray flannel lining. In his other hand, he held a field mouse. He'd befriended the tiny creature with a piece of bread left over from lunch. The mouse rubbed against his thumb. Jinx gave it a halfhearted smile.

He guessed it was close to early evening. In the dim half-light of the vast hall, there was no way to know for sure. Most of the kids had already gone to the makeshift mess hall a few rooms down, under guard, of course. Everything they did was under the watchful eyes of the gun-wielding Core guards and the suit-wearing agents.

Now most of the nearly four hundred kids lay on their pallets or talked in hushed voices. According to Lily, it had been like this for weeks: kids taken outside in shifts to use the bathroom and stretch their legs, back to the main hall, kids taken in shifts to eat, back to the main hall, kids taken outside before it got dark to use the bathroom again.

Occasionally guards patrolled the room itself, but mostly they stayed by the doors. When they did comb the room, it was never good. Sometimes fights broke out among the kids. In those cases, the guards took everyone involved. Most were never seen again. Sometimes they took a kid who hadn't done anything. Those times were the worst. If guards came into the room when it was calm, you knew someone was going to be taken.

Jinx had a sinking feeling as he spotted Slab making his way across the room. He'd seen the giant before, they all had. Usually he came with the guards to pick up a group or older boy they thought might put up a fight. Jinx rubbed his chin. Slab was alone this time.

Jinx watched as the giant picked his way through the crowd. The refugees from the academy scurried out of his way like mice before a hungry cat. Slab's head swung back and forth scanning faces, his own unreadable behind the battered leather mask.

Jacob slipped up next to Jinx and took a seat. "What's Mad Max doing here?" he asked, nodding towards the giant.

"No idea. Just keep your head down and maybe he'll—"

Slab changed courses and headed straight for them. Lily poked her head out of the tent, rubbing her puffy eyes as she took in the scene. "What's going on?"

"Go back inside, Lil. Trevor wouldn't want you to—" Jacob tried to shove her back inside and draw the tent flap, but it was too late. A colossal shadow fell across the tent. The mouse in Jinx's palm squeaked as it jumped down and scurried away. The giant towered over them.

"Friends."

The word hung in the air like a death sentence. Then the giant plopped down on Jinx's sleeping bag, nearly crushing Lily's canvas tent in the process.

"What the hell, man?" Jacob shot to his feet. "We don't want to be your friends!"

The giant cocked his head to the side. "Friends," he repeated, more insistent. Then he grasped his head in both hands and shook it from side to side. The others watched, fascinated, as the giant seemed to struggle with himself.

He pointed at each of them in turn. "Jacob. Jinx. Lily. Bobby. Friends."

Jacob looked around. "What the hell are you on about? Bobby isn't here. Neither is Trevor. Your people took them. So, no, we don't want to be your friend. I don't care how big you are. Get outta' here before I kick your teeth in."

Slab shook his head, clearly bewildered by this response. He stood up as awkwardly as he'd sat. Backing up, he stepped on a corner of the tent, snapping the pole with a loud crack. Head slumped and shoulders slouched, he turned to go.

"Wait, what about Trevor?" said Lily. "For goodness sake, if you know anything about him or Bobby..."

The giant lifted his chin a fraction of an inch. "Don't know Trevor," he mumbled.

"You mean you don't know him at all, or you don't know where they've taken him?"

"Where they've taken him," echoed the giant.

"What about Bobby?" asked Jinx. "Do you know where he is?"

The giant lifted his head, reanimated. "I take you! I take you to friend."

Jacob was on his feet now and in the giant's face, or more accurately, in his chest. "We're not going anywhere with you, freak," he said, herding Jinx and Lily toward the broken tent. "You want to do to us what you've done to all the kids." Placing himself before the tent flap, he spread his feet and crossed his arms. "Not gonna happen."

The giant shrugged and turned to leave. The outburst had already drawn the attention of the guards. Three gun-wielding soldiers left their posts and headed to the small gathering.

"For Pete's sake, Jacob," said Lily. "Maybe we could have gotten him to tell us where they are, but you had to go and piss off the guards."

The lead guard trampled the already battered tent as he made his way to the giant. "Slab, what's going on here?"

"I take them," said the giant, gesturing towards Jinx and his companions.

The lead guard's heavy brow furrowed. "Did the Scarlet Seer command you to get more students? Why didn't she notify us?"

Slab bobbed his head. "Yes, yes. The Scarlet Seer commands."

"Hey, wait a minute," said Jacob. "That's not what he—"

From behind the tent flap, Lily stepped on Jacob's foot. "He said he was gonna take us to get extra blankets for the others," she said.

The guard balked for a moment, then broached a huge smirk. With a wink for Slab, he said, "Extra blankets? Sure. And more food too," he said with a laugh. "Just like all the others."

"Goodness me, we better get going," said Lily, shoving Jacob forward as she grabbed hold of Jinx's arm and pulled him along. "Let's all follow the nice friendly giant."

"The Scarlet Seer commands," parroted Slab.

"Yes, right, we'd best be off," said Jinx, finally catching on. "We wouldn't want to keep the Scarlet Seer waiting."

Slab turned toward the far exit and began picking his way through the crowd, many of whom had gathered around to watch the scene. Kids stood frozen in place, too dumbstruck by the sight of Jinx, Jacob, and Lily being taken from their midst to move out of the way. Slab didn't shove any of the kids or use his hands. His sheer bulk cleared a path.

Jinx spotted Anastasia, the young girl in the polka dot dress he'd seen his first night here. She ran up to them and grabbed Jinx's sleeve.

"Please don't go," she begged.

"We're only going to get extra blankets," he said softly. "We'll be back soon, and we can share them with you, okay?"

The girl stepped back with a brave nod. "Promise you'll come back?"

"I promise," said Jinx in a voice far calmer than he felt. He might have told the girl they were coming back, but believing it himself was a whole other matter.

* * *

The guards watched Jinx the entire way as he and the others followed Slab to the far end of the hall. They continued the charade out in the corridor, where more guards stood watch. It wasn't until they navigated several turns to an empty hallway that Lily grabbed the giant's arm and yanked him into an alcove.

"Please tell me you're really taking us to Bobby."

Slab cocked his head to the side, seemingly confused by the question. "Bobby. Friends. We go now."

Jacob didn't budge. "If this is some kind of trick, some sick game to get us to come along without a fight, I'm gonna stick my foot so far up your ass you'll taste shoe leather."

Slab patted Jacob on his head like an owner might pet a dog. "You funny friend." He looked back and forth between the others. "We go now?"

"I told you, we're not friends, freak. And we're not going anywhere with you without proof—"

Jinx stepped in between. "Excuse us for just a moment, won't you?" He dragged Jacob and Lily off a ways.

In hushed tones, he spoke to the others, "I think Lily's right. We don't really have a choice at this point. If we go back in there, the guards will know something's up. They'll probably take us to Ashley and the others, or worse."

"So then let's ditch the Mad Max wannabe and find a way outta this place," said Jacob. "I mean, seriously, the dude's wearing a freakin' mask."

"And leave Trevor and Bobby?" said Lily. "For heaven's sake, even you're not that selfish."

"We can ditch the giant later and escape if it turns out he's trying to trick us," said Jinx. "For right now, he's our best chance of finding the others. Think about it: you've spent weeks trying to sneak out of that room. He walked us right past the guards. Hell, he can probably walk through this whole place without anyone batting an eyelash."

Jacob's face scrunched up as he thought that over. Finally, he spoke. "Okay, but if Slab shows any signs of deception, I'm taking him out. I don't care how big he is. I'll kick in his knee-caps so bad he'll have to learn to walk on his hands."

"Fair enough." Jinx turned to Slab. "We're ready. Lead us to Bobby."

CHAPTER TWELVE

The hemp ropes tying him to the table chafed his wrists and ankles, but that wasn't what bothered Bobby. What concerned him were the voices in his head. Originally just a single voice, a whole chorus of people now clamored away inside his skull as he lay immobile in the room where Simpkins and Hayward had left him after dragging him from the fighting pit. The voices called to him, begging him to do something, but they were too soft for him to hear what they wanted.

"Go away," he said, squeezing his eyes shut in a futile attempt to shut out the unwelcome intrusion.

The voices elevated, accompanied by a pounding noise that felt like a hammer banging on his inner eardrum. Twisting his arm painfully against the restraints, he thrust a hand into his pocket to grasp Itzamna's talisman. "Get out of my head!"

The voices quieted, all save one. Bobby recognized the spirit of the girl from Maximon's vision, Lingya. Her voice was too powerful to ignore. Wrapping his hands around the Hunhau idol, Bobby took a deep breath and tipped his head back.

"Go on then. Tell me your story."

***

What little food Lingya and Maximon had taken with them ran out in the first two days. By the time they reached the city, they had only their clothes, a handful of valueless personal items, and the skills they'd practiced since birth.

They took up shelter on the edge of the jungle; so far from the temple they could barely see the top of the pyramid in the distance. The area nearest the base was reserved for prayer and ceremony, with the first plateau housing the most powerful members of society. The next few tiers were home to middle-class people and upscale merchant shops: jewelers, weavers, and other artisans in demand by the wealthy. Beyond that were lower-class citizens, servants, and blue-collar tradesmen: blacksmiths, tanners, potters, and the like.

On the farthest outskirts lived the farmers, fisherman, and other peasants who worked the land to survive. They lived in teepees and huts cobbled from the surrounding forest. It was here that Maximon and Lingya lived when they first arrived, with virtually no protection against the predators that lurked in the jungle.

Using bone hooks Maximon had brought when they fled, he caught fish in the nearby rivers, which he then traded in the market for blankets and clothes. Gathering herbs by day, Lingya made poultices and tonics which she sold at night for food, a cook pot, and other supplies.

In time, they were able to afford an actual home, away from the edge of the jungle. Life was difficult but not unbearable, full of hard work and long hours, but also love. They spent many nights lost in each other's arms, dreaming and planning the life they were building with one another.

One day, Maximon noticed Lingya's belly had begun to swell. Elated at the expectation of their first child, the young couple redoubled their efforts. Maximon bought a canoe so he could travel farther from the heavily fished rivers surrounding the city. Lingya rented a booth in the market, garnering favor with the wealthy as her potions proved useful and effective.

With the baby's arrival only a few moons away, the city faced an increasing threat: the Spanish conquistadors and their allies. Every day, more and more tribesmen fled to the holy temple, bringing reports of death and destruction. Foreign warriors carrying strange weapons besieged the Mayan empire, spreading illnesses that killed as surely as any blade.

As the periphery of the Mayan civilization suffered and died, the heart of the city swelled until it was fit to burst. Major cities like theirs were overcrowded with people who had lost their homes, their friends, their families; the people with nowhere else to go. Maximon and Lingya didn't know it at the time, but the end of the Mayan empire had begun.

***

Something grabbed Bobby by the shoulders. He struggled to free himself as hands gripped the sides of his head and held him tight. "It's okay, Bobby. It's us."

He blinked a few times while Jinx, Lily, and Jacob came into focus. Then Slab came into sight, his massive frame dwarfing those of his friends. Bobby bucked up and down, trying to liberate his arms and legs. "Get away from them! You leave them alone!" he yelled.

Jacob cast a nervous glance at the hallway then closed the door. "My God, he's delirious," said Lily. "Whatever they did to him, he doesn't know lollipops from candy canes."

"It's okay Bobby." Jinx placed a reassuring hand on his chest. "We're here to rescue you."

Bobby's eyes rolled. His head banged against the table. "I heard his voice in my head, and then all these other voices…"

"Of course, you did," said Jacob. "The big oaf forgot which room you were in. We've been roaming the halls calling for you. I swear this place makes the Jade Academy look like a Tokyo apartment."

Bobby stared wild-eyed at Slab. "He's with you?"

Lily began unbuckling Bobby's straps. "Dear heavens. Not only did he march us out of the main hall right past the guards, but he led us here. Well, mostly."

The enormous man in the leather mask wrung his hands, his pale blue eyes fixated on Bobby with almost painful intensity. "Bobby. Friend," he said softly.

Bobby met his gaze and a torrent of memories came flooding back. "Torture," said Bobby. "They tortured me. They tortured…*you?*"

Lily freed his arms and Bobby raised his right hand, extending it toward Slab's face. Slab cocked his head to one side, and then bent down, allowing Bobby to place a palm on his masked cheek. Extending his other hand, Bobby reached around and unbuckled the clasp holding the mask. Slab raised two baseball glove-sized hands to his face. Tilting forward, he let the mask fall into his palms and straightened up.

Bobby wasn't sure what he'd expected, but this wasn't it. Slab's face was unblemished, with a button nose and soft, rosy cheeks. His eyes mirrored a kind, gentle expression. It was the face of a cherub.

"My goodness, Jimmy, what have they done to you?" Lily laid a hand on the giant's face. Her palm rested on his smooth cheek, but her fingertips stretched to his neck, where hideous scars and bruises had been inflicted upon unprotected flesh.

Slab reached up and cupped Lily's hand in his own. Then he gently pried her hand away and replaced his mask, securing the clasp in the back. "No Jimmy. Slab," he said. Then he turned to Bobby. "We go now."

"Wait," said Jacob. "We have to get Trev. He may be a freakin' pain in the ass, but I'm not leaving without him."

"Agreed," said Bobby. "Slab, do you know where Trevor is?"

"Bobby. Friend?" asked the giant.

"That's right, my friend, Trevor."

Slab headed for the door. "Follow. Trevor. Friend."

* * *

As it turned out, Slab knew exactly where Trevor was located. Their tall, lanky friend was back down a long hallway they'd passed on their way to find Bobby.

"Why the hell didn't you tell us he was here when we went by the first time?" complained Jacob.

Slab shrugged his massive shoulders. "You say go to Bobby."

Jacob smacked his forehead. "You big oaf," he said, but there was no venom in his voice.

It took a moment for Lily to unlock the door using a hairpin and a little concentration. On the other side, they found Trevor tied to a table, still unconscious. Lily rushed to him, letting out a soft moan as she took in her boyfriend's condition.

"This explains why he didn't answer when we went by calling for Bobby," said Jinx. Bobby and Lily unstrapped Trevor while Slab stood watch at the door. In less than a minute, they had Trevor free and wide awake thanks to an open-palmed slap by Jacob.

"Dude!" said Trevor, rubbing his jaw. "Who hit me?"

Jacob shrugged, unapologetic. "You were sleeping on the job. Besides, I owed you one."

Trevor cocked his head. "For?"

"For…something," Jacob finished feebly. "Screw you, Rasta man. Get your ass up and let's get the hell outta here."

Trevor struggled to stand on wobbly legs. Slab ducked into the room, the top of his head nearly scraping the doorframe. "We go now," he said.

"What do you think we're doing, you big oaf?" said Jacob. "This isn't a picnic!"

Trevor took a baby step and stumbled. "Dude, I'm seriously trippin' from whatever they gave me."

Lily grabbed his arm. "My gosh, you can barely walk."

"We go now," repeated Slab more urgently this time.

"For goodness' sake, he needs time to recover." Lily's voice was thick with worry.

Slab crossed the room in two strides and grabbed Trevor around the waist. With one hand, he hoisted the lanky teenager off the ground and tossed Trevor over his shoulder.

"Hey, wait up." Jinx hurried to catch up to the giant, who had already ducked back out into the hall. "What's the hurry?"

They only needed to step into the hall to discover the answer.

* * *

The look on Willy's face betrayed nothing as he came down the hall toward Bobby and his friends. Flanked by guards and dressed all in white like some debauched angel, Willy's eyes narrowed as he took in the scene. "What's going on here?" he said. For once, Mercy was not on his shoulder but pacing back and forth behind him.

Slab stepped in front of Willy, arms outstretched as if to ward off evil. "I take," said Slab. "Scarlet Seer commands."

The guards took a nervous step back. Willy held his ground. Behind him, his pet pounded the ground and screeched. "Mercy thinks you're lying," said Willy. "You all need to come with the Creep right now."

"Heavens," exclaimed Lily, "we don't want any trouble."

"Speak for yourself," said Jacob.

Willy craned his head to stare up at the towering Slab. "They told the Creep you were acting strange. The Creep might not be able to read you, but he can feel the nervousness from the others."

"Not nervous," said Slab. "Scared of Slab," he said, and thumped his chest.

"Possible, but what about him?" said Willy, gesturing to Bobby. "What's he doing out of his cell?"

Slab gave an incomprehensible high-pitched retort.

"The Creep knows what's going on," said Willy. He turned to Lily and Jacob. "You tricked this simpleton into helping you escape. Well, you failed."

Bobby pushed his friends behind him as the guards brandished their weapons. "Run!" he shouted over his shoulder.

Willy raised his hand, fingers extended. Bobby felt a wave of guilt wash over him, crushing his will to flee with tidal force. He was breaking rules, disobeying orders. There were others to think about, people who wanted and needed him here. Bobby lowered his head, confused and embarrassed by his own actions. Behind him, all of his friends stood frozen in place, staring at their feet as if they too were ashamed of their actions.

Willy gestured to a guard and pointed at Bobby. "Take that one back to his cell." To the other guard he ordered, "Return the others to the holding chamber. The Creep will take Trevor to the Scarlet Seer."

Nobody moved, not even Jacob, whose head hung the least. Instead, Slab reached out and grabbed the two guards, cupping their heads like grapefruits in his gigantic palms. Then he brought his hands together, slamming their skulls into one another. With a loud thunk, both men fell to the ground, unconscious and bleeding.

"I take!" bellowed Slab. Willy stumbled backwards and tripped over Mercy. He turned to run but Slab shot out a hand and caught him by the back of the collar. With his other hand, Slab swiped at Mercy. The nimble primate leapt out of reach. From ten yards down the hall, Mercy stood on her hind legs and howled. Then she turned and raced down the hall.

Meanwhile, Willy wriggled in Slab's iron grip. "Put me down, you big ox!" Slab lifted Willy until their faces were inches apart. For a second, Willy gazed deep into the pale blue eyes behind Slab's leather mask, then his eyes rolled up into their sockets and his head lolled to one side.

Jacob shook his head, as if waking from a dream. "What the hell just happened?"

"I'm not quite sure," said Jinx. "I think Willy tried to hypnotize Slab but it backfired."

"These two are hurt," said Lily, examining the unconscious guards.

"We can do something to help with the bleeding," said Bobby, "then we really should get going."

"Babe, are you okay to walk now?" asked Lily.

Trevor nodded slowly. "I'm not trippin' nearly as bad anymore."

"Probably best to drag the guards into the cell, tie them up, and gag them," said Jinx. "You know, so they can't escape or call for help."

Jacob paused, appraising Jinx. "Damn, Nerd Boy, I didn't know you had it in you."

The tasks were performed in under a minute. They used the same straps that had been used on Trevor, plus a few more from a drawer. When they were done, Bobby turned to the others. "So, where to now?"

They all shook their heads. "No idea," said Jinx. "Honestly, I'm not sure any of us expected to get this far."

"Well, we can't go back through the main hall," said Bobby.

"Oh dear!" exclaimed Lily. "We need another way out."

"Other place?" said Slab. The gentle giant had stood watching the hall as Bobby and his friends tied up Willy and the others.

"Lilster is right," said Jacob. "We need to get the hell outta here."

"I take other place," said Slab.

CHAPTER THIRTEEN

Deep within the temple, the machines thrummed like a continu-ous earthquake. Bobby felt the intense vibrations through the soles of his Vans as he followed Slab, alongside Jinx, Trevor, Lily, and Jacob. The shaking reminded Bobby of the Spine of the World, when the mountain had tumbled down around him. Everyone walked softly and talked in hushed voices. Still, there were no signs of Core guards or patrols, for which Bobby was grateful.

After ten minutes, they came to a huge circular room with a domed ceiling. In the middle, a large, decorative fountain sat on a broad dais. Bobby gawked at the vision before him. Tall, with a narrow base, the fountain appeared almost alive, with gems that glistened along its el-egant curves.

As he gazed upon the radiant splendor, the whispering voices re-turned. They sounded more real than before, not phantoms or figments, but actual voices inside his head. They called to him with promises, beckoning him to come and find them.

He took two steps toward the dais, so that he was level with the flut-ed rim. The crystal water pouring from the center rose three feet into the air, sending up an azure plume that sparkled like starlight before falling back into the bowl. High overhead, missing blocks in the ceiling created beams of sunlight that gave the room a golden aura.

As beautiful as it was, the voices didn't appear to be coming from the fountain. If anything, they seemed to be coming from somewhere below. Bobby tore his gaze from the shining cascades of crystal water and took in the rest of the room. An outer ring of pillars held ancient inscriptions, as did the circular walls. Alcoves provided space to either kneel and pray, or sit and observe the splendid scene.

Set into several niches near the back of the room, portable generators powered a bank of computers set up on makeshift workstations. Here finally, was the source of the rumbling. At the base of the dais, a drilling station produced the constant thumping that vibrated the walls, its mighty piston hammering a long shaft into the floor.

"My god, this place is incredible," Lily said.

"No doubt a tourist destination at some other time," said Jacob. "Now, where's the damn exit?"

"At least we finally know where the banging's coming from," said Bobby, walking over to the drill.

"Maybe it's got something to do with the experiments they're doing on us," said Trevor.

"Goodness gracious," exclaimed Lily. "That must be why the Core came here in the first place."

"We should investigate," said Jinx. "The answers could help us take down the Core once we escape."

"We can spare a few minutes," said Bobby. "Then we need to focus on finding a way out."

The others spread out, each investigating something different. Jinx went to the nearest wall to decipher the inscriptions. Jacob went to the computers to poke around, and Lily searched for another way out. Slab stood guard.

"Yo, I can help translate the glyphs," said Trevor, heading to the wall across from Jinx. "Check me out. I was forced to study Mayan last semester. Seemed strange at the time, but makes sense if they intended to send me here after graduation."

Bobby tore himself away from the radiant fountain and made his way over to Jinx. "What about you? Can you read all this?"

"Most of it, yes," said Jinx. "I was never assigned Mayan studies like Trevor, but I did memorize the three hundred most common glyphs as part of my free study on comparative languages."

Bobby gave his cousin a playful nudge. "Only three hundred? Slacker."

"That's all the textbook contained," whined Jinx. "Unfortunately, there are some here that weren't in my book. And since Mayan is logo-syllabic, I can't be sure if they represent words, syllables, or names. Like this one here," he said pointing to a glyph that looked like a serpent coiled around a tree. "I know what the surrounding glyphs are, but I've never seen this one before."

"Well, keep at it, I guess," said Bobby, already losing interest. He wandered over to Lily and Jacob, who were typing furiously at separate computer terminals.

Bobby came to stand by Lily's shoulder. "I knew Jacob liked computers. I didn't realize you did too."

Lily looked up and gave him a wink. "Back at the academy, I mainly chatted with friends. But I'm a quick study."

"Thankfully, I know more than how to open a chat window," said Jacob. "I ran a search and pulled up the most commonly accessed programs. Check this out."

He and Lily gathered around to peer at a spreadsheet filled with data. The heading at the top read 'Analysis of Water Composition, Sample #327."

"So, all of this equipment is to test the water?" said Bobby.

"Sure looks that way, golden boy," said Jacob.

"My gosh, they're trying to tap into the water at its source," said Lily.

"Yeah, but why?" asked Bobby. "I mean, the fountain is beautiful and everything, but what could possibly be so interesting about the water?"

"I think I know," said Jinx, making his way over. "Most of the glyphs I deciphered are what you'd expect from a Mayan temple: stuff about the various gods they worshipped, crops, harvest, the weather, stuff like that. But I also found a section that talks about this fountain."

Bobby, Jacob, and Lily followed Jinx to the wall across from where they'd come in. "See this right here?" said Jinx. "It's hard to do an exact translation, but it basically says that the water has power. It talks about living forever and witnessing all things, past, present, and future."

Beside him, Lily gasped. Even Jacob's breath seemed to have caught in his throat. "Are you telling me that this fountain…" Bobby's voice trailed off.

Jinx shrugged, a sly grin on his face. "I think it's safe to say we now know why the Core is so interested in this place. They think *that,*" he said, pointing toward the fountain, "is the legendary Fountain of Youth."

* * *

Itzamna pondered the words of the stranger long after his departure. The images shown to him by the raven-haired man were bizarre and disturbing; places where people lived on top of one another like some giant, above-ground beehive; and where massive beasts made of some unknown shiny substance carried people without devouring them, all while moving at incredible speeds on round legs.

The fact that the stranger wanted Itzamna and his hunters to stay away from the temple was clear from both his images and words, but the reason made no sense. The foreigner had seen the two young ones go to the other side. He must know that the Spirit Men would soon find them and devour their souls.

Perhaps the stranger was a coward, too afraid of the net made of lightning cast over the temple by the gods. It was true, they could not pass under the net as the outsider children had done, but that was not a reason to give up.

Itzamna and his men were warriors, descendants of the great and powerful Mayan gods themselves. He, especially, had been named after one of the most powerful gods, one that had taught his ancestors how to grow crops and understand the cycles of the moon and sun. He might not be able to journey to the other side of the spirit realm, but there were others among them who could.

Calling to Tohil and Votan, Itzamna ordered his lieutenants to gather the elders. The stranger could do what he wished, Itzamna wished him god speed, but they were neither powerless nor cowards. They would not wait idle for the outsider's return while two more souls were claimed by the Spirit Men. No, they would not wait. They would act.

* * *

For a few moments, no one spoke. Like the others, Jinx's proclamation rendered Bobby temporarily speechless. He stared at the sparkling, gem-encrusted fountain and imagined what it would be like to live forever.

As usual, it was Jacob and his typical abruptness that broke the spell. "I don't get it," said the short, stocky redhead. "If that's the freakin' Fountain of Youth, then why are all these readings normal?"

Bobby pried his gaze from the fountain and turned to his friend. "What do you mean?"

Jacob pointed to the computer screen. "See this? According to these reports, they've run hundreds of tests and haven't found a damn thing."

Bobby wrung his hands. "Maybe the light from above somehow combines with the gems to transform the water or something. I mean, it's possible right?"

Jacob scoffed, prompting an angry glare from Lily.

"Not really," said Jinx. "Certain gems and stones, like jade, have energetic qualities, but really they just store, reflect, or redirect natural energy. They can't do anything like cause someone to live forever."

"Perhaps if there were people involved, some kind of ceremony," offered Lily.

"My gut tells me there's a reason why this water appears to be normal," said Jinx.

"Perhaps because it is normal," said Trevor. Until then, the oldest of Bobby's friends hadn't been part of the conversation. Instead, he'd spent his time studying the various glyphs in the vast circular chamber. Trevor squatted by the base of the fountain, his lanky arms and legs poking out like broken sticks from his slender torso.

"What do you mean, babe?" asked Lily.

Trevor stood so the sticks fell into alignment and made his way over to the others.

"Are you saying this isn't the Fountain of Youth?" asked Jacob. "Because Jinx just said it is, and even I have to admit that he's a freakin' genius."

Trevor shook his head and handed Jinx a slip of paper. "Gimme a sec. I want him to check something for me."

Jinx read the piece of paper. "Where did you see this inscription?"

"It's below the surface of the water inside the bowl," said Trevor. Jinx rushed over to the fountain and gazed into the bowl, staring long and hard into its misty depths. After a few moments, he straightened up and returned.

"Strange as it is, your translation appears to be correct."

"What does it say?" said Jacob, snatching the scrap of paper from Jinx's hand. Bobby looked over his shoulder and read along with him:

Water is the key, but not the answer
For the pious, gods are in the shallows
For the enlightened, eternity is in the depths
Life starts with light from the East
Afterlife begins with the dark in the West

"Why would the Fountain of Youth say that its water is not the answer?" asked Jacob. "And how the hell can something start in the East but begin in the West? Your translation is obviously wrong."

Jinx shook his head. "All of these glyphs are ones I memorized. The translation is definitely correct."

"So then how come it makes no freakin' sense?" snapped Jacob.

"It's a riddle, silly," said Lily. "We need to solve it in order to understand."

Bobby pointed. "Looks like the Core decided to take a more direct approach. They're probably trying to drill to whatever depths the riddle is referring to."

"I doubt they'll find it that way," said Jinx, leaving the fountain and heading back to the chamber walls.

"For real, what makes you say that?" asked Trevor.

Jinx never got a chance to respond. Instead, his attention was diverted to the entrance where Slab had ducked into the room, his tremendous girth all but obscuring the doorway over which he'd been standing watch.

"What's the matter?" asked Bobby. "Is someone coming?"

Slab nodded vigorously. "People come. Lots and lots of people come."

CHAPTER FOURTEEN

The pounding of the drill all but drowned out the clamor of the approaching soldiers. Now that Bobby knew to listen, however, he could just barely hear it: the distant but distinct sound of people shouting, accompanied by the occasional screech of a monkey. *Well, that explains how they know we're free*, thought Bobby, cursing Willy's bizarre connection with his pet.

Still, the shouts seemed to be far away. "Yo, they're still searching," said Trevor. "Otherwise, they'd be here already."

"Still, we don't have much time," replied Bobby.

"I protect," said Slab. "You go."

Jacob threw up his arms. "And where do you want us to go, you big oaf? In case you haven't noticed, there's only one doorway, and it leads to the people with guns!"

The giant dropped his head and returned to the door.

"Actually, there may be another way," said Jinx. Bobby's little cousin stood by the east wall. "See this glyph?" he said, pointing to a carving that looked like a four-leaf clover with a dot in the middle. "That is K'in."

The others studied the logogram as Jinx traversed the room. "Help me search for it over here," he said.

"You solved it, didn't you?" asked Lily. Jinx looked up, a twinkle in his eye. "Heavens, you know what the riddle means!"

Jinx flashed a grin. "I'll know for sure once we find it."

They spread out. Jacob and Jinx searched low while Bobby looked up above. Trevor and Lily searched together, the two of them only a few inches apart, their hands nearly touching as they moved in sync across the midsection of the wall. Meanwhile, the voices grew steadily louder.

"This is stupid," said Jacob with a glance at the tunnel where Slab stood guard. "We should go meet them and kick their asses." The others ignored him and kept searching.

The voices from down the hall were distinct now. Bobby recognized Sandman's pit-bull growl. The Core guards' captain shouted orders to his troops, sending guards down side tunnels to investigate. Thankfully, the fountain room was at the very end. Plus, they were around a dogleg, which allowed Slab to stand watch without being spotted.

Bobby was searching frantically for the clover-shaped rune when Jacob called out.

"Here. Over here!" Jacob knelt by a deep alcove set into the bottom of the wall.

Jinx rushed to his side. "Where? I don't see it."

"It's on the underside here," said Jacob, pointing to the lip of the alcove and rubbing his head. "Never woulda noticed the bloody thing except I whacked my freakin' head on it. Luck of the Irish, I guess."

The shouts from down the hall changed pitch. Bobby heard Ashley and Willy, along with Sandman calling out to Slab and rushing toward them.

"Dude," said Trevor. "Whatever you found, better make it quick."

Jinx nodded and raised a palm. Then, with a sly smile, he pushed on the rune. Bobby froze, not quite sure what to expect. There was a moment of utter silence in the chamber as everyone held their breath. Even the generators and drill seemed to take a beat off from their perpetual pounding. Then sound rushed back in, bringing reality with it. Bobby wasn't quite sure what Jinx had expected to happen but knew exactly what had happened: absolutely nothing.

* * *

Finding someone willing to talk was not the problem. Everyone wanted to talk. The problem was that Jeremiah hadn't brought nearly enough cash to afford all the "information" the locals wanted to give him. Thankfully, Cassandra knew when someone wasn't telling the truth. It took no more than two or three questions for her to sense when someone actually knew something and when they were just trying to string along the gullible Americans for a few extra quetzals.

Still, after spending two days chasing leads all over town, talking to over two dozen people claiming to have seen the mysterious blonde lady matching Melody's description, Jeremiah was not only exhausted, but nearly out of cash.

They pulled up outside the tiny, one-building excuse for an airport at just after seven o'clock. This would be their last lead of the day. It was getting late and they hadn't gotten any viable intel since noon. Jeremiah wondered if perhaps they were just wasting their time.

Parking their rental car in the dirt lot outside, Jeremiah and Cassandra entered the muggy, unairconditioned lobby. They made their way to the lone counter against the far wall that served as passenger check-in as well as security and administration. A night guard leaned uneasily against the desk, puffing on a Marlboro Red, blowing the smoke out over the empty rows of plastic chairs in the boarding area.

The gaunt, middle-aged man brushed back a thin wisp of greying hair as he watched them approach. His right hand, which held the cigarette, twitched uncontrollably, sending a steady cascade of ash over his faded Timberland work-boots.

"Are you Mario?" asked Jeremiah. It was merely a formality. There was no one else in the entire airport except perhaps the air traffic controller in the tower next door, finishing his logs. No more flights were scheduled for the day, and the custodian wasn't scheduled to arrive for another two hours.

"Not here," said the guard. Dropping the half-smoked cigarette on the linoleum without bothering to put it out, he unhooked a heavy keyring from his belt. Turning to a metal door behind the desk with the words Sólo El Personal Autorizado on it, he unlocked it and signaled for Jeremiah and Cassandra to follow.

They went through the battered door into a narrow, white corridor. Three doors down, Mario opened another door leading to a surveillance room with half a dozen monitors hooked up to live camera feeds.

"Fifteen hundred quetzals," he said, extending a hand to receive the money.

"That's nearly two hundred dollars," exclaimed Cassandra.

"We haven't even told you what we want," said Jeremiah.

"You're los Americanos looking for la mujer rubia," he said.

"That's right, we're looking for the blonde lady," replied Jeremiah. "Your cousin, Eliza at the hotel told us you have access to the security cameras."

Mario turned to the monitors and punched in a series of commands on the keyboard. An image of the airport lobby appeared with a date stamp in the lower right from nearly a month past.

"Fifteen hundred quetzals," he repeated, glancing toward the door.

"Why are you in such a hurry?" asked Cassandra, looking around. "We're alone."

"These people you ask about," said Mario, "they bad people. La mujer rubia y las perididas. I see them. I see them very bad. I no want trouble."

"Wait, that word you used 'las perididas,' it means 'the lost ones.' Why did you say that?"

"Please, 1,500 quetzals. I no want trouble."

Jeremiah fished into his pocket. He had nine hundred and twenty quetzals left.

"I've got it," said Cassandra, producing three brand new five hundred-quetzal notes. "Queue the tape." She handed the money to Mario and gestured to the monitors.

"You watch. I go," said Mario, heading for the door.

"Wait a minute," said Jeremiah, blocking the door. "How do we know this isn't some kind of trick?"

"It's okay," said Cassandra, placing a hand on his arm. "He's telling the truth. I'm not sure why he's so nervous. Maybe he just doesn't want to get fired for allowing us back here, but he's not trying to deceive us. I can tell that much."

Jeremiah stood aside, allowing Mario to pass. The elder watchman was out the door and gone in a heartbeat, already reaching for a new cigarette as he made for the lobby. Taking a seat in the blue swivel chair before the monitors, Jeremiah located the controls and pushed play.

They had to fast-forward for a while until there was anyone on the screen besides airport employees. Several flights came and went. All they saw were typical crowds of tourists, business travelers, and locals returning home. Then, at 2:13 pm according to the timestamp, a charter flight arrived from Turks and Caicos. As the passengers deplaned, a blonde woman was met by a well-dressed man with thick muscles and a shaved head.

Jeremiah backed the tape up, replaying the image in real time. Now he understood Mario's unease. The woman wore some kind of mask or paint over the right side of her face, giving her an unsettling visage.

Dressed in all red, she wore large designer sunglasses that obscured her eyes, making it even more difficult to judge her face. Still, it was enough.

The cheeks and chin were right, but the nose and mouth were all wrong. His beloved had delicate features where this woman had an angular beak and plump lips. The hair was wrong too. His wife had naturally golden locks. This woman had peroxide bleached hair feathered in layers down her back.

Beside him, Cassandra placed a hand on his shoulder. "I'm so sorry, Jeremiah. I know how much you wanted it to be her."

"I don't get it. Why was Mario so scared to show us this video?"

"I think I know." Cassandra pointed to the bullnecked man in the photo. "Look."

Jeremiah, who had only had eyes for the blonde woman, turned his attention to the man.

"That's an Armani suit," said Cassandra, "And he's wearing a Patek Phillippe watch. People around here don't have that kind of money and walk around with a woman like that unless they're drug dealers. That's what made Mario so nervous."

Jeremiah sighed, weary to his bones. That had to be it. There was no conspiracy or deeper reason for the guard's behavior. Occam's Razor: the simplest explanation is usually correct.

"Come on," he said, heading for the door. "Let's go home."

* * *

It took a moment for Jinx to regain his focus. "It's here somewhere, I know it is." The young genius probed and prodded at the K'in glyph, looking for a way to maneuver or manipulate the stone carving.

Meanwhile, the hallway outside had dissolved into raucous chaos. Slab wrestled with a guard who had tried to rush past. Finally, the leather-masked giant managed to grab the guard by the cuff and hurl him back. Bobby heard a heavy thump, followed by several groans as the guard collided with his comrades.

Still, it was only a matter of time. Any second now, the guards would subdue Slab, and then Bobby and his friends would be dragged back to holding cells.

"I've got it!" exclaimed Jinx. Bobby looked over in time to see Jinx jam his thumb into the dot in the rune's center. This time something did happen. With a rumble, the back of the alcove slid away to reveal a narrow tunnel that disappeared into darkness.

Trevor peered into the shadows. "Where ya think it goes?"

"Who the hell cares?" snapped Jacob. "Anywhere is better than here."

"Get in, quickly," said Jinx, "before they break into the room and see where we've gone." With that, he ducked into the hole, followed quickly by Lily and Bobby.

At the chamber's entrance, Slab fought with three guards. One nearly slipped by, but Slab stuck out a knee, pinning the guard up against the wall while he grappled with the other two. He tossed one back. Then, with his free hand, Slab snatched the guard and hurled him back with the others.

Bobby flashed a smile, glad that the big fella was on their side. But Slab's triumph was short-lived. Electricity crackled, followed by a flash of light reflected across the domed ceiling high overhead. From just around the corner, Bobby heard Hayward yelling for the others to get back. Then the tip of an electric cattle prod extended toward the giant, flashing crimson as it made contact with the giant's massive right thigh. Slab bellowed and grasped his leg but held his ground.

Jacob took a step towards the secret passage and hesitated. "I can't leave the big oaf to hold them off by himself."

Lily and Jinx pleaded, but the fiery redhead turned his back on them. With solemn strides, Jacob headed towards the chamber entrance. Slab looked over, his expression unknowable beneath his leather mask. The cattle prod darted in again, setting the room crimson with anger and pain.

"I got your back, big guy," said Jacob, snatching the shaft of the cattle prod as it lashed out again. Slab yanked it free, but not before being swarmed by guards.

Now it was Trevor's turn to hesitate at the tunnel entrance. Lily must have seen the look on his face because she started screaming and grasped for his arm. "You can't. Babe, you can't!"

Trevor pulled his arm free, then reached out and caressed her face. "You know I hate it when Jacob tries to act more heroic than me. Besides, he's right, baby girl. Slab can't hold them off by himself."

Trevor's eyes shifted to Bobby. "Go get help, but more important, take care of her for me. We'll do what we can to buy you guys time to escape."

Lily lunged for him, but Trevor pulled back. With his eyes still locked on her, he reached up and pressed on the dot in center of the clover. The stone slab began to slide back into place. Trevor withdrew from the opening, his eyes never leaving Lily until the door was shut.

CHAPTER FIFTEEN

His name, Taavi, meant "adored" in the old language. The name suited him well, for he was well loved. At only twelve sun cycles, he was the youngest of his tribe to be granted the warrior's blade since his grandfather, Itzamna. Now, after only two full moon cycles as a man, he had been chosen for an important task.

The elders had come to him last night, around the great fire, and explained the need: two more souls had been taken by the Spirit Men. The elders were not content to wait idle while the stranger with the hair like a jungle cat went to get more foreigners: people who knew not their customs or ways, people who who did not honor the spirits.

Taavi knew he had been chosen because of his size, small and lean, with the ability to crawl through the hidden space into the spirit realm, but it mattered not. What mattered was he had been chosen. He was strong and brave. He would go alone into that evil place and rescue the souls of the foreign ones who had gone before him.

Those two were not warriors; they were not strong like him and did not know the ways of his people. The elders would perform the ceremony of warding to protect his soul from being lost in the spirit world. After that, it would be up to him to rescue the others. If he could not save them, he would at least make sure that their souls found peace.

* * *

The darkness would have been absolute if not for Jinx. From a hidden pocket, he produced a flashlight, revealing a narrow stairwell heading down. It also illuminated Lily's face. Her cheeks glistened with tears.

Locating an unlit torch on a sconce just inside the door, Jinx produced flint and tinder from yet another hidden pocket. Lighting the torch, he passed it to Bobby and stowed the flashlight to save the battery. Lily's face seemed even more sullen in the orange glow of the torch.

"Where do you think it leads?" she asked, wiping at her face.

"Only one way to find out," replied Bobby.

They descended the narrow staircase single file, hands balanced on wet walls coated with lichen. Bobby could almost taste the moisture on his skin, not the fetid moisture of rot and decay, but the spongy, verdant wetness of life.

"So Jinxy, how exactly did you know about the passage?" Lily's voice was muffled by the dampness, giving it a strange, distant quality.

"It was the part about East and West," said Jinx. "'Light in the east' and 'Dark in the west' are clear references to the Sun. At first, I didn't understand the part about the afterlife, assuming that it meant death, but then I realized that the translation isn't literal. For the Mayans, afterlife doesn't mean death, it means beyond life or, perhaps a better translation, higher, more evolved life.

"That portion, plus the reference to depths, which the fountain clearly does not have, led me to suspect there was a hidden passage on the west wall, one that only an enlightened visitor would ever think to look for."

"So that symbol you had us look for, K'in, it means Sun, right?"

"Exactly. When we found the Sun symbol on the east side in plain sight, I should have realized it would be in an alcove on the west in the darkness. I was so focused on the symbols for darkness and depths referring to a tunnel. I didn't suspect it also hinted at the symbol's location."

Bobby tousled his cousin's hair. "You did great."

The stairs ended after a few tight spirals, dumping the three friends out in a grotto roughly thirty feet across. Bobby used his torch to light two iron braziers that looked like they hadn't been touched in centuries. Covered with verdigris, they sputtered and coughed as he set torch to oil.

Eventually the braziers caught, illuminating the cave's jagged ceiling where stalactites hung in ropes like saliva from some cavernous maw. A stone well sat in the middle of the room, its circular rim rising three feet above the mossy floor.

The instant his eyes fell upon the well, the whispering voices that had fallen quiet since he saw the fountain returned to life. "Not now!" said Bobby, covering his ears with both hands. It did no good. The voices were inside his head.

"Bobby," prodded Lily. "Is everything all right?"

Bobby nodded and dropped his hands. "Just a headache," he said. "I'll be fine."

"Well, there's 'the depths' from the riddle," said Jinx, gesturing to the well.

Lily walked over and examined the well. Bobby hung back, fighting with the voices seeking to draw him near. "Dear me," gasped Lily. "There's another inscription along the lip."

Jinx walked to the rim and studied the glyphs before translating:

The key lies within,
Yet beware
Those of faith without knowledge
Those of knowledge without faith
Eternity awaits all

"So, you think this is what the Core is really after?" asked Bobby.

"Heavens, didn't the riddle say water is the key but not the answer?" asked Lily.

"Perhaps," said Jinx, "But I wouldn't want to be the one to test that theory. I don't see any steps or rope to pull someone out, do you?"

"Speaking of a way out, does anyone see a way out of the cave besides the way we came in?" asked Bobby.

"Over there," said Lily, pointing to the far wall. Sure enough, a small crack revealed a passage that appeared to lead up and outward, away from the temple. It wasn't long before Bobby felt both his pulse and his steps quicken as he and his friends smelled freedom.

* * *

They would have stood side by side, but there wasn't enough room. Slab took up so much space that Trevor and Jacob were forced to hang back, lest the giant accidentally hit one of them as he wrestled with the Core guards that continued to come at them in waves.

It had been nearly ten minutes since the others had vanished into the secret passage. Trevor looked over at the alcove for at least the hundredth time, reassuring himself that the passage was closed, undetectable from the guards who would surely get past them sooner or later.

Even from the back, Trevor could tell that sooner was rapidly approaching. Slab's shoulders drooped. His arms hung at his sides. Each time a new wave of guards came at them, he was just a half second slower to react, forcing Jacob and Trevor to jump in and help out to hold the line. It wouldn't be much longer now.

Still, they would buy as much time as possible. Trevor glanced at the alcove again. As long as Lily and the others were safe, he didn't care what happened to him.

From beyond the mass of bodies in front of them, Sandman barked orders at his men. "Attention!" he yelled, shoving people out of the way as he and Hayward made their way to the front. Simpkins stood off to the side. Ashley and Willy retreated to the back, as far away from Slab and his indomitable strength as possible.

Hayward rolled up the sleeves on his velour jumpsuit. He carried a cattle prod in his other hand. Trevor called out to Jacob. This would be their third attempt at this tactic. The first time, Jacob had grabbed the shaft, allowing Slab to snatch the electric rod away. The second time it was Trevor who caught it. He nearly fried his left wrist in the process but held on long enough for Slab to smash it to pieces.

"Clear!" yelled Sandman. Hayward stood shoulder to shoulder with the bullnecked captain as the guards retreated behind them. Slab held his ground, watching as the pair advanced. Trevor and Jacob waited behind Slab, ready for Hayward to lash out with the cattle prod.

But Hayward didn't come forth. Instead, Sandman raised his arms.

"Ah, nutballs!" cursed Jacob. The fierce-tempered redhead took two steps toward Sandman, then stumbled and fell. Jacob rolled to the side, his eyes shut, saliva pooling at the corner of his mouth.

Slab tried to rush to Jacob's aid, but Hayward was ready with the electric rod. He extended the prod, making the hairs on Trevor's arm stand as he shoved the tip into Slab's gut with electrifying results. The giant howled and retreated to Trevor.

"You're next," said Sandman, shifting his gaze to Trevor. The guard captain raised his arms again. Trevor felt the world around him grow dim. Images swam before him as he struggled to focus. The last thing Trevor saw was Hayward advancing toward Slab, cattle prod extended.

"You're mine now," sneered the obese agent. Trevor heard Slab howl and felt the hairs on his arms stand up and stay up this time. Then all went black.

* * *

The tunnel leading out of the grotto ended in a steep slope, slick with moisture and covered in moss. Jinx went first, scrambling on hands and knees to find purchase on the slippery incline. It took several minutes but finally he ascended the twenty-foot rise to the small landing at the top.

Lily went next, struggling to find footholds, same as Jinx. Every time she tried to push herself up, her foot would slip, sending her sliding back down.

Bobby came over and cupped his hands together. "Here, let me give you a boost." She graciously accepted his offer, vaulting a third of the way up, where she found a small outcrop to use as a handhold.

She clung to it, inching upward as she pressed against the slope to maintain traction.

"Come on, you can do it," Jinx encouraged from above.

She gave him a weak smile and lifted her right foot, setting it atop the outcrop she'd used as a handhold. When she stepped down, the stone broke loose. Unable to support her weight, she fell, sliding down the slope to land in a heap at the bottom.

Bobby rushed to her aid. "Are you okay?"

Lily grasped at her right knee. "Gracious me, I think it's twisted."

"Ah crap," said Bobby. "Do you think you can still climb?"

Lily tried to rise to her feet and sat back down immediately. "Oh dear," she said, shaking her head. "I can't even bend it."

"Maybe we can pull you up?" said Jinx.

Lily shook her head again. "I'm dead weight and that slope looks as slippery as Willy's grasp on reality." She blushed. "I shouldn't have said that. I'm sure he's a nice person on the inside. Just really, really…really misunderstood."

"What about trying to heal you?" asked Jinx, already scrambling back down the trail. "Want me to give it a go?"

Lily's flinch was almost imperceptible. "Umm, no offense, Jinxy, but maybe we should let Bobby try first."

"I can take a look," said Bobby, "but honestly, I'm not even sure what to do." They rolled up the pant leg of Lily's khakis. Her knee was swollen and red.

"You've gotta channel anima into it," said Jinx. "Here, I'll show you."

Lily grimaced but said nothing as Jinx squatted before her and placed both hands on her knee. No sooner had Jinx closed his eyes than Lily squirmed away. "Okay, that's enough. Thank you, dear."

Jinx balked. "But I was just getting started."

One look at Lily's face and Bobby understood. Whatever Jinx had done, it hadn't helped. She was in more pain now than before but was too polite to tell him.

"Still want me to try?" asked Bobby.

Lily grimaced again. "You said you came with others. Are they nearby?"

"Yeah, Chief should be at the village. Want us to go get him?"

"Dear me, I think that may be best."

From the pockets of his deceptively trim pants, Jinx produced two granola bars and a canteen filled with water. "Here," he said, handing them to her. "In case it takes us a while to get back."

Lily graciously accepted the offer. "You know where to find me."

They said their good-byes. Jinx struggled with the climb again, but Bobby helped this time, following a few feet behind and giving his little cousin a boost when needed. The climb was much easier for Bobby with his upper body strength. He used his arms more than his legs, managing to ascend with relative ease.

The top of the chute ended in a short landing capped by a mossy slab at the far end. A gentle push revealed a pivot point on the left of the slab, allowing it to tilt outwards just far enough for them to squeeze through. Bobby pushed aside the stalks of a giant hydrangea to reveal the electric fence a few feet away, buzzing every few seconds as some unknown insect or animal met an untimely demise.

If Jinx was disappointed the secret passage hadn't taken them beyond the fence's perimeter, he didn't show it. "Guess we gotta find the hollow log," he said.

The task was easier said than done. Using the position of the sun, which had just begun to crest over the temple, Jinx determined their approximate location. Still, they didn't dare step out onto the open terrace surrounding the temple where a Core guard patrol might spot them. Instead, they clung to the dense jungle, moving slowly and with as little noise as possible through the heavy foliage. Even once they'd traversed to the north side of the perimeter, where they knew the log to be, it still took a while to locate it.

The blazing sun had long passed its zenith by the time Bobby and Jinx found the partially submerged tree trunk hidden beneath the thick vegetation. Bobby glanced up at the tree where he'd spotted the jaguar, but the upper canopy was devoid of life, without so much as a bird to rustle its branches.

Jinx went first, with Bobby giving him a boost from behind to help propel him quickly to the far end. As the boys climbed out of the hollow and brushed themselves off, they heard noises off in the distance.

"That sounded like gunshots," said Bobby.

Jinx nodded. "It came from the direction of the village."

The cousins exchanged worried glances. Without another word, they broke into a run.

CHAPTER SIXTEEN

The jungle was deadly silent as Bobby and Jinx raced toward the village. For the past hour, the trees had echoed with the sharp retort of gunfire. Now, however, they heard nothing. Bobby urged Jinx to pick up the pace.

The air filled with the iron taint of blood and gunpowder as the first thatch huts came into view. Bobby and Jinx stood transfixed, horrified at what lay before them. The village lay in ruins, its wood hovels smashed to pieces. Roofs and walls were riddled with bullet holes, leaving nothing but empty husks. The inhabitants of the village lay everywhere, their bodies bloodied and broken. Some he thought he recognized. Others were too mutilated to be sure.

Bobby gingerly picked through the carnage, one hand holding the neckline of his shirt up over his nose. He caught Jinx's eye and saw his own worry mirrored back at him. *If Chief lay here someplace...* Bobby swallowed hard, unable to finish the thought.

He returned to searching faces, giving each body only the most cursory glance, just enough to assure himself it wasn't the man who'd brought them here. More often than not, it was a woman. Sometimes it was the twisted remains of a child.

"I don't see any men," he called out to Jinx. "Do you?"

"I saw a couple of old men, but no warriors. They must have been out hunting when this happened."

At that moment, Bobby became aware of another presence. There was someone or something else with them in the village. He closed his eyes and listened intently. There were no voices in his head. Instead, he heard grunting, shouts, sounds of a struggle, almost as if the violence that had befallen the village were being replayed in the spirit realm.

Bobby thrust a hand into his pocket and pulled out the idol of Hunhau. Lifting it to his forehead, he opened his eyes. A spirit stood ten feet away. Dressed in animal skins and carrying a staff capped with bright feathers, Bobby's first thought it was one of the natives killed in the attack. But this man was larger and darker than the villagers he'd met, his visage more primitive.

Bobby blinked and took a step back. He recognized this spirit from Maximon's memories. This was Ek Chuaj, the son of the Mayan chieftain; the teen who had brutally assaulted and raped Lingya.

Ek Chuaj moved through the village, searching for something, just as Bobby and Jinx had done moments before. Bobby watched, confused as Ek Chuaj stumbled around the village, faltering in his search as if confused by the landscape. Then he turned and saw Bobby watching him. Ek Chuaj's eyes grew fiery. His face twisted with rage. Raising the staff, he shouted words Bobby didn't understand.

Bobby stood frozen as the specter advanced on him. Ek Chuaj stopped less than an arm's length away. He continued shouting, pointing at Bobby, and gesturing at the idol clutched in his hand. Bobby didn't need a translator to know the angry spirit wanted to share his story. Bobby just wasn't sure he wanted to hear it.

"Why do I feel like I'm gonna regret this?"

With a deep breath, Bobby took a small step forward and extended his hand.

***

It was the Spanish conquistadors, led by Pedro de Alvarado, who destroyed Ek Chuaj's village. They attacked in the middle of the night, murdering most of the men in their sleep before an alarm could be raised.

When Ek Chuaj woke, it was to his father's hand clamped over his mouth. The memory felt strange to Bobby, full of shadows, as if Ek Chuaj were trying to hide something from him.

Bobby saw a blurred image of the village leader ordering Ek Chuaj to hide in the forest. The teen argued, saying he wanted to stay and help defend the village. Nohchil and his men fought bravely, buying time while the women and children fled into the jungle. But the conquistadors had metal armor, superior weapons, and military training.

Bone-tipped arrows bounced harmlessly off bronze breastplates; wooden spears shattered against steel swords. Mayan warriors fell easily to the Spanish conquerors, while the Mayans were unable to take down even a single enemy.

Outnumbered and wounded, Nohchil ordered his warriors to surrender.

In some memories, a shadowy Ek Chuaj stood at his father's side. In others, the teen watched from a distance as events unfolded. Bobby saw both images at the same time, almost as if experiencing two different versions of the same event.

Nohchil and his men were forced to their knees. The leader of the Spaniards came forward; a ginger-haired brute the natives called Tonatiuh, or Red Sun. Ek Chuaj was dragged into the middle of the clearing, a sword put to his throat.

The scene in Bobby's head went dark. He couldn't make out what occurred next. Words were exchanged. Conquered natives from other tribes were brought forth to act as interpreters. The memory went dark again.

For long moments, Bobby waded through the murky shadows of Ek Chuaj's memory. When it finally became clear again, Ek Chuaj stood alone in the middle of a razed village, just as his spirit now stood among the ashes of Itzamna's clan.

Nohchil lay dead, slain by a sword through his spine. By his right arm lay the chieftain's staff. Bending low, Ek Chuaj picked up his father's scepter and straightened.

Beside his father lay a pile of weapons and armor worn by the invaders. Ek Chuaj loaded the items into a sack. Then he shouldered the satchel and headed toward the temple city.

***

Jinx tapped Bobby on the shoulder, pulling him from his vision. Bobby blinked a few times, regaining his bearings. His cousin pointed to a banyan tree behind the closest hut. Something moved in the shadows. Bobby blinked again. The spirit of Ek Chuaj was gone. This was something else, something human.

"Chief, is that you?" called Bobby. "Please tell me it's you."

The figure that detached itself from the shadows made Bobby's heart leap with joy. It wasn't Chief, but it was the next best thing.

"Itzamna!" exclaimed Jinx, rushing toward the bone-clad shaman. One look at the dark eyes of the village's leader and Jinx pulled up short. Itzamna extended his carved staff, now smeared with tar and covered with feathers. He barked a series of harsh, guttural phrases that could only be condemnation.

Other figures detached themselves from the cover of the forest. Warriors encircled the boys, forming a tight net, just as they had the first time in the jungle.

"What are you doing?" asked Bobby, instinctually raising his hands as one of the hunters pointed a spear at his chest. "It's us. We're your friends, remember?"

If the hunter understood, he made no reply. Instead, the ring of warriors advanced steadily, bows and spears aimed at the boys.

"I don't get it—" Jinx broke off midsentence, his eyes growing wide as realization hit him. "Ohh…"

"What is it?" asked Bobby. "Don't tell me they think we did this. We don't even have guns."

"I doubt these people have ever seen a gun," said Jinx. "Even if they have, they wouldn't understand it. They undoubtedly think Spirit Men did this using magic."

"Okay, so then why are they treating us like this?"

"They saw us go into the temple, right? Where the Spirit Men devour souls. Ergo, they think we are some sort of ghosts or demons."

"That's ridiculous," said Bobby. Turning to Itzamna, he tugged on his own forearm. "Look, skin and bone. Human. Real people just like you, not demons." He said the last words carefully, as if pronouncing each syllable slowly would make the shaman understand.

Itzamna's jaw tightened. His eyes narrowed as if he sought to peer into their souls. He said something to his band of hunters and the spears drew closer.

"Yup," said Jinx. "We're screwed."

* * *

In Trevor's nightmare, he was strapped to the table again. Two doctors wearing surgical caps and gowns hovered over him with shiny scalpels but did not touch him. Instead they moved to the table next to him. He craned his head and saw Lily strapped to an identical table at his side.

The surgeons nodded to one another, their eyes cold and dead, their faces hidden behind pale blue masks. Lily screamed. Trevor called out, losing sight of her as the surgeons swarmed over her prone form. She tried to kick but her legs were restrained. The surgeons continued their grisly work as though she were sedate.

The screams seemed to last an eternity, ringing in Trevor's ear until he thought he would go deaf from heartache. Then they abruptly ceased. The surgeons stepped back and removed their masks. Simpkins and Hayward wore satisfied grins, their rubber-gloved hands covered in gore and dripping with blood. Trevor looked past them to the motionless body of his beloved. Then it was Trevor's turn to scream.

* * *

Trevor woke with a start. The foggy tendrils of his nightmare clung to his dulled mind. It had been a dream, a horrible dream to be sure, but still just a dream. Lily was safe, he'd seen to that himself.

He started to close his eyes again, when realization came flooding back. Lily might be safe, but he and Jacob had been knocked out by Sandman and taken captive.

Trevor snapped upright, his eyes wide open. He sat in a chair, his wrists and ankles unrestrained. One look at the woman seated in the straight-backed wooden chair across from him and he wished he were still asleep.

The woman's features were attractive enough: white blonde hair, angular cheeks, but her visage was horrific. The entire left half of her face had been painted crimson, with a twisted upturn at the corner of the mouth drawn in white that gave her a hideous, devil's grin. And then there were those eyes…the eyes of a surgeon: cold, calculating, devoid of emotion. Dressed in spiked heels and a high-neck red leather dress, it didn't take much to know who sat before him.

"So, you're the Scarlet Seer." Trevor faked a yawn. "Truth? I'm not impressed." She returned his neutral stare. He shifted uncomfortably in his chair.

"Where are the others?" The woman's voice was the rustling of dry leaves in a cold breeze.

Trevor shrugged. "Got no idea what you're talking about."

The Scarlet Seer rubbed her temples. "I have no desire to hurt you unnecessarily. Please just tell me what I want to know."

"Yo, do what you gotta do. I ain't scared of you."

The Scarlet Seer winced as if she'd been struck. "You're only making it worse, Mr. Williams. Tell me what you were doing in the fountain chamber."

"Truth? I was thirsty. Slab took me and Jacob there to get a drink."

The Scarlet Seer grit her teeth. Her face contorted, and she pinched the bridge of her nose. She sat there, unmoving for a moment. Then something flashed in those dead-pool eyes. In his mind, Trevor heard Lily's screams. He saw her lying on the table, just as it had been in his nightmare. The screams grew louder and louder until he thought his ears would burst.

Trevor clutched at his head. "Tell me what I want to know," said the Scarlet Seer.

Trevor thrashed from side to side. "Yo, you're messed up."

"Where are the others?"

Unable to stop himself, Trevor thought of the alcove within the fountain chamber. Lily's screams quieted a little but did not cease.

"So, there is a secret passage in the chamber." It was not a question. The woman was inside his mind, able to see what he thought. "How do I open it?"

This time Trevor kept his thoughts under control. He pictured the journey to the temple, where the kids had clustered together. As horrific as the entire ordeal had been, he and Lily had been together. He pictured how they'd sat together on the long bus ride from the airport to the edge of the jungle, holding hands in secret under a blanket with guards from the Core sitting just a few feet away.

He remembered her soft tears over the absence of Bobby and Jinx. As sad as she had been, she glowed with an inner strength. Never once did she complain about their own situation, instead worrying only about their friends and the need to be strong. It was then that Trevor knew how much he loved her.

The Scarlet Seer's eyes flashed again.

In his mind, Lily turned to look out the window of the bus. When she turned back, her eyes were gone, replaced by burnt out husks. What remained of her skin was scaly and green, sloughing off in patches to expose hoary bones beneath. Even her lips were gone, rotten away to reveal black and decayed teeth.

"Peace!" yelled Trevor. "I'll tell you whatever you want. Just get outta my damn head."

In an instant, Lily's face was her own again: warm, beautiful, and full of compassion. Quickly, Trevor conjured up the image of the K'in symbol, envisioning the spot on the underside of the alcove where the release trigger was hidden.

"How did you come by this knowledge?" asked the Scarlet Seer. Trevor showed her the inscription inside the rim of the fountain.

"I see," said the Scarlet Seer. "Do you know of anything else, anything you would like to add?"

"That's all, f'real," Trevor panted as the woman continued to torment him with images of what she would do if he was lying. "I don't know where the passage leads or what's down there."

The Scarlet Seer leaned back in her chair and steepled her hands. "I believe you," she said at last. "Which leaves only the matter of your punishment."

Trevor gave an involuntary shudder but held his tongue. He might not be able to fight her, but he would not beg for mercy. He curled his hands tight into fists, bracing for whatever came next.

Before she could begin, a sharp knock came at the door behind him. The Scarlet Seer lifted her dead stare to the door, a slight downturn at the corner of her painted smile.

"Enter," she commanded.

Sandman stepped into the room. "I'm sorry to disturb you, commander. There's been an incident by the north perimeter and I wanted to give you a report."

"What kind of incident?"

"One of the guards spotted a young native boy covered in paint and dressed in a loincloth attempting to sneak into the temple."

"And where is the boy now?"

"We have him surrounded in the brush near the fence, commander. Shall we eliminate him?"

The Scarlet Seer stood and made her way to the exit. "I will see to the boy myself. I want to discover where he came from, what it is he's looking for, and how he got past the fence."

"Very good, commander. What about this one?" The captain of the guard gestured to Trevor.

"Take him back to his cell and sedate him. I will decide what to do with him and the other when I return."

The Scarlet Seer swept from the room, taking her ruthless eyes and horrible visions with her. Trevor had no idea who the young native boy might be. Whoever he was, his future looked extremely grim.

CHAPTER SEVENTEEN

From their guarded location by the fire, Bobby and Jinx looked on as Itzamna and the members of his hunting party examined the remains of the village. Tohil stood nearby, watching the boys with a fearsome stare. The deep gash that ran from just below his left eye to the corner of his mouth gave him a dark, almost sinister expression.

"I guess this guy doesn't have any family," said Bobby, hooking a thumb toward their watchdog. Indeed, all the other men, including Itzamna, were combing the camp, sending up howls of rage and wails of despair in equal measure as they uncovered the bodies of wives and daughters, mothers and sons.

"We need to do something," Bobby whispered to Jinx.

"What we need is a way to communicate," Jinx whispered back. "So, they know we aren't demons."

"Or we could try to escape," offered Bobby. "We could run into the forest." He glanced at the bald warrior. The corner of Tohil's mouth drew up into a snarl.

"And go where?" asked Jinx. "These men are trained hunters. Even if we managed to escape, they'd track us down in minutes. That's assuming we don't stumble into quicksand or get bit by a poisonous snake first."

"Good point," said Bobby with a sigh.

"I've picked up a few words of their language," said Jinx. "It's not much, but maybe I can sense the right words if I try to read his mind."

"Worth a shot."

Jinx closed his eyes for a few seconds, then turned to Tohil and spoke. The scar-faced hunter tilted his head to the side as he listened, then he reversed his spear, and slammed the butt into Jinx's stomach.

"What did you say?"

Jinx let out a groan and gripped his midsection. "I tried to tell him we're sorry for his loss, but his thoughts are so foreign, and I couldn't find all the words. I think what I actually said was 'your pain is so much.'"

"I can see how that might piss him off, especially if he thinks we did it."

Now the men were gathering the bodies. Bobby and Jinx watched as the warriors dragged their loved ones into the clearing at the middle of camp. When they were done, they began to chant, performing what Bobby could only assume was some sort of mass burial ritual. Afterward, they tossed oil on the corpses and set them on fire. Then they took torches to the huts, setting the entire village ablaze.

As the fire spread, Bobby feared the natives intended to leave him and Jinx to burn among the ruins. Instead, Tohil gestured for them to rise to their feet. He pointed to the far side of the village, where the other hunters were gathering.

Bobby and Jinx rose and joined the others, watching the flames spread, trying hard not to look at the faces. The acrid sting of burning flesh made Bobby's eyes water. He wanted to wretch. Instead, Tohil prodded him in the back with the butt of his spear.

With the village sufficiently ablaze, the hunters struck out into the jungle. Bobby was all too happy to leave the grisly scene. He fell in single file behind Jinx, following a game trail he knew all too well.

"We're headed back to the temple," said Jinx over his shoulder.

"This is insane," said Bobby. "Don't they realize that the guards from the temple are the ones who did this?"

"These people have no idea about guns or people at the temple. They think it's occupied by Spirit Men, remember?"

"So, what do you suggest?" asked Bobby.

"Maybe I could try talking to them again."

"Don't you dare," said Bobby. "They might kill you if you use the wrong word."

"There may be another way. Remember back at the Eagle's Nest when you communed with the deer in the meadow? Remember how you were about to sense its thoughts? Well, I think I can do that in reverse."

"You want to show a deer how you feel?"

"Not a deer, obviously, and only as in intermediary. If I can convey my feelings to an animal, a bird perhaps, then all we need to do is convince Itzamna to read the bird. He should be able to sense our innocence, or at least the fact that we're not demons."

Bobby's face turned sour. He shrugged. "Given where we're headed, I don't see a whole lot of other options."

* * *

Bobby followed Jinx as they descended a small hillock, turning the damp earth into marsh. Itzamna picked a path around stagnant pools and murky streams, avoiding the sinkholes as he carved a circuitous but steady path toward the temple.

Jinx waited until they passed through a clearing, the ground made firm by the roots of a giant ficus, then he stopped walking. Expecting something like this, Bobby stepped to the side, but Tohil kept going. The warrior almost stumbled into Jinx, leaping back at the last moment as one might from the edge of a cliff.

Shouts went up and the other warriors stopped as well. Itzamna doubled back, curiosity painted across his face alongside the green and black hunting dye. He jabbed his staff at Jinx, shouting at him and pointing off into the bushes.

In response, Jinx raised his hands, palms open in the same expression of parley that Chief had used during their first encounter. The shaman took a step back, shaking his staff at Bobby's cousin.

"He doesn't want to touch me," said Jinx. "He must be afraid that my tainted soul will somehow corrupt him."

"So, what now?"

"I expected this," said Jinx. "It's okay. I don't need to touch him for my plan to work. I just need to find an animal. He'll understand after that. I'm sure he will."

Jinx lifted his hands, gesturing to the trees high overhead. Then he sat down, crossed his legs and closed his eyes.

The warriors shouted and stomped their spears on the ground. Several came forward, intent on poking Jinx until he moved. Bobby stepped in between, keeping them at bay with his mere presence. He and Jinx might be their prisoners but none of the warriors wanted to risk physical contact.

"Better hurry," said Bobby over his shoulder.

"Just a little bit longer," said Jinx, unmoving and with his eyes still closed. "I'm searching for a bird. There, I found something. It's a wild parrot, I think. It should be coming now."

Bobby scanned the trees but saw no sign of a bird. Most of the natives followed his stare, looking up into the canopy. Tohil shouted and pointed into the quagmire. Bobby shifted his gaze. "Umm, Jinx…"

"Give me a sec, it's almost here."

Now all the natives were shouting and gesturing wildly, pointing beyond the tree to the mud and muck of the swamp.

"Jinx, stop!"

Jinx opened his eyes with a scowl. "I can't commune with the parrot while you're shouting at me. You don't want it to fly off, do you?"

"I don't think that's gonna be a problem." Bobby pointed behind his cousin.

Jinx turned to gape as a huge, green anaconda with brown spots shaped like figure-eights emerged from the bog. Its head was the same size as Jinx's, its torso nearly as wide, and over twenty feet long.

The warriors scattered as the enormous reptile slithered to Jinx and coiled itself around the young boy like a cocoon made of carnelians and emeralds. The snake brought its head around to hover above Jinx, its forked tongue darting in and out.

Momentarily speechless, Jinx finally stammered, "Umm, that's not a parrot."

"Perhaps it can still work," offered Bobby. "See if you can get Itzamna to commune with the snake."

"Are you kidding me? I can't even commune with this thing. Maybe when I thought that it was a sweet, little, colorful parrot... Now that I know it's a humongous, man-eating snake, all I can think about is how it can swallow me whole."

"We've gotta do something," Bobby countered. "The natives are freaking out."

Indeed, both Tohil and Votan had already crept forward, spears raised to their shoulders, ready to attack at the slightest twitch. In response, the snake rose up and hissed, revealing razor-sharp teeth.

Votan pulled back his spear and jabbed, but the bone-tipped spear might as well have been made out of rubber, glancing harmlessly off the reptile's iron-like scales. Another hunter let loose an arrow. Like the spear, it didn't make a scratch. One hunter threw down his spear and fell to the ground. Another ran off into the forest.

"So, umm, what do we do now?" asked Jinx, sitting motionless, hands pinned to his sides by the coils around him.

"Somehow I don't think we can shoo it away," Bobby answered.

Itzamna came forth, his staff held before him like a shield. He looked first to Bobby and Jinx, studying their faces, then to the snake. The snake rose up again, but it did not hiss. Instead it hung there, slatted eyes staring back at Itzamna with a cold, predator's gaze.

The shaman spoke and the snake wavered back. Without taking its eyes from the shaman, it uncoiled itself from Jinx, heading back to the marsh. Tohil remained perfectly still as the creature slipped between his feet, forcing the hunter's legs open with its girth. The anaconda paused, lifting its massive diamond-shaped head level with the hunter's neck. Then it sank back down and slithered into the water. In moments, it had disappeared.

Bobby helped Jinx to his feet. His cousin took a huge breath. "So, what now?"

Itzamna provided the answer. The shaman pointed toward the trail and drew a finger across his throat. The message was clear. Either keep going or be killed.

CHAPTER EIGHTEEN

It felt strange being in the house without her. The modest two-bedroom cottage sat on a hill overlooking a park. With its neat herb garden and white picket fence, it was the kind of home he and Melody had always talked about buying together.

Instead, Jeremiah was here with Cassandra, looking for clues as to Melody's whereabouts. Of course, they'd been over it all before. In their first sweep of the house Cassandra discovered the internet search of Guatemala which had turned out to be a wild goose chase.

Now they were going through everything again, looking for anything they might have missed. Before seeing the tape from the airport, Jeremiah had tried calling Chief on the satellite phone. Unfortunately, it didn't seem to be working and he had no idea why. The first time he'd called it, it had rung several times before the line simply went dead. Ever since then, all he got was an error message that the subscriber he was trying to dial could not be located.

That message concerned him mightily. After all, both his grandsons were with the man. But Cassandra had assured him that Chief was the most competent man she knew. Plus, she claimed to have a psychic link that would allow her to know if any harm had befallen any of them. Jeremiah wasn't sure he truly believed this last part, but he had to admit it made him feel better.

They poured over the mail first. Two weeks' worth had arrived since they'd last been here, but none of it was of any interest. Junk mail, coupons from Bed, Bath and Beyond, and a bill from the Department of Water and Power littered the table. They went over the phone bills next. None of the calls were to anywhere unusual, mostly neighbors and a few friends from the various places Melody had lived over the years.

There were no calls to Jeremiah or their son, Nate. That wasn't unusual. Whenever it was safe, Melody came by in person rather than call. Still, she hadn't been to see them since shortly after Bobby was taken to the academy. That seemed too suspicious to be coincidence but didn't prove anything or give him a lead to go on.

Jeremiah had just stepped into the backyard to get some fresh air and clear his head when Cassandra came out. She held a copy of a credit card statement in one hand and a bank statement in the other.

"What is it?" asked Jeremiah.

"There's a line item here for two hundred and fifty dollars." Cassandra pointed to the expense in question.

Jeremiah took the statement from here and examined it. "I saw that transaction before, but all it says is 'consultation fee.' There's no way to know exactly what it's for.

"I know that, but look at this other statement," said Cassandra. "The day after that consultation, whatever it was, she visited the bank and made a small withdrawal."

"Yeah, so? She only took out two hundred dollars. It was probably just to cover groceries."

"I've gone back over ten months. All of her other withdrawals were by ATM."

"You think she had another reason to go to the bank besides the withdrawal?" asked Jeremiah.

"Didn't you tell me the two of you keep a safety deposit box with the items you took from the Spine of the World? Maybe the real reason for the trip to the bank was to visit the box. Perhaps she left something for you to find in case there was trouble."

"That's brilliant!" exclaimed Jeremiah, dashing back up the porch steps to get his coat and car keys. "Come on. We can be there in ten minutes."

* * *

At first, Bobby was confused about why they'd stopped. They stood in a clearing perhaps twenty yards across. The apex of the temple was visible beyond the closest trees, but this was not the clearing with the hollow log. The electric fence stood nearby, its buzz accompanied by high-pitched zaps as a low wind carried unwitting birds and insects to their deaths, but there was no gate.

He scanned the ground. It was flat and undisturbed, no sign of another rotten tree or other means by which to slip under the fence. *What are we doing here? Why return to the temple, except to be vanquished back to the other side?*

Then Bobby spotted the body. Roughly the same age as him, the native boy lay on the other side of the fence, not twenty feet from where they stood. Covered in red and white paint, he wore nothing but a loincloth with a bone knife strapped to his waist. At first Bobby thought the boy was asleep. His expression was serene, his hands resting loosely at his sides. Then Bobby noticed the bullet hole four inches below his left collarbone.

"Taavi," said Itzamna, pronouncing the name slowly and pointing to the boy. The shaman's expression was a mix of pride and pain.

"They must have sent him through the log to try to rescue us," said Bobby.

"Or to ensure our souls weren't stolen," said Jinx, pointing to the knife. "My guess is he had orders to kill us if we couldn't be saved."

Bobby shuddered at the thought. "Looks like one of the Core patrols spotted him first. But why is he over here and not by the log?"

"The guards must have spotted him. He ran, and they shot him," said Bobby.

"Once they saw him, they knew they had to do something about the natives," replied Jinx.

"Which explains the massacre," finished Bobby. "Sandman or the Scarlet Seer must have thought Taavi was an advanced scout for an attack and decided to strike first."

"Poor kid," said Jinx. "He probably thought all that war paint would protect him."

Bobby scratched his head. "What I don't understand is why they brought us here. They still think we're missing our souls, right?"

"Which may be the point, not to mention the reason we're still alive." Jinx turned to Itzamna and spoke a few words Bobby didn't understand. In response, Itzamna reached out his arms, made a cupping gesture and drew his arms back into his chest.

"Just as I suspected," said Jinx. "They believe that, in order to save Taavi's soul from eternal damnation, they need to perform the same ritual that they performed on the others back at the village. And in order to do that—"

"They need his body," Bobby finished for him.

Jinx nodded. "It's why they spared us back at the village. They think that, since we are tainted, we can pass through the fence. They want us to retrieve Taavi's body and bring it back."

Bobby rubbed his face with his palms. "This day just keeps getting better and better."

* * *

A gust of wind sent a howl through the branches high overhead. Bobby looked up and saw dark, pregnant clouds swarming about with the promise of heavy rain. A slight drizzle had already begun, coating the upper canopy enough to send fat drops splattering down on his head. Bobby let them hit him, rooted as he was by his dilemma.

Obviously neither he nor Jinx could walk through a fence, electric or otherwise. However, one look at the grim faces of the natives, painted black and red and lined with determination, and Bobby knew they would accept no substitute.

Taavi's body lay far beyond the fence. There was no way to reach it from this side, even with a rope or long pole. Even if they could, there was no way to draw it through the fence.

Bobby turned to Itzamna, hands clasped together to beg for their lives, for understanding, for patience, as he and Jinx sought a way to explain. The medicine man, however, was not looking at the boys. Head cocked to one side, he seemed to be listening to something in the forest too subtle for Bobby's untrained ears.

Another gust of wind, this one accompanied by a clap of thunder. The warriors were moving now, gliding like wraiths out of the clearing. In seconds, they had slipped into the shadows and disappeared.

Jinx glanced around. Only Itzamna, scar-faced Tohil, and claw-wearing Votan remained. "What the hell is going on?"

Itzamna stood there, his body rigid, his countenance stern. For a long moment, he stared at Bobby with jet-black eyes that seemed to bore holes into Bobby's very being. Then he spoke. Immediately after, he turned and slipped into the forest with Tohil and Votan close behind.

After Bobby finally took a breath, he turned to Jinx and asked, "What did he say?"

Next to him, Jinx looked ashen. "The Spirit Men come."

* * *

The wind howled. For a second, Bobby thought a giant bolt of lightning had torn the sky. Then a warrior staggered into the clearing, clutching at a hole in his chest. That's when Bobby realized the truth.

Grabbing Jinx, he dove to the ground as gunfire erupted all around them. A Core guard broke into the clearing, an arrow protruding from behind his left shoulder. Another burst forth, grappling with a warrior with a bone knife angled for the guard's throat. The warrior's right arm hung limp and useless at his side, his spear nowhere to be seen.

Bobby dragged Jinx behind a giant fern as more gunshots rang out. From between wide fronds, Bobby saw Sandman accompanied by four Core guards, all dressed in black fatigues and carrying M-4 assault rifles. There was no sign of Itzamna or the others.

Right behind Sandman, a woman dressed all in red strode into the clearing. Bobby knew instantly it had to be the Scarlet Seer. With half her face a stoic facade and the other half painted in a horrible grin, she reminded Bobby of a hyena, laughing on the outside while inside wanting to rip your throat out. Two of Itzamna's warriors rushed at her, spears extended, ready to skewer her where she stood. She turned to each. Bobby saw her eyes narrow ever so slightly. Both men fell to the ground, grabbing at their heads, screaming as blood poured from their eyes, nose, and ears.

When the men on the ground grew still, the Scarlet Seer turned to Sandman. "Find them," she ordered.

Did she mean the natives, or me and Jinx? Either way, Bobby had no intention of sticking around to find out. Tugging on Jinx's sleeve, he pointed off into the jungle. Jinx nodded, his eyes posing a wordless question that Bobby could not answer. Neither of them had any idea what to do next.

CHAPTER NINETEEN

A million shades of green blended together to form a never-ending carousel of heavy fronds and clingy branches that slapped at Bobby with every step. The sounds of gunfire and shouting were distant now, mere echoes he kept at his back. He had no idea how long he and Jinx had been running, or in which direction, only that the light drizzle had turned into a true rain and that his boots were becoming harder and harder to lift.

At some point, they'd crossed a bridge. Bobby remembered breaking through the bushes to find a ledge overlooking a broad tributary. To the west, a rope bridge had spanned forty feet of wild rapids fuming with piranha.

Neither he nor Jinx said a word. They crossed as quickly as possible and trekked on, eager to put as much distance between themselves and the carnage behind them as possible. The rain had turned even the high ground to mud that sucked at their boots, draining their energy with every step. With the sky darkening and downpour intensifying, both boys were ready to quit.

"We need to find shelter," said Jinx.

"Back to the village?" Even before he asked the question, Bobby knew the answer.

"It's the first place they'll look."

"We could hide inside the hollow log," suggested Bobby.

"That also means going back." The weariness in Jinx's voice conveyed what he thought of that idea. "Besides, if this rain keeps up, that log is gonna fill up like a swimming pool."

"Got any suggestions?"

"Only one," said Jinx. With a tug on Bobby's coat, he drew his cousin to a stop. Shielding his eyes from the rivulets pouring off his forehead, Jinx pointed up.

Bobby sighed, an audible rumble over the constant pattering of the rain. "Like I said before, this day keeps getting better and better."

* * *

What Bobby at first took to be a near impossible task proved to be relatively simple. The trees were wet and slippery, but there were so many it wasn't long before they found a cluster with broad, low hanging branches that were relatively easy to climb. In the end, it was not dissimilar from ascending a spiral staircase. They went from one limb to the next until they were twenty feet off the ground.

The boys settled on a large kapok tree with limbs wide enough to sit comfortably. From their treetop perch, Bobby saw ruins scattered below them: squat stone structures that might have once been merchant stalls at a marketplace on the outskirts of the city. He also saw across the river, where thin wisps of smoke rose from the smoldering ashes of the village.

The wind shifted, bringing with it the foul stench of the Core's misdeeds. Bobby closed his eyes and breathed through his mouth until the wind shifted back. Thankfully, it wasn't long before the smoke and smell disappeared, buried beneath sheets of water and the veil of growing darkness. Bobby leaned against the kapok's trunk and waited for the storm to pass.

"Think the Core can track us up here?" asked Bobby over the noise of the now torrential flood.

"The rain will wash away any tracks," answered Jinx, shifting an overhead branch to redirect the flow away from his head. "Besides, no one wants to be out in this weather. They're probably already back at the temple."

"What about leopards or snakes?" asked Bobby,

"Even predators seek shelter from storms like this," said Jinx.

Bobby couldn't think of anything else worth talking about, so he settled back against the trunk and closed his eyes. It wasn't long before he fell asleep.

***

The spirit of Maximon visited Bobby in his dreams. The forlorn ghost of a long-dead empire showed Bobby images of the temple as it had been before its collapse. With immigrants pouring in every day, the jungle surrounding the city transformed into a makeshift refugee camp.

With the birth of their first child less than a moon cycle away, Lingya was so swollen that she was could barely walk, let along forage in the jungle. For this same reason, Maximon couldn't risk the increasingly long fishing trips needed to find waters not already picked clean. Instead, he took Lingya's place in the market, selling what few dried fish and poultices they had available.

It was there, in the marketplace that eventually became the ruins where Bobby slept, that Maximon encountered Ek Chuaj again. The brute carried a satchel over his shoulder and held his father's staff as he approached Maximon's nearly empty stall.

"I figured you might have fled here," said Ek Chuaj.

Tending to one of the few patrons Maximon had seen all day, he stiffened as he looked up and discovered the broad-shouldered youth from his home village towering over him. For a moment, Maximon flashed back to the night he and Lingya had run away, wondering if Ek Chuaj was here for revenge.

"Relax," said Ek Chuaj, as if reading his mind. "I am not here to hurt you. I just thought you'd like to know that our village was destroyed."

Maximon froze. He felt no ties to his home village. Still, Ek Chuaj delivered the news with such nonchalance that Maximon shuddered at his cousin's callousness. Ek Chuaj jingled the satchel on his shoulder. "Souvenirs from the Spaniards I slayed. Proof of my honor and bravery."

"But you said the village was destroyed."

Ek Chuaj smiled as if delivering good news. "I was away hunting when it happened. But don't worry, I took care of the invaders when I returned."

"What about your parents?"

Ek Chuaj shrugged. "Dead. Lingya's too, I'm afraid. Speaking of Lingya, where is my bride-to-be?"

"Not here," said Maximon. "And not yours. Lingya and I married right after we moved here."

Ek Chuaj stepped back in surprise. "Well, look at you! I didn't think you had it in you! I mean that quite literally. Of course, I knew how you felt about her, but I never thought you had the nerve to do anything about it. Too bad the marriage won't stand. We both know the village leader didn't give you permission."

"Your father would have approved if he knew the truth about what you did."

"I took only what was mine!" said Ek Chuaj. He raised his father's ceremonial staff. "Lingya was always meant for me. I had her before and will have her again!" Ek Chuaj took a deep breath, grasping the staff with both hands to calm himself. "Just as soon as I take care of a few other matters."

Maximon felt his face grow fiery with rage. He wanted to jump over the stall and murder Ek Chuaj. Instead, he folded his arms.

"Well, I must be off," said Maximon's cousin. "Time to declare myself to the priests and receive my reward for slaying these foreign devils," he said, jingling the bag on his shoulder. "But don't worry, now that I know where to find you, you can be sure you'll see me again."

***

Bobby woke to the unexpected sound of absolute stillness. The rain had stopped, washing away the physical events from the day before but not the haunting memories.

With a loud yawn, Jinx unfolded himself from the branch above and slid down next to him. "What's our next move?"

"The way I see it," said Bobby, "we have two options. We either try to walk outta here and get help, or we sneak back into the temple and try to rescue the others ourselves."

"They'll be expecting us to come back. Then again, I doubt we have much chance of getting outta here without a guide," said Jinx. "Not without falling into quicksand or being bitten by a poisonous snake."

"Then it's settled. We head back. Lily is still alone in the grotto and needs to know what's happened. Let's find some food to bring her and maybe a rope. Together, we'll figure out what to do next."

Finding food turned out to be incredibly simple. A nearby red-leaf fig tree was bursting with ripe figs. They stuffed their faces, then their pockets, supplementing their breakfast with the fresh rainwater pooled on leaves and the remains of a granola bar produced from yet another of Jinx's hidden pockets.

When they'd had their fill, they descended the trees and headed back toward the village. Upon reaching the river, however, they discovered a problem.

"Where's the bridge?" asked Bobby, scanning the riverbank in either direction.

"It must have torn free during the storm last night," said Jinx.

"Or was cut loose by the Core to strand us on this side," replied Bobby.

They searched for twenty minutes in either direction but found no other suitable place to cross. Bobby studied the rapid current, constantly broken by the white foam of treacherous rocks lying beneath the surface. As he watched, half a dozen fist-sized fish broke the surface, their razor teeth glinting in the morning sun.

"Those are piranha, the most dangerous creature in the entire rainforest," said Jinx.

Bobby stared at the infested water. "Jinx, this is it! This is the first trial Itzamna mentioned. Remember he talked about crossing the water made of teeth?"

"He said we had to do it without a boat yet remain perfectly still. I've been thinking about that mystery," said Jinx. "I haven't figured out how to do it. Maybe if we had an escalator. I think that would qualify as us remaining perfectly still."

"I'm gonna go out on a limb and say that we aren't likely to find a river-crossing mini-mall any time soon."

"I suppose we could use a log to float across," said Jinx.

"Even if we could keep from falling off, the current would carry us downstream and smash us on the rocks. Besides, I don't see any logs, and we have no tools."

They stood there, pondering the puzzle for some time. Bobby took a seat, drawing random squiggly lines in the soft clay of the riverbank with a stick. "I've got it," he said leaping to his feet.

"What is it?"

"Don't be mad, but I think I should be the one to do it."

"Do what? What are you talking about?"

Bobby grinned at his cousin. "Just promise me you won't scream." He sat down and assumed the lotus position, closed his eyes, and settled into a meditative trance. Performing the desired task was much like trying to have a private conversation in a noisy, crowded room. Thankfully, the voice he needed was one of the loudest.

To his credit, Jinx didn't even flinch when the water began to ripple. Something moved through the muddy river, something so big that even the piranhas left it alone. Jinx's mouth fell open when the giant diamond-head emerged, but he seemed more impressed than afraid.

"I should have known," said Jinx, as the anaconda slithered out of the fast-flowing river, its wet scales glistening like fresh grass laden with dewdrops in the warm morning sun.

"It's like we always say—" began Bobby.

"Everything happens for a reason," finished Jinx.

"If you hadn't summoned the snake, I never would have had the idea."

The green and brown behemoth coiled in the mud at Bobby's feet, its head resting lightly on top. Bobby held the mental link, projecting the image of what he wanted into the reptile's mind. In response, the serpent lowered its head and turned back for the water, stopping at the shoreline, its body poised.

"I guess now we find out if I'm clever or just insane," said Bobby.

"I just hope I don't wet myself," said Jinx. "And I'm not talking about the river."

Together, the boys walked down to the water's edge, stepping to each side of the snake's foot-wide torso. Lifting a leg, Bobby stepped across the snake, straddling it like a horse. Behind him, Jinx did the same. Before either boy had a chance to chicken out, the snake rose up, lifting their feet off the ground.

The massive serpent slipped into the river, angling southeast against the current. Elevated as they were, Bobby and Jinx found themselves gliding across the water, feet dangling inches above the surface. In the muddy depths of the churning waves, Bobby saw the darting arrowheads of piranha, tracking their movement. The merciless predators swarmed all over but did not attack.

Bobby gripped the snake's rock-hard side. Behind him, Jinx clung to Bobby's waist to keep his balance. Together, the two boys held on, breathless as the serpent worked its way steadily across the wide, frothing river.

Halfway to the shore, a piranha leapt out of the roaring water and snapped at Bobby's leg. It clamped on to the bottom of his pant leg, dangling there by its teeth. The giant snake slowed for just an instant. Its neck came around and the head shot out. Bobby felt something brush his leg and when he looked back, the sharp-toothed fish was gone. The great snake crunched down, then swallowed before resuming its course.

* * *

On the soggy shore of the far riverbank, Jinx fell to his knees, bowing over and over again to the great snake. Bobby looked over his shoulder at the river with its thrashing tides of man-eating piranha and added his own silent thanks. He still had no idea what the other two trials were supposed to mean, but he couldn't imagine them being any more terrifying than that experience.

Tugging at Jinx's jacket, Bobby signaled that perhaps it was time to go. Jinx rose from the muddy banks and brushed himself off, adding one last thanks before moving away. The emerald serpent sat there, watching them through reptilian eyes the color of the jungle itself, but made no move to leave or follow.

Making their way into the rainforest, Bobby and Jinx moved rapidly through the brush. Locating a game trail, they followed it until Jinx recognized the path that would lead them back to the village. It took nearly half the morning but finally they spotted trees blackened by the fire set by Itzamna and his warriors.

Heavy rains had contained the fire, but not before the village itself, along with the surrounding area, had been charred to ash. Slowing as they approached the center, Bobby forced his shoulders to relax. Not only was there no trace of the Core, the water had washed away most of the gore. He tried to avoid staring at the pile of bones in the middle of the clearing as he let out a deep breath. It was still gruesome to behold but the stench was gone.

Reluctant at first, they searched the wreckage, looking for an undamaged rope that could be used to hoist Lily up from the well chamber. They stuck to the perimeter of the village where there was less damage. Jinx found a long rope made from braided vines below a fishing net he guessed had been wet when the fire started because it was barely singed. Bobby coiled up the rope and hooked it over his shoulder. With a last look, he and Jinx departed the silent clearing.

They walked quickly at first, happy to be away from the village, then slowed about an hour later when the temple began to draw close. They passed first by the clearing where Taavi had been, but the boy's body was gone, probably removed by order of Sandman or the Scarlet Seer. Bobby wondered about the warriors who had fought with the Core guards at this very spot. He saw no bodies and, again, the rain had washed away all tracks. Still, he didn't peer too closely into the bushes.

Roughly ten minutes after leaving the clearing where Taavi had been, Bobby and Jinx arrived at the sunken log. It took only a moment's glance to know something was wrong. In the low light, the hollow looked to have filled with water.

Jinx dropped his pack and slumped to the ground. "What the hell? It'll take hours to dig this out."

"What choice do we have? Lily's been trapped in that grotto for over a day now and is expecting us to come back with help. We have to get back in there and tell her what's happened."

As it turned out, only the top layer was water. Dipping a hand in, Bobby discovered that the log had been filled in with dirt. Jinx looked ready to burst into tears as he inspected the hole. "The Core must have realized that Taavi snuck through the fence and searched until they found the hole," he said.

"Which means they're also probably gonna patrol more regularly from now on," said Bobby.

"Which effectively eliminates this as an option," said Jinx. "Even if we could dig it out, they'd spot us for sure. Hell, for all we know, they have motion detectors and cameras set up watching us right now."

That raised the hairs on Bobby's arms. One glance at Jinx and he knew his cousin was thinking the same thing. They retrieved their packs and retreated into the jungle. Without waiting to know if they'd been discovered, they headed out once again.

CHAPTER TWENTY

The bank manager, Gordon "The Gordster" Kawolski, had a helmet of sandy brown hair that looked like you could strike it with a bat and not make a dent. Early forties, with a spray tan that left orange streaks down his neck, he wore pants two sizes too small in a futile attempt to hide his increasing potbelly.

The former insurance and real estate agent looked from Jeremiah to Cassandra with desperate, watery eyes. "Please try to understand. It's not my rule. It's corporate's. We aren't permitted to allow anyone inside the vault who isn't a holder of a security deposit box."

"I'm on the signature card," said Jeremiah. "I showed you my ID."

"Oh, you're not the problem," said Gordon Kawolski. "It's your... ahem...girlfriend, who we are not able to allow inside."

Cassandra shot Jeremiah a glance. He looked bedraggled from all their running around, and no telling what they might find in the vault. She could see from the grim look on his face that he needed her now.

Taking a moment to gather herself for what she was about to do, she took a deep breath, then leaned in close to the bank manager. Crossing her legs, she placed a hand lightly on his arm and batted her eyelashes. "Gordon, right? I'm not his girlfriend,' she said in the most sultry, seductive voice she could muster. "I'm his sister."

Kawolski blushed so hard he would have turned beet red if not for the painted orange hue of his skin.

"So then, you're related?" He said it as a question, leaving Cassandra to wonder if perhaps she hadn't overdone it with the charm.

"In fact, we are," she said when it became clear he wanted an answer.

"She's also single and only in town for a few days visiting," said Jeremiah, "You could use someone to show you around town. Isn't that right, sis?"

To Gordon he added, "Older women can be quite sophisticated, wouldn't you agree, Gordon? I'm sure my sister would love the companionship of a proper gentleman such as yourself."

Gordon Kawolski's eyes travelled all over Cassandra, from her Prada dress-jacket to her respectable but inviting mini-skirt.

"I couldn't agree more," he said, practically drooling on his desk. "I suppose we can make an exception as long as we have positive proof of ID and get an authorization form." His eyes were glued to the hemline of Cassandra's skirt.

Cassandra pretended to fish around in her purse for a moment. "Oh shoot, I seem to have left my ID back at my hotel room. Couldn't I show it to you another time? Say, over dinner tonight?"

Gordon Kawolski swallowed hard and shifted in his chair. No doubt, the Gordster was already fantasizing about events at the hotel room, adding them to past conquests, however imagined they might be.

"I...I suppose that would be acceptable, as long as I'm able to make a copy for our files."

"I've got a printer with a copier in my suite," she said.

"Among other things," added Jeremiah, clearly relishing his role.

"In that case," said Gordon, standing up from his desk and taking a moment to adjust his suit, "Follow me. I'll show you to the vault where we house the deposit boxes."

* * *

The instant they were alone in the vault, Cassandra wheeled on Jeremiah, striking him in the shoulder with her purse so hard he'd have a bruise for a week.

"Don't you ever do something like that again!"

"What?" said Jeremiah. "You were already flirting with him."

"I was only doing what I needed to do to so that I could accompany you. I don't know if you realize it, but you've been preoccupied ever since we left Melody's cottage."

"Alright, I'm sorry. I just thought the story would work better if I helped sell it a little."

Cassandra was not smiling. Her face brimmed with unbridled rage. "By telling him I'm single and that I'm only in town for a few days, like some cheap floozy?"

"You're the one who invited him back to your hotel room."

"Where you basically promised him that I'd have sex with him!" exclaimed Cassandra.

"Cass, you don't even have a hotel room!" countered Jeremiah.

Cassandra glared at him. "That's not the point."

"Okay, you're right. I'm sorry. Now can we please do this?"

"Fine, but don't think for one second that I've forgotten about that 'older women' comment either."

Locating the deposit box, Jeremiah withdrew the long, slender gunmetal grey container and set it on the high-standing marble table in the middle of the vault. Opening the lid, he began to withdraw the contents, taking mental inventory as he set each item off to the side.

"Several of the larger gems are missing, but that doesn't mean anything," said Jeremiah. "Melody probably took those to pay for the house. The jewelry, her will, the deed to the house, even our real passports when I changed our last name to Ether after we fled the academy; everything appears to be in order."

"There isn't a note or anything? What about on the deed, maybe she wrote something on it?"

Jeremiah shook his head. "Melody would never leave something so obvious. We've learned to take precautions over the years, in case the academy ever tracked one of us down," he said, removing the last items: gold coins from the Spine of the World's treasure room. All that remained was a sheet of newspaper, cut and placed as a liner on the bottom of the box. "If she left us a clue, it will be something subtle that can't be directly tracked back to either one of us."

"Wait, what's that?" said Cassandra, pointing to the newspaper. "It looks like the personal ad section."

Withdrawing the paper, Jeremiah flipped it over. "There's nothing on the back."

"Maybe one of the ads means something," she said, scanning the small boxes with their tiny print. "There, look at that one," she said, pointing to the box in the lower right corner. "Private Consultation: $250."

"There's no phone number and no description what kind of consultation it is. It could be anything."

"Just like Melody's credit card statement, and the amount is the same."

"The address is in Downey. We can be there in an hour if we beat traffic."

"Then you'd better let me drive," said Cassandra, helping Jeremiah toss the items back into the lockbox and place the box back in the wall.

"I'd love to," said Jeremiah. "But don't you have a date back at your hotel?"

Cassandra shot him a dark look full of malice, but the corners of her mouth upturned. "One more word out of you, old man, and I'll make sure the Gordster finds his way to your room tonight."

For the first time in weeks, Jeremiah roared with genuine laughter. He hid his mirth when Cassandra gave Gordon Kawolski a fake hotel room number, written in lipstick on the back of a deposit slip. Out in the parking lot he let loose again as they settled into Cassandra's Porsche.

Finally, things were starting to look up. They had a solid lead, something that had definitely been left by Melody intentionally for him to find. *What are you up to, my angel?* Only one way to find out.

He settled back into the soft leather seats of the Porsche Spyder and held on tight. Cassandra tore out of the parking lot, heading to Downey with all of the fervor of a Le Mans racecar driver.

* * *

The second night Bobby and Jinx spent in the trees was nearly as bad as their first. It didn't rain, and there was little wind, but fatigue and hunger weighed heavily on each of them.

The figs from the day before were all gone, as was the last of Jinx's secret stash. The boys scavenged in the late afternoon for fruit, berries, and anything else they could find. Bobby didn't mind too much. The granola bars had been brittle and stale, and the figs had given him the runs. Still, both had been better than an empty stomach.

As true night descended, Bobby settled into their new roost, a banyan tree whose branches had grown close to a kapok to form a broad, level platform on which to rest. In his lap, he cradled the bounty he'd collected: three small green bananas, four wild pomegranates, and a large papaya-like fruit Jinx identified as some type of sapote.

Jinx added his score: a bushel of overripe, yellow loquats, a mango that looked like a monkey had eaten half of it before throwing it away, and a shirt full of macadamia nuts. Once again, they drank water collected in leaves and ate what they could.

The hard, green shells of the macadamias were nearly impossible to crack. First, Bobby tried smashing them against the trunk of the Kapok, but the wood proved too porous, yielding rather than cracking the nuts' thick outer layer. The only way to get to the rich creamy nutmeat, he discovered, was to cup his hands and squeeze two shells together until one of them cracked. It was slow going and hurt his hands, forcing him to quit long before he'd had his fill.

Eventually, he leaned back and tried to rest. Fear and anxiety sat upon his shoulders like a troop of monkeys. What if something had happened to Lily while they'd been gone? What if Chief lay dead somewhere and no one knew they were out here all alone? What if Grandpa and Cassandra never came looking for them? Or worse, what if they did come into La Muerte Verde and the natives killed them?

The only people he didn't worry about were Trevor, Jacob, and Slab. Something told Bobby that the Core wouldn't be using Slab to test students again any time soon and, as long as the Core still hadn't figured out the temple's secrets, the others would remain unharmed. Right about now, Bobby would have gladly swapped places with any one of them, trading freedom for a warm sleeping bag and a hot meal.

"Man, what I wouldn't give for a double-bacon cheeseburger and some sweet-potato curly fries," said Bobby. "I wouldn't even complain there was no ketchup."

Jinx nodded his agreement, but Bobby could tell his cousin was far less disturbed by their limited diet. Perhaps it was just that he was smaller and ate less, but his younger cousin seemed in an almost chipper mood, keeping up a constant stream of conversation about the various plants and animals they'd encountered. He talked about the domestic and medicinal uses for various woods and fibers, as well as the seeds, oils, pollens, and other resources found all around them.

Bobby suspected that Jinx talked so much to distract himself from their situation, so he kept quiet and let Jinx chatter about whatever he wanted. Only when it got truly dark did Bobby start to worry about the noise. Jinx seemed to sense this as well, lowering his voice to hushed tones.

It was during an explanation about the migration and feeding patterns of the Guatemalan black howler monkeys, of which they'd several several throughout the day, that Bobby spotted the eyes.

From the deep shadows of a neighboring tree, two slits of golden amber reflected brightly in the dim light. There could be no doubt the feline eyes belonged to a panther. The jungle cat gave a low growl from the back of its throat. Jinx rushed to Bobby's side, clinging to him while reciting everything he could about melanistic Panthera onca, black jaguars, and their feeding habits.

"The jaguar is a solitary, opportunistic, stalk-and-ambush predator," stated Jinx. "However, unlike all other species in the Panthera genus, jaguars rarely attack humans."

"Where did you learn that?" asked Bobby, amazed by both the information and his cousin's photographic memory.

"Wikipedia," said Jinx. "Chief gave me a laptop with a hardline connection when I was with him at the Eagle's Nest over the summer."

Bobby watched the feline eyes for a long time. After nearly an hour, he occasioned to blink and they were gone. He waited for a long time for the eyes to reappear, but they never did. Eventually, he grew tired, closed his eyes and dreamed.

* * *

He sat upon a misty white cloud, high above the verdant rainforest. Far below, monkeys howled, and birds cried, filling the air with their vibrant and abundant songs of life.

For a while, Bobby floated above it all, content to enjoy the view. The rainforest looked so tranquil from up here. Down below, it seethed with violence and chaos: animals devouring one another, from tiny insects to large predators, cunning reptiles to poisonous amphibians, killing and dying in the eternal cycle of life. There was no death up above, merely the calm and beauty of the canopy, masking the frenetic competition for survival that took place every second of every day below.

He felt at peace so high up. No trouble could touch him up here, not even his own. And then smoke began to rise from the forest. At first, he thought it was another village on fire, but no orange glow accompanied the dark tendrils. He watched as four thick columns of black smoke rose up and headed toward him. As they drew closer, he realized there were people atop each column.

Simpkins rose up on his left. The skeletal agent wore a gray cloak and heavy cowl in place of his customary seventies attire, granting him the appearance of death itself. Hayward came up on his right, his clothes entirely absent, replaced by the gelatinous body of a giant green slug.

Sandman stood behind. The guard captain's body was a hideous Minotaur combination of man and bull, swollen with muscles and complete with bovine torso, legs, and tail.

The Scarlet Seer was in front. She wore a blood-red wedding dress. Over her face, she wore the split masks of comedy and tragedy, with the tragedy side painted a brilliant white, the comedy side a deep crimson. She laughed and Bobby felt malice deep in his bones. She and the others had come to pull him down from the sky and drag him low.

Hayward pointed at Bobby, and a bolt of lightning shot forth. Bobby tried to swerve but Simpkins raised his arms. Bobby was unable to move. Sandman fixed his gaze upon him and suddenly the cloud beneath Bobby's feet was thinning. With each lightning strike, it dissolved from pearly white to translucent until there was nothing left.

And then he was falling, tumbling down from the heavens and their calm to crash into the jungle and madness below. All he heard as he fell was the lady in red, laughing and laughing, the horrible sound echoing in his ears until he thought he would go mad.

CHAPTER TWENTY-ONE

T he eyes were there in the morning. Bobby spotted them high in the treetops, only now, he saw the faint outline of the jaguar as well, gray on black in the dense shadows of the trees. The magnificent jungle cat stepped into the open with measured strides.

It stopped, majestically posed fifty feet above the jungle floor on nothing but a branch the size of Bobby's wrist. Then it lowered its head.

"Come on," said Bobby, shaking his little cousin awake urgently. "I know what we need to do."

Jinx blinked at him, his own dreams still heavy on his eyelids. "What's going on?" he said sleepily.

"I'll explain when we get there. Right now, we gotta get going."

They scrambled down from the kapok and ate the fruit left over from the night before as they travelled through the jungle once more. When they emerged into the familiar clearing near the hollow log, Jinx huffed and said, "We've been over this before. It'll take forever to dig that tree out again. Besides, the guards are probably watching the whole area."

"I just needed to get my bearings," said Bobby, groping through the heavy brush until they came to a sandbox tree with a trunk as big around as his house back in LA.

"Time to climb."

Thick black spikes protruded from all over the tree, making it difficult to scale. Instead, they used lengths of the braided vine scavenged from the village to hoist themselves up one branch at a time. Bobby went first, helping to pull up his smaller and less athletic cousin.

Huffing and wheezing as he was, Jinx still managed to bombard Bobby with questions about the plan. When Bobby finally told him, Jinx lost his grip on the branch he was holding. Bobby caught him by the back of his jacket, hailing him up by the scruff of his neck like a lioness with a cub in her mouth.

"You know this is insane, right?" said Jinx, bear-hugging the tree trunk as he regained his composure.

"You got a better idea?"

Jinx huffed and reached for the next branch. They were high now. The canopy lay like a spongy green blanket below. Only a few other trees poked out, like groundhogs checking the weather. Off to the south, the electric fence surrounding the temple reached its limit, its top slashing a perpendicular line a few feet below them.

"This is the spot," said Bobby, pointing off to the south. "I recognize that tree on the other side."

"So, we're doing all this because you saw a jaguar when you woke up this morning?"

"It was the same one we saw leap over the fence when we came out of the hollow log. I know it. He was trying to show me how to get across."

"Not that I'm doubting you, but maybe next time you could ask him to show you how to pick the lock on the main gate or distract the guards by imitating a panther growl or something."

Bobby couldn't help but laugh at his cousin's nervous attempt at humor. "Next time, for sure."

"So, now what?"

Bobby gazed out over the divide to the narrow branch of the banyan tree on the other side of the fence.

"Now we jump."

* * *

Bobby couldn't remember the last time he felt so nervous. Here he stood on a slender tree branch over fifty feet in the air, contemplating leaping to another tree well over ten feet away. All the moisture had left his mouth, apparently transferring to his hands and brow. From the sweat pouring off his forehead, it felt like it was raining again.

Maybe he really was going crazy. Somehow, though, he knew he wasn't. He'd correctly read the signs leading to the first trial, which allowed them to cross the river.

He remembered Itzamna's words about "walking across the sky, high up where the birds fly." Clearly, this was the second trial. He just had no idea how to do it.

Handing his backpack to Jinx, Bobby sat down and straddled the branch, gripping it with his thighs to maintain his balance. Behind him, Jinx leaned against the trunk, his expression quizzical.

Everything was different above the canopy. Bobby heard rustling leaves, accompanied by the occasional squawk of a wild parrot. He felt the glowing warmth of the sun on his cheeks. Up here water evaporated rather than drip down to the forest floor.

Even the wind was different, carrying the sweet fragrance of fresh air rather than the ubiquitous smell of damp earth found in the underbrush. As he sat there feeling the breeze, a giant feather floated down from the sky. The feather floated softly in the breeze, swinging back and forth like a baby in a cradle. Then a gust carried it out over the divide where it danced in the wind before disappearing from view.

"I know what I have to do," said Bobby, standing up and extended his arms out to either side to keep his balance. He stood there for a moment, feeling the breeze swirl around him. *It will work, I can feel it.* He closed his eyes, waiting.

He waited for a long time, perfectly balanced on the slender branch high above the forest floor. Jinx remained by the trunk, quiet as the breeze, spellbound by Bobby's bizarre actions.

Now! With a start, Bobby opened his eyes and took off running along the branch. Beneath him, the limb grew slimmer and slimmer with each step. He barely noticed. In fact, his feet barely touched the bough at all.

The branch narrowed until it was nothing more than a twig with a handful of leaves on the end. Bobby took one last step, right before the end. And then he was leaping out over the gulf into empty space.

* * *

When asked later, Bobby swore he felt so light that the breeze literally lifted him, allowing him to float across the gap. All Jinx could say was that he'd never seen or heard of anything like it. For nearly five seconds, Bobby hung in the air, his arms and legs churning in the aftermath of his mad dash. Then he slowly began to fall back down.

Even floating the way he did, he barely made it to the other side. His right foot grazed the tip of the branch, buoying him ever so slightly. It was enough. He leaned into his landing and got his left foot down. Three more steps and he reached the trunk, hugging it as he caught his breath.

"OMG, that was amazing!" called Jinx. "I can't believe that just happened!"

Bobby grinned. The last time Jinx had been that excited was when Bobby had described his encounter with the badger back at the academy.

"When I saw that eagle's feather, I thought of this game I used to play as a kid: light as a feather, stiff as a board," said Bobby. "I focused on making myself as light as possible, then waited until I felt the breeze at my back."

"I will make sure to consult the instructions for that game as soon as we return to civilization," said Jinx.

"There's no rule book. It's just something kids do on sleepovers." Bobby saw the blank look on Jinx's face. "Never mind. Come on, your turn."

Even from across the divide, Bobby could tell Jinx had turned as white as the clouds overhead. He hugged the tree trunk, shaking his head vehemently. "This is insane!"

"Jinx, listen to me. I can't really explain it, maybe it's the prophecy, but I know you can do this."

"I... I can't. I'm afraid to even leave the trunk. What if I fall?"

"We'll use the rope," said Bobby, then sheepishly added, "Actually, I probably should have thought of that before I jumped."

Bobby tossed the rope across the gap to Jinx. They formed a loop and tied the packs to it. Together, they shuttled their gear across like a conveyor belt.

With their meager supplies safely on the other side, Jinx tied the rope around his waist. "I don't know about this," he said. "With my history, trying to imagine myself light as a feather could have catastrophic results."

Bobby nodded his understanding. "Give me a sec. I'm gonna climb up above so that, if you fall, I've got better leverage to catch you."

"Knock on wood," said Jinx, with a nervous laugh for his unintended pun.

Bobby scrambled up two branches, secured himself around the waist, and propped himself against the trunk.

"Here goes nothing." Jinx blew hard through his mouth as he left the comfort of the trunk and ventured out onto the branch. When he stood a good five feet from the end, he carefully placed his hands on the bough above him. Then he stopped.

"Before I actually jump, let's see if I can decrease my weight the way you did."

Jinx closed his eyes. Bobby waited. After a few moments, he felt the energy around Jinx begin to shift. "You're doing it, buddy!"

With a loud crack, the branch snapped. Jinx tried to jump back, but it was already too late. The branch sent up a thunderous roar as it crashed its way to the forest floor. For a second, Jinx clung to the limb above him, but a spike dug into his wrist and he lost his grip.

Time seemed to slow as Jinx fell. Bobby frantically took up slack, but the rope had been loose for the jump. Two agonizing seconds passed before the rope finally grew taut. Unfortunately, it also pulled Jinx out over the divide and straight toward the electric fence.

With mere moments before Jinx got electrocuted, Bobby did the only thing he could think to do. Grabbing the rope firmly in both hands, he jumped out of the banyan tree.

As he'd hoped, his counterweight lifted Jinx, but not by much. Jinx's feet barely cleared the fence. His right boot dragged, catching the top links. Sparks flew and the air filled with the noxious smell of burnt rubber. And then Jinx was over. His pendulum swing carried him into the tree on the other side.

Bobby let go of the rope and Jinx landed on a branch several rungs below. Bobby scrambled down to his cousin. The right side of Jinx's face was scratched and bloodied from where he'd struck the tree. His hiking boot was a blackened mess, the thick rubber sole all but melted away by the contact with the electric fence.

"Somehow, 'I told you so' doesn't quite cover it," said Jinx.

"I am so sorry!" said Bobby. "I should have had more tension on the line. I thought you were going to jump."

"Yeah well, me trying to become light as a feather made me heavy as a ton of bricks."

"Agreed. Next time we'll string the rope between the trees, and you can cross hand over hand."

Jinx shot him a look of utter disbelief. "You really are crazy. There is never, ever going to be a next time."

* * *

It wasn't until they were on solid ground that Bobby looked back at where they'd crossed. The panther stood on the uppermost branch, resplendent with its glossy black coat and brilliant amber eyes. The jungle cat dipped its head low for a moment and then it was gone, leaping from limb to limb as swiftly as the wind.

CHAPTER TWENTY-TWO

B ack on the temple grounds, Bobby and Jinx moved cautiously through the heavy undergrowth near the edge of the uppermost terrace. It wasn't long before they'd worked their way to the west side and located the mossy boulder that concealed the underground passage leading to the secret grotto.

Prying the boulder aside, Bobby peered into the tunnel. The landing above the grotto lay in complete darkness. Like voices in the night, Bobby heard whispers from the well below. He ignored them as he took out a flashlight and shined it over the lip of the slope.

Not wanting to risk being heard by a nearby patrol, he called softly into the darkness. "Lily, are you down there?" Nothing.

"Perhaps she's asleep," suggested Jinx.

Bobby slid down on his rear with Jinx close behind. When he got to the bottom, Bobby panned the light around. "Lily, where are you? We brought food, and a rope to pull you out."

Only the muted echo of his voice returned from the dark. He went to light the brazier. As Bobby fumbled in his pocket for the lighter, his hand brushed the idol of Hunhau. He leapt back in surprise. A woman stood in the middle of the room, but it wasn't Lily.

"Lingya!" said, Bobby seeing the spirit of the Mayan woman standing by the well. She wore the full-length linen robes of a servant woman, her lustrous brown hair bundled tight. In her arms, she cradled an infant boy.

"What are you doing here?" asked Bobby.

"I remember now," said Lingya.

Bobby held up a hand, as if a mere gesture could ward off a ghost. "I don't have time for this right now."

As she drew close, Bobby saw that she was distraught. Whatever memory the spirit wanted to share, it had drained the color from her normally ruddy cheeks and set her full lips tight with despair.

Still cradling her child with one arm, the teary-eyed ghost lifted her other hand and placed it on Bobby's forehead. "Listen to my story."

***

After her son Bahlam was born, Lingya went to work in the temple full time. The pregnancy had been hard on her back and legs, making it difficult to forage, especially with an infant strapped to her chest. At the temple, there were other maids to help look after the baby whenever she needed to run to the market or assist one of the priests. The rest of the time, she was able to perform her tasks of serving meals, cleaning the prayer chambers, and mending clothes with Bahlam nearby.

She was cleaning the fountain room when Ek Chuaj found her. She turned from sweeping under the prayer benches to find the thick-browed ruffian standing in the doorway. Lingya screamed and dropped her broom. Maximon had told her about their encounter in the marketplace. Still, it caught Lingya by surprise to find Ek Chuaj here, in the inner sanctum of the temple.

"You had to know it was only a matter of time before I found you," said Ek Chuaj with hands on his hips. Her first thought was for Bahlam, but her son was with Maximon at the market today. Lingya clutched both hands to her robe, pulling it tight.

Ek Chuaj snorted. "We really need to take care of this timidity of yours. It won't do to have my wife so nervous all the time, especially in public."

Lingya forced her hands to her sides. "Maximon told me all about your meeting. I will never marry you!"

Ek Chuaj detached himself from the wall and sauntered over to the prayer bench beside Lingya. It was after visiting hours, with no chance of being disturbed. Setting one foot on the bench, he offered a smile full of chipped and crooked teeth. "Not even to a wealthy and powerful man?"

Lingya clutched her stomach; the thought of Ek Chuaj with power made her physically ill.

"I told them I know the foreigners' weaknesses, how to kill them," said Ek Chuaj. "As a reward for my service, they have made me a captain in their army. I'm to begin overseeing security of the farmlands and commerce roads immediately."

Lingya flung her hands in the air. "There's no way you killed the foreigners. You're a bully, and like all bullies, you're a coward at heart."

"Ah, but I had proof of my heroism: a bag full of armor and weapons taken from the soldiers I defeated at our village. Now I have a position of power and deserve a beautiful woman at my side."

Lingya shrank back into the corner. Grabbing the broom, she brandished it like a sword. "Stay away from me. Stay back!"

Ek Chuaj retreated, hands up. "I have no need to use force. Not anymore. You will offer yourself to me willingly soon enough." He turned, heading for the chamber entrance. He stopped and glanced over his shoulder. "Just don't take too long, my betrothed. This city may not be safe for you if you aren't by my side."

* * *

Bobby woke to rough hands grabbing him by the shoulders. He stood in the grotto, one hand leaning against the well. Lingya's spirit was gone, replaced by a larger and entirely corporeal figure. Sandman was accompanied by two burly Core guards, both equipped with Tasers.

The captain of the guard gave a wicked grin as he dug his fingers into Bobby's neck. "Welcome back, cadet."

* * *

By the time Cassandra pulled the Spyder into the empty parking lot outside the address listed on the ad, Jeremiah's jovial mood had all but evaporated. His wife was still missing. Time was wasting and a nervous twist in the pit of his gut told him he needed to find Melody, and fast. He got out of the car, leading Cassandra to the building.

The property stood in disrepair, with patches of weeds sprouting between the concrete slabs that led from the parking lot to the dour, one-story office building. Off to the side, a row of untrimmed hedges squatted below a faded blue-on-white sign that read OmniCorp, Inc.

Jeremiah checked the address before pulling open the double glass door and gesturing for Cassandra to enter. She did so with a look of obvious distaste for the surroundings. They passed into a narrow, dim lit hallway with an unmarked door at the end.

Jeremiah tried the handle and found it unlocked. They stepped through together, discovering a reception area that belied the building's exterior.

Cassandra all but swooned at the white on white décor, the egg-shell leather couches, and the fossilized seashell centerpiece surrounded by a spray of white orchids atop the frosted glass and steel coffee table. The fossil itself might not have been her style but the colors suited her perfectly.

"That's an original Patrick Nagel," she gasped, gesturing to the large art deco painting of an elegant woman with black hair and bright red lipstick. "Do you have any idea how much that's worth?"

Jeremiah had no interest in the artwork. With long, determined strides, he crossed to the sliding glass window on the far wall. Ringing the service bell, he waited until a statuesque brunette with startling blue eyes slid the panel open.

"May I help you?" the woman asked.

"I'm looking for a woman who came here for a consultation, Melody Ether."

"I'm sorry, sir, but all of our client information is strictly confidential."

"I know she was here. What is this place? What do you do here?"

The woman's voice was congenial but held a tone of iron that clearly conveyed what she thought of this line of questioning. "I'm sorry, sir, but I'm not at liberty to discuss the nature of our services."

"What about this ad I found in the paper? How can I know if I want your services if you don't tell me what they are?"

"I'm sorry, sir, but you must be mistaken. We don't advertise. Our business is by referral only."

"Then how did I get this address?"

"May I?" asked the woman, extending a hand. Jeremiah handed her the paper. "Ah, yes, I recall this case. We placed this ad after the client had already retained our services. A strange request, but you know what they say: the customer is always right."

"So, she was here. Do you have her records? What address did she give you? Did she leave a current phone number?"

"I'm sorry, sir, but as I stated before, I am not at liberty to—"

Jeremiah reached through the sliding window, snatched the woman by her designer blouse, and yanked her halfway through the opening.

"Now you listen to me," he said, panting as he fought to control his temper. "My wife left me this," he said, waving the personal ad in front of the woman's face, "so that I would find this place. I am not leaving until I know where she is. Either you tell me now, or I will break down this door and come back there and get the answers for myself. Am I clear?"

The woman appraised him calmly with her arresting blue eyes. Jeremiah saw neither fear nor anger in her gaze, merely curiosity.

"Jeremiah, let go," said Cassandra, laying a hand gently on his arm. "There are better ways to do this." He released the receptionist.

"Perhaps there is a supervisor we can talk to?" suggested Cassandra.

The receptionist took a moment to straighten her blouse. "One moment." She slid the glass panel shut, leaving Jeremiah and Cassandra alone in the lobby. Cassandra sat on the cream-colored couch, admiring the art, while Jeremiah paced back and forth like a caged tiger.

Moments later, the receptionist returned. "I've been instructed to give you this," she said, handing him a brochure, "And to tell you that all further inquiries need to be directed to our main office."

Jeremiah opened the brochure and realization began to set in. "These aren't your main offices?"

"This is where we do some of our initial consultation and follow-up appointments."

"Where are your main offices?"

She told him.

"Come on," Jeremiah said to Cassandra, grabbing her hand and dragging her to the door.

"Where are we going?"

"Back to the airport. I think I finally know what's going on."

* * *

The first stop for Bobby and Jinx was a pit much like the one where Bobby had fought Slab. Over twelve feet deep, the main difference was that this pit had no door up above and no gate down below. It was just a hole in the ground. Separating the boys, the guards fastened a rope around Jinx's waist and lowered him down, then pulled the rope up again after he reached the bottom.

Sandman turned to leave and one of the guards prodded Bobby in the back, signaling for him to follow.

"Where are we going? You can't just leave Jinx here," said Bobby. His cousin hadn't said a word since their capture back in the grotto, but Bobby could tell from his wide eyes that Jinx was scared out of his mind.

"The commander has other plans for you," said Sandman.

With no other options, Bobby followed him through the stone corridors until they came to a massive archway over which a modern steel door had been constructed, fitted perfectly against the stone to provide complete privacy for whatever lay on the other side.

The guards stationed themselves to either side of the entrance. Sandman gestured for Bobby to enter. Cracking open the thick metal door, Bobby discovered a majestic solarium. Exposed to the sky, an assortment of trees and flowers bloomed in the vast, circular chamber. Bobby spotted a wild apple tree, along with some banana stalks and a red leaf fig tree like the one he and Jinx had eaten from during their first night alone in the jungle.

For a moment, he wondered what he was doing in this picturesque garden. Then, from behind the apple tree, a woman appeared. She wore all red and the right side of her face was painted in the mask of comedy. Bobby recognized the Scarlet Seer from when he'd last seen her in the forest by Taavi's body.

The woman's eyes went to the door behind him. Bobby realized it was still ajar, with Sandman peering through the opening.

"That will be all," said The Scarlet Seer.

"Commander, this boy is the one I told you about, the one we tested—"

"We will be fine. Won't we, Bobby?"

The question sent a strange chill creeping across the surface of his skin. He didn't know why, but for some reason, he believed her.

Sandman snapped to attention. "Yes sir, commander." He saluted and closed the door behind him.

Alone with the woman who'd dropped men to their knees with only a glance, Bobby gripped one hand in the other. She made her way slowly toward him. He began to tremble as she drew close, but the woman's eyes where not on him. Instead, she strode past him to the door.

Bobby stood there, transfixed as she flicked the deadbolt, sliding it home with a dull thud. She paused for a moment. Bobby felt a tingle of anima ignite the air. Then it was gone.

Finally, she turned to face him. "Alone at last," she said. The bare half of her face drew into a smile to match the painted side. "Tell me Bobby, do you know who I am?"

"They call you the Scarlet Seer," he said slowly. "You run this place, looking for the secret of the Fountain of Youth. You're experimenting on kids brought here by the Core, injecting them with serums derived from the water in what, I assume, is the hope of triggering enhanced metaphysical abilities in the subjects, most likely prolonged or even eternal life."

The Scarlet Seer left her place by the door, walking up to him until she stood just a few feet away. "That is all very insightful, and correct, but that's not what I asked. I asked if you know who I am?"

Bobby stood there, uncertain how else to reply. She studied him, her forest-green eyes watching him with the intensity of a hawk, registering every move, every facial expression.

"Follow me," she said, breaking eye contact. She walked past him again, this time heading toward the back of the solarium. When he made no move to follow, she stopped and turned back around. "I assure you, everything will become clear in a moment."

He followed her past the apple tree, then past a small garden where an assortment of wild roses bloomed. They stopped at a slender, crystal stream that ran from under the stones on the east wall, trickling a delicate path through the garden to a pool in the northwest corner.

The Scarlet Seer knelt down beside the pool, her back to him. A loose stone lay by his feet. He bent to pick up the rock then stopped. He watched as she pulled the sleeves on her scarlet gown up over her elbows, then plunged her hands into the water. Cupping her palms, she brought the water to her face and scrubbed at her cheeks. She performed the motions again, this time tilting her head to the right so that the water hit only the side covered by paint. The crystal waters at her feet turned red as the paint wore off, running in rivulets down her elbows to drip into the pool. She performed this routine several more times until the water ran clear once more. Then she stood up and turned to face him.

The difference was striking. Devoid of her painted mask, the woman before him was neither terrifying nor intimidating. In fact, she looked somehow familiar. Bobby re-examined her angular features, her thick lips and indelicate nose. Then he gasped. She looked almost like...except for...

Slowly, the Scarlet Seer lifted a hand to her right eye. She pinched her fingers and closed her eyelid. She repeated the gesture with her left eye. She stood before him now with her eyes closed. Then she opened them. Bobby took an involuntary step backward. Her eyes had changed. No longer were they the piercing green of the Scarlet Seer. Instead, they were blue, the kind, gentle blue of...

"That's right. Bobby. It's me. It's your grandma."

CHAPTER TWENTY-THREE

Aboard the private G6 bound for Guatemala, Jeremiah sat back and tried to relax. Next to him, Cassandra, who'd insisted upon chartering and paying for the jet to get them there as quickly as possible, had dozed off after her second glass of champagne. The waitress entered the spacious cabin to offer him beluga caviar and a glass of Dom Perignon. He refused. Instead, he flipped open the brochure, reading through the contents yet again. Inside the leaflet, colorful photos of shapely women advertised discrete, image-altering cosmetic surgery.

He swore under his breath for at least the hundredth time. He should've known when he first saw the woman on the video. He should have recognized his own wife, regardless of the changes. Instead, it had taken this brochure. Even then, he hadn't put all the pieces together until the receptionist mentioned the location of their main office: Turks and Caicos, the departure location of the woman on the airport video.

The bag at his feet buzzed and Jeremiah jumped. He'd nearly forgotten about the satellite phone. Restoring his seat to upright, he located the heavy black phone and answered it.

"Chief, is that you?"

"Sorry I haven't been in touch with you sooner," said the old Navajo. "We ran into some technical difficulty." Chief caught Jeremiah up on what he'd discovered in the jungle with Bobby and Jinx, including how the natives had accidentally smashed his phone, as well as the discovery of the temple and the electric fence protecting it.

"You're telling me that my grandsons went into this temple alone?" said Jeremiah, his voice somewhere between incredulous and irate.

"It seemed like the right call at the time," said Chief. "They were only supposed to perform a quick reconnaissance and come right back. I didn't sense any danger, and we wanted to know if the kids from the academy were really there."

"You can be sure of it," said Jeremiah, sharing what he'd deduced about Melody and her transformation. "I'm not sure what she's doing there, but there's no way it's a coincidence."

"Agreed," said Chief. "I'm going back to the temple to disable the electric fence and find out what's going on inside as soon as the rest of my team arrives."

Jeremiah checked his watch. "Our flight touches down in a little over four hours. If your team gets there first, go on without us. Something tells me they might all be in terrible danger. Cassandra and I will catch up as soon as we land."

Chief gave him the location of the temple and then hung up. Leaving the phone on the seat next to him in case Chief called again, Jeremiah sat back in the high-backed leather seat and tried to get comfortable. Tracking Melody had been emotional enough. Now his grandsons were missing as well. Saying a prayer for his grandsons and then one for his wife, he willed the plane to fly faster. *Hang in there, my angel. I'll be there soon.*

* * *

They walked the garden for a long time. Bobby had so many questions for Melody that he didn't know where to begin. He couldn't take his eyes from his grandma's face. Some of her features were alien: her cheeks and nose, the set of her mouth. Others were so familiar it made him want to cry with joy. Melody's eyes filled him with delight, just as they had since he was toddler when she'd held him in her arms, tickled his tummy, and smiled at him while making cooing noises.

Melody was telling him again how she'd come to be working for the Core.

"Your grandfather has never had a premonition that hasn't come to pass. So, when he had his vision about you at the academy, we both knew we couldn't prevent it from happening. Instead we had to do something to save you after you'd gone.

"Jeremiah's plan was to leave clues for you to find once you got there. That's what led you to the diary in the bear's den. He also tried to send you help, which is how Chief and Cassandra got involved."

Melody paused, her expression grim. "I took a different approach. Having grown up at the academy, I knew what those people were capable of and wasn't convinced that a rescue effort would be successful. So, I developed another plan. Working in secret so that your grandfather wouldn't try to stop me, I began to track Simpkins and Hayward whenever they left the monastery to hunt down new students. Even when they were searching for us, I was spying on them.

"I spotted Cassandra with them numerous times and had to be very careful to keep my distance. Even without you or Jeremiah around, my aura nearly gave me away. I did all this while you were growing up, eventually tracking Simpkins and Hayward to a base of operations in the United States.

"Over time, I identified their cars, their safe houses, the agents they used in the field. It was this surveillance that led me to discover the existence of the Core. Once I realized they had other operations besides the academy, I made a plan. I would infiltrate the Core: work for them so that I would be on the inside, prepared for the day when you would need my help.

"I didn't change my appearance right away because I knew your grandfather would try to stop me. Thankfully, the Core is structured like a terrorist organization, each cell gets only the information it needs to carry out its missions, with no interaction with other cells. That helped insure that I never bumped into Simpkins, Hayward, or Cassandra.

"I worked small jobs for the Core at first, 'internal interrogations' they call them. Over the years, I developed a reputation for extracting information. I've always had the ability to sense other people's emotions. I applied that skill until I learned how to turn these emotions back on the subject. I felt no sympathy for most of the people I tortured. These were evil people: criminals and psychopaths who deserved what they got.

"Of course, there was the occasional innocent victim, someone simply in the wrong place at the wrong time. But those situations were rare. I am not proud of some of things I've done. But I did what I had to do.

"Throughout the entire process, I adopted a new persona: the Scarlet Seer. I hid my emotions behind a façade. I also learned to control my anima. I knew eventually I would encounter Simpkins and Hayward, so I masked my energy so well not even Jeremiah could sense it. I disguised myself and bumped into him in public. He never had a clue," she giggled.

Bobby paused, taking a seat at the base of the apple tree. They'd walked around the tiny garden three times as Melody told her tale. It felt like the whole world was spinning. "The entire time I was growing up, you were infiltrating the Core, torturing people, and planning my rescue?"

She knelt next to him and took his hands in hers. "You're my grandson. There is nothing I wouldn't do for you."

Bobby stared at his grandmother. "You had all that done after the Core took me?" he said, gesturing to her face.

Melody nodded. "I'd already worked my way into a position where I could be promoted to virtually any location within the Core, except the academy, that is. I puzzled out long ago that the Headmistress was my daughter. I didn't trust myself to be that close. Plus, Jeremiah had already sent Chief in undercover. So, I waited for another opportunity. When the academy collapsed and I heard the kids were being transferred here, I convinced the Core to appoint me to oversee the operation. In reality, my only goal was to find you and bring you home safe."

"I escaped the academy," said Bobby. "I'd been back home for months with mom and dad. Grandpa even came to see me."

"I had no way of knowing," said Melody. "I was deep undercover. After the academy collapsed, they appointed Simpkins and Hayward as my lieutenants. I couldn't exactly walk out of here with those two right under my nose."

They sat in silence, lost in familial bliss and the joy of being in each other's company.

"So, what now?" asked Bobby.

"Now we get you out of here."

"I can't just leave. My friends are still here. Your men are holding them. They have your grandson."

"I know about Jinx. He's safe for the moment. We can get him on the way out. As for the others…" His grandmother's voice trailed off. "Bobby, they've done something to me. After I recovered from my surgery in the Caribbean, the Core sent me to a facility in the Ukraine. They did things before they sent me here…they got inside my head. Not like what I do. I have ways of getting people to tell things they don't want to tell.

"They had no idea I had secrets. They just wanted to ensure that when they put me in charge, I would carry out my mission as instructed. Whatever they did is still inside me. I can feel it in the back of my head like floodwater. Whenever I try to do something against my mission, the water rises and threatens to drown me."

"Is there a way to fix it?"

"Believe me, I've tried. If I even think about ordering your friends released, I'll get a terrible headache, like someone drilling inside my brain. Besides, even if I managed it somehow, Sandman and the guards would know something was wrong. I think Hayward is already suspicious of me."

Bobby folded his arms and stared at his grandmother. "I won't leave without the others."

"Bobby, it is going to be next to impossible to sneak the three of us out of here without getting caught. Not to mention the pain," she said, gripping her head. "We can't possibly take anyone else."

A rustling in a nearby tree brought their heads up. A large shape moved in the shadows. Bobby saw the switch of a tail and thought perhaps it was the jaguar again, following him for some unknown reason. Then the shadow stood on its hind legs, appraising them with almost human eyes.

"Isn't that the boy's pet?" asked Melody. "Mercy, right?"

"We gotta catch it," said Bobby in a hushed tone, "We can't let it escape."

"What's the big deal?"

Bobby stood up and tried to act casual as he crept toward the fig tree. The branch was low enough that he could reach Mercy if he jumped.

"The monkey has a bond with Willy that allows him to know everything it knows. I don't know how long it's been in that tree, but if it overheard our conversation…"

The white monkey stood motionless, watching him with those human eyes. Bobby took another small step and coiled himself to jump. Even before he'd left the ground, Mercy sprang nimbly from her perch to another several feet higher.

Bobby caught the branch and pulled himself up, but already the monkey was moving higher in the tree. The beast stopped for a moment, letting loose a primal screech. Then she pulled back her cheeks into a hideous grin.

"Stop it!" said Bobby. "It's going to warn Willy."

Melody stared at the creature, her eyes narrowed. Bobby knew she was attempting to invade the animal's mind. What worked on humans apparently did not work on primates. Mercy lifted her arms, pounded her chest, and screeched again.

Mercy sprang to a limb near the upper lip of the solarium. A second later, she appeared on the roof, dashing along the rim until she disappeared from view.

* * *

"We must act fast," said Melody as she helped Bobby down from the tree. "If we go now, we should be able to get to Jinx and get out of here before the others find out."

"We need to find my friends, too," said Bobby.

Melody grabbed him by the wrist and pulled him towards the door. "There's no time. We need to go now."

Bobby pulled free. "I told you, I'm not going anywhere without the others."

His grandma turned to him and sighed. "I want to help, I truly do. But you have no idea what'll they do to us, what they'll do to me, if they catch us."

"I know it's dangerous but I think I know a way to even the odds."

When he told her, Melody nodded approval. "I suppose it's as good a plan as any. Come on."

From the folds of her full-length dress, Melody pulled out a kit and reapplied her make-up. Satisfied with her transformation back into the Scarlet Seer, she led Bobby to the door. The guards at the door stood on either side, oblivious to what had transpired within. Sandman was gone, likely off dealing with some security matter. In his place, Simpkins and Hayward waited off to the side. As the Scarlet Seer came through the door accompanied by her most recent victim, a wide grin broke over Hayward's face.

"It's about time that one got what was coming to him," said the obese agent. Bobby kept his face intentionally neutral.

"Report," commanded the Scarlet Seer, her voice authoritative.

"We followed up on the leads about the two strangers in town asking about you. We weren't able to catch up to them before they left town. However, from the descriptions we got from the guard at the airport, it appears it may have been our old colleague, Cassandra, and a man who has ties to the academy."

Bobby felt Melody stiffen. "Tell me about the man."

"You wouldn't know him," said Simpkins. "He was a student at the academy a long time ago. His daughter became headmistress. We believe he may be searching for clues to the location of his grandchildren."

"Which includes this one here," said Hayward, gesturing to Bobby. "I hope you fried him nice and good. I still owe his grandfather."

Bobby did his best to look zombified as his grandmother went rigid.

Hayward sniffed the air. "Do you sense that?" he asked. "It smells like…"

"It's just the fragrances from the garden," said the Scarlet Seer.

"It reminds me of something," said Hayward. "Something I haven't smelled in a very long—"

"You will pay attention when I am giving you instructions," snapped the Scarlet Seer. "I have no time for your fantastical reminiscences."

"What are your orders?" asked Simpkins. "Should we remain here and assist at the temple, or track the man with Cassandra and see if we can capture him?"

"Neither," said the Scarlet Seer. "I want you to head south into the jungle. See if you can locate any more native villages."

"But Sandman and his men are already out dealing with the natives," complained Hayward.

She silenced him with a look. "I have reason to believe they are planning an assault on the temple. I have seen inside this boy's mind," she said gesturing to Bobby. "They believe we are evil spirits that must be vanquished in order for their ancestors to find peace."

Now it was Bobby who had to hide his reaction. How did she know that? Had she read his mind without him knowing?

"The fence is more than sufficient," replied Hayward. "If they try to attack, they'll be fried like turkeys at Thanksgiving dinner."

"They've figured out a new way in. The boy doesn't know where it is, but they're building a new village in the south to use as a base. Find it. Destroy it. Do I make myself clear?"

Hayward opened his mouth to respond, but Simpkins stopped him. "Yes, mistress," said the cadaverous agent. "We will take care of it at once."

"Good. Now go." The Scarlet Seer clutched her head as if in pain. "Do not return until you've dealt with every native within a hundred miles."

CHAPTER TWENTY-FOUR

Alone in the halls, Bobby followed his grandma through twists and turns to the pit where Jinx was held captive.

"How did you know the villagers think this place is full of evil spirits?" Bobby asked.

"We captured their leader, the shaman named Itzamna, in the forest," said Grandma. When she saw the look on Bobby's face, she added, "Don't worry, I put on a show for Sandman and the guards but left him unharmed. I told them to let him accidentally escape in order to follow him back to their other village."

"But there is no other village," protested Bobby. "Your men burned their only home."

"That was unfortunate. Sandman acted without my permission. And I know there are no other villages. I saw that in Itzamna's mind. I also showed him an image of the guards following him. No doubt he will evade them."

"If you knew there weren't any other villages, then why did you send Simpkins and Hayward to look for them?"

"To get them out of the temple, of course. You saw how Hayward picked up on that scent. That wasn't the fragrance from the garden. That was our anima, Bobby. With you close to me, I'm not sure how much longer I can keep the scent masked. So, I sent them as far away as possible in order to buy us time to escape."

"Very clever," he said. "Let's just hope they don't realize they're on a wild goose chase until it's too late."

They traversed one corridor after another in rapid succession. They passed several guards, all of whom stepped aside to let them pass. After a few minutes, they came to the pit where the guards had dumped Jinx.

The pit stood empty, as did the room above, without so much as a single guard at his post for them to question.

"Jinx should be here," said Melody. "The guards were told to hold him until they received further instructions."

"Who else has the authority to take him?"

"No one except Sandman and…"

"What is it?" asked Bobby, noting the concern in his grandmother's voice.

"As you know, Ashley and her friends have been put in charge of selecting subjects for our studies based on their knowledge of the academy personnel. I never approved, especially after I found out Ashley is my granddaughter, but the decision came from over my head."

"How is that possible? I thought you were in charge here."

"I am, but unlike all the other students, Ashley went to another Core facility immediately after the academy's collapse. Apparently, she impressed whoever she met there. She was given training and a special assignment before being assigned here. That's all I know, but she may very well have the authority to countermand my orders."

"If Mercy got to Willy and told him about your secret, it's a sure bet he told Ashley."

"The guards won't turn against me easily, not without evidence. But with Ashley's power, there are few who would stand in her way."

"Then we need to get to the others before word spreads," said Bobby.

"Come on," said his grandma. "I know where they are. I just hope we aren't too late."

* * *

At first Bobby thought they were headed for the fountain. Then, two intersections before the dogleg, his grandmother made an abrupt right turn. It was a section of the temple Bobby hadn't seen before.

"There's a lab," she explained.

"Do I even wanna know what's in the lab?" asked Bobby.

His grandmother left the question unanswered except for a sheepish, almost apologetic tightening of her mouth. "I'm not proud of a lot of what I've done in order to be here with you."

Bobby felt sudden heat flush his cheeks. "I'm sorry," he said. "I didn't mean...I'm sure it's been hard..." He let his voice trail off. They continued on in silence.

All his previous journeys through the temple had taken him inexorably down. This time they went up. They came to a broad staircase, ascending until they were near the top of the ziggurat. The stairs ended in a wide stone archway. Beyond lay a large chamber, with carved pillars supporting the roof and gaps in the walls, allowing daylight into the otherwise dim interior.

Rows of metal tables divided the room into neat rectangles, like cribs in a maternity ward. The occupants, however, were not infants swaddled in soft linen. They were students from the academy, strapped down at their wrists and ankles, hooked up to machines with tubes and needles swarming all over them.

Bobby walked over to the nearest gurney, staring down at the sedate face of a pre-teen girl with rosy cheeks and strawberry curls. Even unconscious, her face was twisted in agony.

"My God, what are they doing to her?" he asked, tracing the tubes to long, thick needles injected into her upper arms and thighs.

"These are all subjects who were administered serums derived from the fountain. With Slab no longer available to test subjects, we've been forced to analyze living samples, looking for changes at the cellular level."

"These aren't subjects," said Bobby. "These are children; kids who trusted the academy to look after them."

"You're right, of course," said Melody, shaking her head. "I've been undercover for so long that it's gotten into my head. I hardly ever come up here. It's too painful for me to see, but I had my orders. If I had disobeyed, they would have known I was a fraud and likely had me executed."

"We need to free these people. Help me get these straps off," said Bobby.

"Look around, there are over fifty people on these tables," his grandmother replied. "Guards may already be on the way here. We don't have time to free everyone."

Bobby lifted his gaze to the rows of tables, each containing an adolescent in similar circumstances.

"Fine, we stick to the plan," said Bobby, "but we come back for the rest after we're done."

They split up, searching for Bobby's friends as they made their way slowly to the far wall. Bobby saw many faces he recognized, but none of them were who he was looking for. With only three gurneys left before the wall, he found Trevor, splayed out like a frog on a dissection table, arms and legs spread wide, his head lolling to the side.

"Over here," Bobby called to his grandmother. She came over and placed a hand on the chest of his unconscious friend. She checked his pulse and raised his eyelids to see the whites of his eyes.

"He's sedated but not heavily. I should be able to enter his mind and—"

Trevor's eyes fluttered, taking in Bobby's face through unfocused pupils as Bobby unstrapped his left wrist and ankle. Melody did the same on the right side. When Trevor saw the Scarlet Seer, he bolted upright.

Bobby grabbed his friend's shoulders, restraining him. "It's okay," he said, filling in his friend about his grandmother's secret.

The terror in Trevor's eyes diminished but did not extinguish.

"I'm sorry for what I did," said Melody. "I didn't realize you were a friend of my grandson." She gave a regretful sigh. "Not that it should have made a difference."

Trevor watched her warily, not saying a word as Bobby continued to explain how Grandma had revealed herself to him, only to be spotted by Mercy. "We need to get Jacob and Lily and get out of here before the guards show up."

At the mention of Lily's name, Trevor was on his feet and moving. They found Jacob the next row over, with Lily a short distance away. Melody repeated her actions, evaluating each in turn before reviving them by entering their dreams. When they were all awake, they headed for the exit, with Trevor helping to support Lily, who was still a bit drowsy and whose knee had not yet been properly treated.

They were halfway across the room when they heard a groan. They all stopped, craning their heads to see where the noise had come from. The groan came again, this time accompanied by the rattling of chains. Lily pointed to the north wall, adjacent to where they'd come in. Two thick, iron chains hung down from the limestone walls. Bobby spotted a pair of enormous hands, barely visible above the rows of tables.

"It's Slab!" said Jacob, rushing to the giant's side. Their hulking friend sat on the ground, his tree trunk legs folded beneath him. His mask laid in front of him, discarded, his bare head hanging in his lap.

Jacob reached down and cupped the giant's chin, lifting his head to reveal the unblemished, innocent baby face that so drastically belied the rest of his physique.

"He's heavily sedated," said Jacob, slapping his friend on the cheek. "Come on, big guy, snap out of it."

Bobby showed his grandmother how to breach Slab's protective barrier. Melody placed both hands on Slab's forehead and began to rub. A moment later, the giant's eyes flickered open. Bobby noticed that his gaze held none of the fear that Trevor's had when he saw the Scarlet Seer. Melody looked over her shoulder, noting Bobby's surprise.

"I was always nice to Jimmy," she explained. "I couldn't read his thoughts the way I can others, but it isn't hard to see he's a tortured soul."

Slab groaned again and pulled on his chains so feebly they barely rattled. "I'm not sure I can fully revive him," said Melody. As if to prove her point, Slab's head dropped back down.

"We need the big oaf if we're gonna bust outta here," said Jacob. "Besides, he's my friend. He risked his life for us back in the fountain room. You shoulda seen what they did to him, but he kept fighting to buy time for the others to escape."

"Heavens, if he's coming with us, we gotta get those chains off," said Lily. They spread out to search for the key while Melody worked to revive Slab. They were still searching when the first guards appeared.

With his back to the entrance, Bobby didn't realize the guards were there until he heard a crash. He turned to see his grandmother sway on her feet, knock over a mobile IV stand, and topple to the ground. He looked past her to the door and saw Sandman, accompanied by two Core guards.

The bullnecked captain's chest heaved in and out, his cheeks and forehead puffed red with rage. The way he snorted through his nose, Bobby thought he might drop onto all fours and charge them like a mad bull. Instead, Sandman's gaze shifted from Melody to Trevor, who began to waver.

Bobby rushed to his lanky friend, reaching his side at the same time as Jacob and Lily. "Fight the bastard!" said Jacob, but Bobby could already see the fire in Trevor's eyes growing dim, glossing over with the dull haze of sleep.

Bobby felt drowsy as well. An inexorable force pulled his eyelids down. He fell to his knees, his head drooping to the floor. Fighting to lift his chin, he turned to Lily. "Take my hand," he told her. "We have to fight him to—"

Arm outstretched towards his friends, Bobby slumped to the ground, unconscious.

***

The ghost of Ek Chuaj refused to let Bobby dream. As he searched for a way out of the darkness, the angry spirit dragged him toward a vision from the past. Struggling against the ghost, Bobby searched for a path to the real world. *My friends need me!*

It did no good. Ek Chuaj, his face contorted with rage, thrust Bobby into the past, forcing him to relive the ancient Mayan's memories.

***

Having just left Lingya in the fountain room, Ek Chuaj stormed through the halls of the temple. Volcanic anger boiled inside of him, his hands curled into fists as he navigated his way to the council chamber. All the senior priests were present, discussing logistics for the upcoming lunar festival. Excellent. This would make delivering his message much easier.

He waited impatiently off to the side, pacing back and forth until the meeting was finished and the scribes had departed. Despite what he'd told Lingya, his new position within the city's council was not so elevated that he could interrupt the priests without ample cause.

As the scribes scurried off to carry out their instructions, Ek Chuaj made sure to catch the eye of Kukulkan, the high priest and ruler of the city.

"Ah, Ek Chuaj," said the rotund priest, "What news of the city's defenses?"

Ek Chuaj hadn't been lying when he told Lingya he'd been put in command of the city's roads and outer territories. His bag full of conquistador trophies had been more than enough to convince these fools he had the skill to protect them against the Spaniards.

Ek Chuaj performed an exaggerated bow, touching his head to the floor. He straightened up slowly, a pained expression on his face. "It is worse than I had feared," he said. "The invaders continue to raid our outlying villages, killing our men and taking our women and children captive."

High Priest Kukulkan adjusted the gem-encrusted crown on his brow, a gesture that made his jowls swing from side to side. "But you can stop all this, can you not?" he asked. Taking Ek Chuaj by the elbow, Kukulkan guided him along his chosen path. "You have beaten these foreigners before. You know how to defeat them."

Ek Chuaj gave a solemn nod. "I know their tactics, yes, and how to defeat them on the battlefield," he said. "But that may not be enough."

High Priest Kukulkan grabbed his arm, pulling Ek Chuaj up short. "I've given you everything you asked for. We have drastically reduced our warriors here at the temple in order to provide you the men you claim you need to safeguard our territory. What more could you possibly want?"

Ek Chuaj tore his arm free then quickly put his palms together as Kukulkan's eyes narrowed dangerously.

"Forgive me, your Holiness," said Ek Chuaj. "I am simply eager to live up to your expectations. Unfortunately, the number of warriors is not the issue. I have reason to believe the Spaniards have spies among us: people sent to infiltrate our city and scout our defenses."

The corpulent priest's expression was stern, his voice thick with tension. "What reason do you have to suspect such a thing? Surely no citizen of the Mayan empire would conspire with these barbarians."

"There is a man from my village. I knew him as a child. He is a fisherman. The foreigners must have captured him while on his journeys and compelled him to spy on us. I saw him in the market, spreading rumors about our destruction. He even takes trips into the jungle, supposedly to fetch herbs for his wife but, in truth, he is spying on our soldiers, studying their deployment to report back to his masters."

High Priest Kukulkan scratched at his chin. "That is not much proof. Surely many people spend time in the jungle and gossip about the invaders."

"Ah, but this man fled our village just before it was attacked. How else could he have known the attack was coming if he is not in league with them?"

The priest turned apoplectic, his ruddy face splotched with white. "I command you to apprehend this man. We will interrogate him and discover what he knows of our would-be conquerors."

Ek Chuaj cupped his hands in supplication. "As you wish. Once we have uncovered everything he knows, might I humbly suggest that you sacrifice him to the gods? Certainly, the blood of a traitor will appease them more than any other."

Kukulkan's expression turned from consternation to pride. With a broad smile, he patted Ek Chuaj on the back. "The gods will surely rejoice at such a gift. Truly great are their blessings, bestowed upon all through me."

Ek Chuaj dipped his head to mask his annoyance at the man's arrogance. "Thank you, Your Holiness," he said. "I promise I will not let you down. I will capture the traitor at once. After which, I pray you will use the judgement of the gods to punish him."

High Priest Kukulkan reached out and cupped Ek Chuaj's chin, lifting his head until they stared eye to eye. "Do not fear, my son. Righteous wrath and fury shall rain down on all who deserve it."

***

Lily grabbed Bobby's unconscious body and dragged him behind the pillar holding Slab. Bobby had been trying to tell her something right before he passed out, something about holding hands. Did he know something or was he just desperate?

Lily peeked around the pillar. Sandman was advancing down the hall, trying to get a line of sight on her. Meanwhile, the two guards were walking slowly down either aisle, Tasers drawn.

"Wake up, Bobby!" She shook him by the shoulders, but he remained fast asleep. Lily looked on with fear as the guards continued to press into the room. Trevor was passed out in the aisle, too far to reach, but Jacob was only an arm's length away.

Keeping her head back, she stretched out and grabbed a hold of Jacob's ankle. It took all of her strength to pull the stocky boy behind the pillar with her. *My God, you're heavy!* She gave the fiery redhead a slap across the face that felt better than it probably should have.

Jacob woke up screaming and brushing at his clothes. "Sucking bastards! Get them off!"

Lily set both hands on his shoulders. "Relax, Jakey. It's okay. Well, not really, but—"

Jacob shook his head a few times, pulling himself together. "Is it just me or are butterflies freakin' creepy?"

Lily blinked at him a few times. "Concentrate, Jacob! We have a situation."

"Right, sorry," said Jacob, glancing down the hall. "What do we do?"

"Take my hand," said Lily.

"I knew you had a thing for me!" He gave her a wink. "I promise not to tell Trevor if you don't."

Lily shot him an icy glare. "Don't be silly. Right before Bobby passed out, he said something about holding hands."

With a mischievous grin, Jacob set his hands on hers. "Well, if Bobby said so…"

His hands were far softer than she would have expected. They felt warm, but not from sweat. She closed her eyes, probing deeper. His pulse was strong and steady, not fast and panicked like her own. She felt his chi, his lifeblood coursing through his body.

She opened her eyes. The two guardsmen were nearly upon them. "Grab Bobby," she ordered Jacob. "We need to pool our anima. We can fight off Sandman together."

"And what about the goons with the guns?" said Jacob. "Pretty sure they're not gonna join hands and sing 'Kumbaya.'"

Despite his protest, Jacob did as Lily requested. Grabbing Bobby by the wrist, he scooted them both further behind the pillar.

"I have an idea," said Lily. "Just stay connected."

Stretching Jacob's arms to the max, she stood and stepped from behind the pillar. With a tiny side-step, she positioned herself in front of Slab, who lay slumped against the base.

The Core guards were only a few yards away, with Sandman a short distance behind. "Stop!" said Lily, thrusting her hand out in front of her. "Don't come any closer."

The hefty guards lumbered to a halt. They might not know everything about the kids at the temple, but clearly, they knew enough to heed her warning.

"I have the ability to melt stone," said Lily. "Take another step and, heaven help me, I'll dissolve the ground at your feet."

The guards exchanged worried glances. The bigger of the two took an involuntary step backwards. "Shoot her. That is a direct order!" yelled Sandman, but he was advancing up the aisle much slower than before.

Lily felt Sandman's eyes on her and knew the guard captain would try to put her to sleep. She kept a tight grip on Jacob's hand, which fed her strength through the link.

The lead guard pointed his weapon at her chest. *Took you long enough*, thought Lily. She waited until she saw him squeeze the trigger, then dove to the side.

The prongs of the Taser whizzed past Lily's head and hit Slab instead. The leads sank deep into his chest, sending their massive electrical charge into his torso. The giant's body convulsed for a moment, then his eyes popped open.

The guards jumped back as the giant reached up and yanked the wires out of his chest. Releasing Jacob's hand, Lily dropped to Slab's side. Snatching a hairpin from her head, she jammed it into the shackles holding Slab's wrists. A tiny flow of anima and—*pop*—the lock sprang open. Three quick repeats and Slab was free.

Her giant friend stood up, stretched his arms out wide, and glared at the men in front of him. The first guard dropped his now defunct Taser, turned, and ran. The second guard just stood there, the Taser dangling from his hand.

Slab took a step toward the guard. The soldier's hand began to tremble. Slab took another step, the corner of his mouth curling into a Cheshire grin. The guard threw down his weapon and ran, following his companion toward the laboratory's entrance. With an angry roar, Slab took off after him, barreling down the rows of unconscious test subjects. The first guard passed Sandman without slowing. The bull-necked captain let him go, his eyes locked on the angry giant lumbering towards him.

Lily felt a tingle in the air and knew Sandman was trying to lull Slab. Instead the giant picked up speed like a runaway locomotive.

"This isn't over, cadets," yelled Sandman. Then he turned and followed his men in full retreat. Easily outpaced by his smaller adversaries, Slab broke off pursuit and doubled back to Lily and her friends. Jacob helped Trevor to his feet while Lily revived Bobby. Melody had woken up and was making her way over to the others.

"Oh dear," said Lily, shaking Bobby by the shoulders. Melody set a hand on her grandson's forehead. "He seems to be under some sort of trance. It's not Sandman," she explained. "Something or someone is keeping him under."

Lily took Melody's hand, joining her with Jacob and Trevor, who had fully regained consciousness. After a long moment, Bobby opened his eyes.

"What the heck happened?" he asked, rubbing at his head.

Melody sighed as Lily and Jacob took turns explaining how Sandman and the guards had nearly subdued them.

"Quick thinking, beau," said Trevor, giving his girlfriend a kiss on the cheek.

"We'll need to stay alert," said Melody. "If I see Sandman coming, I should be able to stop him, but if he gets the drop on us again, we may not be so lucky next time."

"I don't think his little sleeping trick is gonna work on us anymore," said Bobby. "Not as long as we stick together."

"Either way, we gotta get outta here before Captain Minotaur comes back with reinforcements," said Jacob. "All the power in the world won't matter if the goon squad comes at us from all sides."

They left the lab in swift order. Lily limped on her sore knee until Slab reached down and scooped her up in his muscular arms. He hoisted her as easily as a toddler might carry a doll, her feet dangling high off the ground. The look on Trevor's face was priceless. Bobby couldn't tell if he was jealous or angry for not having thought of it first.

Jacob roared with laughter and applauded Slab while giving Trevor a hearty slap on the back. "And here I thought I would be the one to sweep Lily off her feet!"

CHAPTER TWENTY-FIVE

Bobby led the way down the stairs to the ziggurat's main level. As they approached the central chamber, Core guards dressed in black uniforms began to appear, stationed at various intersections and doorways.

No one gave them any trouble. Some saluted the Scarlet Seer as she passed with her misfit entourage. Clearly, word had not yet spread about their leader's false identity. Perhaps Sandman hadn't bothered to tell all his troops, or perhaps there was some other reason.

The guards watching the main chamber were the first to show any signs of concern. As the Scarlet Seer approached, a muscular soldier with an eagle tattoo on his right bicep gestured at Slab and the kids. "Ma'am?" he inquired, warily eyeing the giant, who was now dressed in a pair of black trousers and mesh shirt taken from the guard quarters. Without his mask and tattered clothes, Slab was a strange sight indeed.

"The giant has been cured, and is once again under my control," she said curtly. The guard waited, clearly expecting more details. When none were offered, he shifted his attention to the children. "What about them?"

"I've come to placate the children. It's easier than torturing them into submission. I've brought back these four," she said, gesturing to Bobby, Lily, Trevor and Jacob, "to show that those who have been taken have not been harmed."

"A clever idea," said the guard with a wink. "No harm at all."

To both guards, she said, "I want you stationed at the exits. Do not let anyone else into the main chamber while I am meeting with the children. We are not to be disturbed for any reason."

Without waiting for a reply, the Scarlet Seer swept through the door and into the great hall. Her ragtag crew followed at her heels.

* * *

Bobby gasped upon seeing the vast hall so depleted. One in every four sleeping bags lay empty, their former occupants taken for testing. The tents, which had held three or four kids apiece, now housed one or two at the most.

Off to the side by herself, stood the young girl who had been crying the night Bobby and Jinx first arrived. Upon seeing Bobby, the girl's face lit up. Tucking her doll under her arm, she ran over to him. "Is Jinx with you?" she asked.

Bobby knelt down on both knees. "Anastasia, right?"

The girl tugged on a ponytail and stared at the hem of her pink dress. "People just call me Ana," she said softly.

Bobby lifted her chin with the crook of a finger. "Well, Ana, Jinx isn't with us right now, but we're going to get him back. Would you like to help?"

Ana hugged her dolly and gave him a brave nod.

"Great," said Bobby. "Go tell the others we want to talk with them. Do you remember where my friends' camp is?" he asked, pointing to Jacob, Lily, and Trevor. Ana nodded again.

"Perfect," said Bobby. "Tell everyone to meet there in five minutes."

Ana ran off toward the nearest camp. Bobby saw her duck into a makeshift lean-to made from wool blankets propped up by sticks. She whispered a few words to the kids inside, and then rushed off to the next camp.

"I'm going to see what I can do about thinning out the guards," said Melody. "Assuming they still think I'm in charge, I should be able to reassign most of them someplace else without arousing too much suspicion."

"I go too," said Slab. "No trouble."

Melody looked up at the giant and smiled. Given her recent encounter with Sandman, Bobby felt certain she welcomed the protection. After their departure, kids began to arrive. Bobby recognized Jacob's friend, Mikey Blanchert. The grungy, pimple-faced, long-haired teen looked as surprised by their presence as they were to see him.

"I guess looking like a loser has its perks," Mikey offered by way of explanation. "I kept my head down after you disappeared. I even stopped pranking the guards."

"You poor thing!" teased Jacob. "Come on, loser. Time to put those pranking skills to use again."

Mikey beamed at his friend. "Now you're talking!"

Bobby told him briefly about his plan as more kids continued to show up. Finally, Ana poked her head in. "That's everyone," she said. "The others are too scared to come. Some think you're all going to get caught. The others saw the Scarlet Seer with you and think it's a trick."

"Alright," said Bobby. "You should go back now before the guards see you. We'll take care of it from here."

"I want to stay," said Ana. "I can help."

Bobby took in her huge blue eyes, full of fear and adrenalin. With a solemn nod, he waved to a place for her to sit. "I suppose we're all in this together."

They waited until Melody and Slab returned. The giant took up a position outside the tent, looking out over the entire chamber while Melody went inside. "I've sent half the guards to protect the lab," said Melody, who took a seat next to her grandson. "I told them that Sandman went rogue and to apprehend him if they see him."

Jacob laughed. "That should keep Captain No-Neck busy for a while."

"I'm not so sure," said Melody. "The report I got was that he's out on the perimeter, responding to some kind of disturbance."

"Then we should hurry," said Mikey, turning to Bobby. "Tell us this big plan."

"I've given it a lot of thought ever since I first snuck out of here," said Bobby. "There's no use making a break for the outside. The area is surrounded by a fifty-foot high electric fence. Even if we did manage to get past it, we're in the middle of the jungle with no food, no water, and no place to go with this many people."

"Is there an actual plan in here somewhere?" asked Mikey. "Because your motivational speaking skills suck."

"I see why you and Jacob are such good friends," snapped Trevor. "I'm sure Bobby has a point. Right bro?"

Bobby nodded. "There may be another way to get everyone out of here. Like I said, we're in the middle of the jungle. Which means all the equipment, the generators, the computers: it all had to be brought in by helicopter."

"That's right," said one of the boys in the back. "I saw them yesterday when we went out to use the bathroom. Big twin propellers, Chinooks, I think. I recognize them from my dad's old army photos."

"Perfect. Then all we need to do is get everyone out of the temple, find the pilots, and force them to fly us out."

"There are crews stationed there around the clock," said Melody. "I should be able to convince them to cooperate without much difficulty."

"Then we're all set. Grandma, if you and Slab handle the guards by the west exit, we should be able to deal with the guards at the east to open a path to the central corridor. From there, we make our way to the terrace. After that, we lift everyone out of the temple in shifts, and we're home free."

* * *

From behind a pillar, Bobby, Jacob and Trevor studied the doorway marking the exit to the main chamber. On the south side stood the guard they'd encountered before, the burly one with the eagle tattoo. Across from him stood another soldier, this one with a short-cropped, black goatee. Both men wore army fatigues and combat boots like the guards who had attacked them in the lab.

Bobby swore under his breath. These men were well-trained. Their impassive eyes never strayed from the milling crowd of kids. That was bad news.

Mikey Blanchert and two other boys from the meeting were supposed to create a diversion by pretending to start a fight. If the guards didn't leave their posts to break it up, Bobby and his friends wouldn't be able to get past them to the next set of guards in the hallway. Someone would undoubtedly call for back-up and their whole plan would be shot to hell.

"Yo, maybe we should get the Scarlet Seer to order them off their post," suggested Trevor.

"Not afraid of a little action, are you, Trev?" asked Jacob.

"Bite me, Jack-Up."

Jacob sneered at the disparaging nickname.

"Quit, both of you," snapped Bobby. "We can't have Grandma order these guys away. It would cause too much suspicion. Besides, she and Slab are clear on the other side of the chamber. Every second we delay, we risk that word will get out about her real identity."

"A'ight, what's the deal?" asked Trevor. "I know those two. They're not gonna leave their posts over a fight."

Bobby was pondering the situation when Ana walked into the open and right up to the guard with the eagle tattoo. She carried her dolly tucked under her arm and wore a pensive look on her face.

Trevor pulled Bobby's shoulder, spinning his friend around to face him. "Dude, what's she doing?" asked Trevor. "She's not part of the plan."

Bobby shook his head and watched as Ana extended her doll toward the guard. "Can you hold Masha?" she asked. The guard gave her a baffled look as if she'd spoken Russian. Ana stood there, arms outstretched, eyes pleading with the guard for assistance.

"Go away, little girl," he said.

"Please," begged Ana. "Just for a second. I want to scratch these nasty bedbugs and don't want to drop Masha in the dirt."

"What are you talking about? There are no bedbugs here," said the guard.

"Really?" asked Ana. "You mean you don't feel them, crawling all over, biting your skin?"

The tattooed guard shoved the doll aside. "No, now go away." The guard's voice was full of iron, but even from a distance, Bobby saw him twitch, like a person fighting to keep a straight face while being tickled.

"What about you?" said Ana, turning to the guard with the goatee. "Can't you feel them?"

The guard's right hand shot to his neck, where he began scratching. He brought his left hand up to his right forearm and scratched some more. Within seconds, he abandoned all decorum, recklessly clawing at every inch of his body in an effort to rid himself of invisible attackers.

"What the hell, Parker?" said the tattooed guard. "Get a hold of yourself."

"Shut up, Franklin. I can't help it," said Parker. "They're everywhere."

The guard named Franklin absently rubbed his arm. "See, I told you," said Ana. "They even get into your shoes. You'd better take them off so you can scratch better."

"What did you do to us?" asked Franklin, but his voice held none of the metal it had before. Instead, he was busy trying to strip off his gun belt with one hand while peeling off his jacket with the other. Beside him, Parker dropped to the ground and tugged at his high-laced combat boots.

"Now's our chance," said Jacob. Mikey and his team burst into the open and rushed at the hapless guards. Bobby, Trevor, and Jacob ran past the guards, who lay sprawled on the ground with Mikey and his friends dogpiled on top of them.

Meanwhile, Ana nimbly sidestepped the melee and retrieved Franklin's weapon belt. Extracting the slender canister of mace, she deftly flipped off the cap and unloaded the spray into the face of the supine guard. Franklin rolled on the ground, screaming as the girl switched to Parker, where she unloaded the remaining contents.

Trevor cheered her on as they raced by. "I haven't seen anything that bad ass since Bobby blazed Siphon like a joint at a reggae festival."

The acrid sting of mace clogged Bobby's nose and made his eyes water. He covered his face and set his sights on the next pair of sentries, who were leaving their posts to investigate the commotion.

Jacob took down the first soldier without breaking stride. Bobby was shocked to see the soldier's movements slow down as Jacob drew close. Jacob flashed a wicked smile as he ducked inside the man's guard and landed a vicious kick to his groin. The soldier doubled over and fell to the ground, grabbing his privates.

Meanwhile, the other guard didn't draw his weapon or raise a hand as Trevor closed to within a few feet. For a second, the guard extended a hand as if to greet Trevor. Then Bobby's tall, lanky friend grabbed the man's wrist, twisted it savagely and torqued it up behind his back. The guard's eyes went wide with surprise.

Bobby paused to stare. "Woah, Trev. Where'd you learn to do that?"

"Dope, right?" Trevor tapped his forehead. "Jacob's discovered how to slow people's reaction time. I'm learning to calm peoples' minds, give them a false sense of security until it's too late," he said with a crooked smile.

"You two are regular superheroes," grinned Bobby, as a group of people came around the corner at the far end of the hall.

Ashley led the way, followed closely by Willy, with Mercy on his shoulder. It was the person at Ashley's side, however, who drew Bobby's attention. Jinx walked beside his sister as if in a daydream, his face expressionless, his eyes glazed and unfocused. He wore a charcoal grey sweatshirt similar to the robes worn by the acolytes at the academy, with the hood pulled up over his head.

Upon seeing Bobby's questioning gaze, Trevor shrugged. "Don't ask me, bro."

"Willy must be doing something to his mind," said Bobby.

Indeed, the creepy bald boy wore his usual impassive expression, but his eyes were glued to Bobby's little cousin.

"We've gotta help Jinx," said Jacob, rushing forward. He got only two steps before a mighty force flung him backward like a leaf in a storm.

"Not so fast," said Ashley. "We have business to attend to." She raised her arms and gale winds ripped through the hallway. Bobby and his friends tried to hold their ground, but it was no use. The unrelenting wall of air pushed them back toward the main chamber with unstoppable force. Meanwhile, Ashley strode forward unfettered, a smug grin plastered across her face. "Let's take this inside where everyone can witness your defeat, shall we?"

With no real choice, Bobby and his friends retreated, taking refuge behind the pillar they'd hidden behind moments before. Ashley and her entourage stopped at the entryway. Everyone in the main chamber looked on as she took up position in the door. Jinx and Willy flanked her on one side; a pair of guards stood on the other.

"The time has come," declared Ashley, "for those of you who are of no use to be swept aside. Your inability to further the great cause makes you no different than mundanes without the Gift.

Those of you who would oppose the inexorable march of progress have even less value," she said, directing her comments to the pillar. "You seek to destroy us, to betray us from within, but we will not be stopped. Your resistance is that of a sandcastle soldier in the face of a tsunami, and I have brought the storm to your shore. And now I will show you weaklings how we deal with those who would defy the Core."

She turned to Willy, who in turn spoke to Jinx. "This place is weak," Willy said to Jinx. "Its walls are crumbling, its stones broken and cracked. The Creep commands you to strengthen the structure.

Feed your power into the fractures in the walls and ceiling and make this place strong!" On his shoulder, Mercy jumped up and down, pounding her chest as if to emphasize Willy's instructions.

Jinx pulled back his hood and lifted his glazed eyes to the high vaulted roof. The tremors were small at first, barely registering over the distant din of the generators. Nothing happened except a few grey clouds of mortar dust drifting down from the ceiling. Then the walls began to shake. The rumbling grew, overpowering the noise in the chamber until it felt like a bullet train barreling past them at three hundred miles an hour.

Cracks appeared along the walls. Small at first, they spread like a nest of spiders spinning webs of destruction as they went. A piece of the pillar above Bobby's head exploded, showering him with stone shrapnel and limestone powder. A fragment tore through his pant leg but missed hitting flesh.

"What the hell is Nerd Boy doing?" cried Jacob. "Willy told him to fortify the building, not pull it down around us."

"I'm sure that's what Jinx thinks he's doing," said Trevor. "Willy's in his head, remember? Lil' dude probably doesn't even realize he's trippin'."

"We've gotta stop him," said Bobby.

"Obviously," said Jacob. "But how? We can't get close with Ashley there."

Just then, Lily rushed up to them. "The other children are panicking. We've gotta get everyone out of here."

"Can't beau," said Trevor. "Ashley and her goons are blocking the exit."

"What we really need to do," said Jacob, "is stop Creep-edition Nerd Boy from bringing the whole place down."

"There's gotta be a way to reach him," said Bobby. Stepping out from behind the pillar, he raised his hands to his mouth and called to his cousin. "Jinx, you've gotta fight it. We're your friends. Don't let the Creep control your mind."

Ashley thrust out her hands and an invisible wall slammed into Bobby, tossing him into the air to land unceremoniously onto his rear. A chunk of limestone dislodged itself from the ceiling. Bobby rolled to the side as the fist-sized rock crashed to the ground inches from where his head had been.

"Yo, that worked really well," said Trevor, helping Bobby to his feet, but Bobby could see that, for at least a moment, the expression on Jinx's face had changed from a sleepwalker's daze to confused and conflicted.

"We just need more time to get through to him," said Jacob.

The group exchanged solemn glances. Then Bobby spoke up. "I've got an idea." Quickly, Bobby told Trevor and Jacob the plan. When he was finished, Jacob raced off to the far exit while Trevor headed for the jumble of tents in the southwest corner. A few minutes later, Jacob came running back with Slab.

"I sure hope you know what you're doing," said Jacob. "The goon squad knows your grandma's not on their side anymore. Some seem resistant to her power, and she's weakening. She was barely holding them off before I went and got this big oaf," he said gesturing to Slab.

Bobby frowned at the news. "Take Mikey and his team and go help her."

"Now you're talking," said Jacob, rubbing his hands together. He raced off, clearly pleased with his new task.

Meanwhile, Slab bent down to Bobby's level. "Bobby friend need help?"

"That's right, big guy. It's time for you and me to kick some butt."

CHAPTER TWENTY-SIX

I t didn't take long for Trevor to return. Arms full, he dropped a jumble of nylon rope at Bobby's feet. "I hope this is what you wanted," said Trevor. "I pulled down half the tents in the chamber to get these."

"They're perfect," said Bobby, sorting through the pile. "Give me a hand."

They ducked behind a pillar where they separated the ropes and fashioned them into a crude harness they then strapped around Bobby's upper thighs, waist, and chest. Slab knelt down, and Bobby climbed onto his back. Then they tied the remaining strands over Slab's shoulders and fastened them around his chest, effectively tying the two of them together.

"You understand the plan?" asked Bobby. Slab nodded his massive head and stood up. Bobby rose with him, hanging off Slab's shoulders like a baby in a carrier. Slab stepped out from behind the pillar. Instantly, Ashley shifted her gaze to them. Bobby felt a terrible force trying to rip him from Slab's back.

Slab brought his hands up to cover his face and took a step forward. The pulling sensation shifted. Wind rushed past Bobby's cheek. He ducked his head against Slab's shoulder and held on tight as the giant took a few laborious steps toward Ashley.

Ashley turned toward Willy and Jinx. "Stop them! Don't let them reach us!"

The ground heaved and Slab stumbled, nearly losing his balance as the room roiled. All around them, children ran and screamed as pieces of pillars and chunks of ceiling tumbled down.

"Jinx, don't listen to them," yelled Bobby. "You can beat them, you've just gotta fight."

The heaving stopped for a moment. Slab took another tenuous step. Another blast slammed into them, but Slab leaned into it and managed two more small steps. Mercy pried a loose stone out of the crumbling wall and flung it at Slab's head. He batted it aside and took another step. They were nearly halfway to the door now.

Two huge stone blocks directly overhead trembled in their mortar. "Jinx, I believe in you. I've always believed in you," called Bobby. "Remember when I summoned the snake to get us across the river? I never could have done it without you. You're the one who did it first. You're the one who showed me that it was possible. We're a team, you and me. I know you don't really want to do this. Fight them with me."

The blocks above stopped shaking. In fact, the entire room stopped shaking. With only the force of the wind to contend with, Slab managed two more long strides. Ashley's eyes flashed to Willy and then to Jinx. From over Slab's shoulder, Bobby saw panic in her eyes. She glanced at Slab as he got yet another step closer, then she turned and bolted for the hallway. Her guards followed a split second later.

Willy's mouth fell open in mute surprise. Mercy screeched and leaped from his shoulder. Jinx shook his head and blinked a few times. Turning to Willy, he cocked a fist, pulled it back, and punched Willy square in the nose. Only then did Jinx's knees buckle. He wobbled for a moment and fell over, out cold.

The wind died almost instantly, but the room still groaned with the occasional tremor. Bobby had just finished extricating himself from the harness when Trevor and Jacob came running up.

"We've taken care of the goons at the other exit," said Jacob. "Where's Ashley?"

Bobby hooked a thumb down the hall.

"What are you waiting for? We've gotta go after her."

"Wait," said Bobby, but it was already too late. Jacob took off at a full sprint in pursuit of Ashley.

To Trevor, Bobby said, "Stay here and take care of Jinx. When my grandma and Lily get back, tell them to evacuate everyone from the temple. Get as far away as you can in case the whole place comes down."

"Where are you going?"

Bobby glanced down the hallway after Jacob. "I'm not sure who will need saving, Jacob from Ashley, or Ashley from Jacob. One way or the other, I've gotta go after them."

"F'real," nodded Trevor, his braids bobbing. "I'd come with, but Lily's knee is jacked up."

Bobby put a hand on Trevor's shoulders. "Take care of everyone here. I'll handle this."

The two boys slapped hands. "Respect," said Trevor, as he bent to pick Jinx up off the floor. Bobby gave Jinx one last look, assuring himself that his cousin was unharmed. Then he turned and took off running.

* * *

Racing through the halls, Bobby relaxed his breathing and fell into the long, easy stride of a long-distance race. Neither Jacob nor Ashley were in sight. It didn't matter. Somehow, he knew where they were going. The whispering voices of the temple had returned and this time he understood them. They guided his footsteps until he spotted Jacob up ahead.

Laboring on short stocky legs, Jacob slowed when he spotted Bobby behind him. "I just saw her," he grunted. "She went around that corner." Bobby didn't need the guidance. He'd already figured out where Ashley was headed, even without the voices.

"I'll stop her," said Bobby, racing by his friend, who looked both irritated and relieved that his friend was taking over the chase.

"Give her hell," said Jacob, doubling over with his hands on his hips. "Just make sure to leave some for me."

The corridor doglegged to the left. Then the fountain room appeared, with its sparkling centerpiece dazzling in the fading glow of midafternoon. Ashley knelt by the east wall. She reached under the alcove and pushed the secret lever to open the hidden tunnel.

Bobby heard the grinding of stone on stone. The door was closing again. He crossed the dais at a dead sprint. He heard a loud crack and knew that Ashley had broken the control lever on the inside to prevent it from opening again. He dove through the gap with barely an inch to spare. The stone block slid home with a thud of finality.

As he picked himself up, he caught the moist fragrance of thick moss. Down below, the muted echo of footsteps announced Ashley's arrival at the base of the steps. He took the stairs two at time, oblivious to the treacherous moisture that made the walls slimy and the narrow steps dangerously slick. The voices in his head were screaming now, bombarding him with a cacophony of pleas and demands, threats, and promises.

He ignored them as he leaped down the final three steps to the grotto's landing. On the other side of the well, Ashley had reached the slope marking the back exit and was scrambling on hands and knees to reach the surface. Bobby took two strides, intent on catching her before she was out of reach, then stopped. Inside his head, the voices had united into a single, commanding presence.

"Help us," said the presence from the depths of the well. Bobby abruptly abandoned his pursuit of Ashley, coming to a halt beside the ancient well covered in cryptic runes. Looking over the edge, he stared down at the shimmering water ten feet below. He thought perhaps he saw a faint light flickering in the depths, but it might have been a reflection from the braziers set around the walls. Bobby ran his fingers over an inscription he hadn't noticed before, somehow able to decipher the ancient words:

The spirit of time
Is the essence of eternity
When knowledge and wisdom collide

Past and present will become one
Granting life never-ending
To those who grasp it

"Hello?" he called down into the darkness. Halfway up the slope, Ashley stopped and looked back. Bobby stood motionless, leaning out over the water.

"Too easy," she said. She raised her arm and sent a blast of air ripping through the cavern. Bobby teetered on the lip of the well, then tumbled headfirst into the water.

* * *

Bobby's arms and legs flailed wildly as he went over the side of the well. He hit the chill water ten feet below with a splash, tumbling dizzily until he lost all sense of direction. Gasping for air, he noticed bubbles rising diagonal to his fall line. Righting himself, he followed the bubbles, kicking and groping until his head broke the surface.

All was deathly quiet below the grotto. He heard a scraping noise and knew Ashley had triggered the mossy boulder atop the slope and made good her escape. He needed to focus on his own escape, on finding a way out of the well.

Lingya's presence was all around him, more urgent and powerful than before. Try as he might, it was impossible to drown her out. Her emotions swirled around him, as if her spirit infused the water. Unable to resist her, the distraught Mayan invaded his mind, drowning him in her memories.

***

It had only been minutes since Ek Chuaj had convinced the high priest to capture and interrogate Maximon, but gossip spread fast in the back halls of the temple. Lingya raced from the ziggarat to the market, only to find Maximon's stall vacant.

Panic rose in her chest like a viper poised to strike. Sweat drenched her robes. *Where is Maximon? Where is my son?* She put both hands on her cheeks, forcing herself to take slow, deep breaths. There were no herbs on the shelves, no dried fish in the baskets. If Ek Chuaj's soldiers had taken Maximon here, surely there would be something left of their wares.

Hiking up the hem of her skirt, she raced through the market, shoving aside anyone in her way. Some people shouted at her, others offered curses. She ignored them as she reached the main road and headed west. By the time she got to their tiny one-bedroom hut, she was so winded she could barely speak.

"Maxi, are you here, my love?" She paused for a moment. "Bahlam, where are you?" she cried out.

She dashed from the living room to the tiny bedroom. Broken furniture and a dent in the wall revealed a struggle. She turned over the fallen dresser, afraid of what she might find, but neither Maximon nor their infant son lay beneath.

Lingya sank to her knees at the foot of their bed. "What a fool I've been," she cried as hot tears rolled down her cheeks. Angering Ek Chuaj had always been dangerous, not for Lingya, but for anyone she cared about.

"I should have known!" She lay on the floor, pouring her tears onto the unyielding earth. "I should have known," she cried into the shadows.

A noise from behind her brought Lingya to her feet. She spun to find her neighbor standing in the doorway. The old crone cradled a bundle in her arms. Lingya leaped to her feet and raced to the door. Tears of sadness turned to joy as she accepted her son.

"Someone at the market warned him they were coming," said the old woman. "They searched the house, but it never occurred to them to check next door."

Lingya smiled at the old woman, thanking her over and over again while staring into the face of her infant son. Bahlam was fast asleep, a content smile on his lips, as if he had not a care in the world. The exact opposite was true for Lingya.

Wiping away the last of her tears, Lingya extended her arms, offering Bahlam back to her neighbor. "Can you watch him just a little while longer? There is something I have to do." The old lady accepted the bundle with a solemn nod.

"I'll be back as soon as I can," said Lingya. With one last look at her son, Lingya left her home and headed for the temple.

***

Lingya stormed through the corridors of the temple. All the maids she asked knew where Ek Chuaj could be found. Some merely pointed. Others shouted encouragement as she headed for the garden.

She burst through the double doors to find Ek Chuaj standing by the apple tree that grew at the garden's center. His head bent low in conversation with a pale man who looked too young to be a priest and too frail to be a warrior.

When Ek Chuaj saw her, he dismissed his companion. The man ducked his head, casting a furtive glance as he passed Lingya. She took a deep breath, taking a moment to smooth her robes before moving deeper into the garden.

Ek Chuaj watched her approach with the predatory gaze of a tiger stalking its prey. With measured steps, Lingya dipped her head in supplication. Stopping ten feet away, she threw herself to the dirt. Clasping her hands in front of her, she raised her chin just enough to see his smug grin.

"Please, I beg you," said Lingya. "Let Maximon go!"

Ek Chuaj folded his arms across his chest, a twinkle of delight dancing in his eyes. "I have no idea what you're talking about."

Lingya gripped the hem of her robe, forcing herself to keep her tone neutral. "Please, Ek Chuaj. Do not punish Maximon for my crimes."

Ek Chuaj cocked his head to the side. "And what might those crimes be, exactly?"

His dark eyes bore into Lingya so fierce that she wanted to dive into the nearby bushes to escape. Instead, she forced herself to take a deep breath. "I never should have run from you," she said. "It is a woman's duty to do as her chieftain commands. I was chosen to be your wife. It is my responsibility to obey."

"You're right. It was your obligation to obey. Just as it was my right to bed you. Instead you chose to fight me. So why should I help you now?"

"Because I have learned my place," said Lingya. Clasping her hands together, she bowed repeatedly. "Please, I will marry you. I am so sorry. Just leave Maximon alone."

Ek Chuaj scratched at his chin. "Your apologies don't change the fact that Maximon has lived with you, laid with you, bore a bastard child with you. Even if I ignored the other charges against him, Maximon has already committed crimes punishable by death."

Lingya glanced at Ek Chuaj. "Please, no!" she screamed from her knees. Her heart was beating out of control. The garden fell silent, save for the chirping of a resplendent quetzal in the top of the apple tree. "I'll do anything," she cried. "Anything."

"You know what I want," Ek Chuaj said with a smirk. Passion burned in his eyes. Lingya's hands went to the front of her blouse. With trembling hands, she began to open her robe.

"No, not here," said Ek Chuaj. "The priests would not approve if they found us. Besides," he said, coughing gently as he gathered himself. "I will have you after we are wed. On our wedding night, and every night after that if I desire."

Lingya turned her head, hoping her revulsion was masked by the hair that swung in front of her face. When she found her voice, it was weak and soft. "Then we have a deal? You will free Maximon if I agree to marry you?"

Ek Chuaj sighed, a grating sound like tearing at the bark of a tree with her fingernails. "Perhaps I can convince the priests that Maximon is just a clueless pawn. In that case, I may be able to convince them to set him free," he said. "If I do, what's to keep the two of you from running like you did last time, fleeing to some other city?"

Lingya fell flat onto the dirt. "We would never do that! We only fled the village because we feared for our lives."

"Even so, I have no assurance you won't do it again. There is only one way I can know for certain you will keep your promise."

Ek Chuaj paused, allowing silence to fill the garden once again. He took a deep breath, clearly enjoying every second of the delay. Walking over to her, Ek Chuaj cupped her chin, lifting Lingya's face until they were eye to eye.

"Before I release Maximon," said Ek Chuaj, "you must bring me your son."

***

Lost in Lingya's vision, Bobby had no idea how long he'd been in the well. Somehow, his body had remained afloat while his mind relived Lingya's past. But reality would not be denied indefinitely. Through the veil of dreams, he felt the ache in his arms and legs from treading water. How much time had passed since Ashley pushed him in? Minutes? Hours?

His breath grew quick and shallow as he searched for a way out. He reached up, but the lip of the well was far beyond his reach. The inner walls were smooth and slick, with no handholds or footholds to climb out.

Dark spots loomed before his eyes. Lingya's spirit flowed all around Bobby, a spectral reprieve from the agony of drowning at the bottom of the well. With arms too heavy to lift and legs too tired to kick, Bobby tilted his head back and allowed the Mayan ghost to reveal her memories once more.

***

Lingya left the garden in a daze. She could barely see through the veil of tears in her eyes. There was no way she could give Ek Chuaj her child. But Ek Chuaj had sworn that Bahlam would be handed over to the priests at the temple, delivered into the care of the servants she knew and trusted. Bahlam would be raised at the temple, under their watchful eyes where she could also be close to him.

Of course, she had no intention of accepting those terms. Bahlam was her son and belonged with her and Maximon. But what else could she do? Lingya stumbled along the path towards her home. By the time she got there, an idea had begun to take form. If her plan worked, handing over Bahlam would be only temporary.

Retrieving Bahlam from her neighbor, Lingya returned to the temple with a lighter step. Bahlam giggled in her arms, grasping at her fingers and wiggling his feet. By the time she reached the garden, she was in decent spirits. Wiping away the last of her tears, she threw open the garden doors, but Ek Chuaj was not there. Instead, she discovered the thin pale man who had been with Ek Chuaj when she first arrived. The frail man had a stern expression as he approached Lingya.

"I will take the child," he said, extending his arms.

Lingya pulled her son tight to her chest. "Where is Ek Chuaj?" she asked.

"He had urgent matters to attend to," said the man. "He left me to handle the matter."

"We had a deal. Where is Maximon?"

She heard shuffling feet. She spun to find Maximon, accompanied by two guards. Lingya threw herself into her lover's arms, causing the baby smushed between them to whimper. Maximon looked haggard, with bruises on his face and purple bags under his eyes. His cheeks were sunken and sallow, as if he hadn't eaten in days.

"Are you okay?" she asked. "What have they done to you?"

Maximon's eyes went to their son. "What have you done?" he asked.

"They've been torturing you, haven't they?" proclaimed Lingya. She put a hand to his face, but he pulled away.

"Tell me you didn't make a deal with Ek Chuaj," he whispered.

"I did what I had to do to free you," said Lingya.

Maximon's face contorted in pain.

Lingya stepped closer again. Lowering her head, she whispered, "I have a plan. I can get you out of here and save our son, but you must trust me."

Maximon's eyes found hers. For a long moment, they stared at one another. With trembling arms, Lingya turned towards the pale man and extended Bahlam.

The pale man took a step forward. With desperate eyes, Maximon grabbed her by the elbow. "Trust me," she whispered.

Lingya placed Bahlam gently into the pale man's arms. Crying once again, Lingya took Maximon by the hand and left the garden. Only when they were safely far away from the pale man and the guards, did she explain her plan.

***

Deep in the heart of the rainforest, Hayward and Simpkins stopped in a clearing to rest. Hayward bent over and rubbed his thighs. This little chore for the Seer had proven to be more exercise than he'd had in nearly twenty years. His bellbottoms were soaked, and his wingtips were buried beneath layers of mud.

"I'm telling you," he said to Simpkins, "this is a complete waste of our time. We must be halfway to Honduras by now."

Simpkins tore a branch off of a tree and used it to beat at the bushes. "The Scarlet Seer wouldn't have sent us out here for no reason," replied the ghoulish agent.

"It's all your fault," replied Hayward. "If you had let me experiment on the Ether boy instead of throwing him in the pit with the simpleton, none of this would have happened."

Simpkins stopped swatting the bushes and thrust the tip of the stick at Hayward. "Just how, exactly, do you figure that?"

"Clearly the Scarlet Seer sent us on this wild goose chase because she thinks we're expendable," explained Hayward. "If you'd allowed me to experiment on the boy, I likely could have discovered something of value."

Hayward continued. "Instead, the simpleton went crazy and, again, you failed by letting that inept guard captain handle it. None of those kids would have escaped if I'd been the one in charge of catching them."

Simpkins withdrew the stick, gripped it in both hands and bent it into the arch of a bow. "I still don't see what any of this has to do with our current situation."

"If it wasn't for that fiasco, the Scarlet Seer would've kept us close, putting us to use on important tasks at the temple. Instead, she sends us out here to wallow around in this stink hole. I'll tell you something—" Hayward was interrupted as a mosquito landed on his neck. The corpulent agent rose up onto his toes and dropped back down. The motion sent the fat on his neck bouncing. The rolls above and below the mosquito collided, squashing the bloated insect and sending a spray of twitching legs, brown bits, and blood splattering all over the collar of his dress shirt.

"You seek to anger me," said Simpkins, "I will not be provoked and allow you to use my emotions against me."

Hayward casually wiped at his collar and then rubbed his hand on his already ruined bellbottoms. "You haven't been able to do so much as read a Ouija board since the Ether kid got inside your head," said Hayward. "I'd say we're at a stalemate."

"I still believe that the Scarlet Seer had a valid reason for sending us on this mission."

"For shit's sake, use your senses," Hayward countered. "You may be better at tracking, but I sense emotions, and I'm telling you there isn't a single creature out here with an emotion more complex than hunger, except for that damn jaguar that's been following us for the last three miles. Too bad it hasn't attacked," he sighed. "At least then I'd have something to kill."

"It does seem odd that I can't sense these natives," pondered Simpkins. "They must have ways to mask themselves."

"I'm telling you, there's something fishy going on. Which reminds me: there was definitely something wrong with the scent I picked up outside the garden."

Simpkins relaxed his grip on his stick, thrusting the tip down into the mud. "It is strange she didn't ask us to pursue Jeremiah," he said, "but the Scarlet Seer is our new mistress. If she said the scent was nothing than we must trust her."

"That's it," exclaimed Hayward. "That's where I remember that smell from! It's the scent we used to track Jeremiah years ago when we took his daughter."

Simpkins snapped the branch in half, then doubled the halves and snapped them again. "If the scent is the same, then that means that the Scarlet Seer is really…"

The two agents exchanged startled looks. "Holy crap," said Hayward.

"We've got to get back to the temple," said Simpkins. "Now!"

CHAPTER TWENTY-SEVEN

It felt as though a lifetime had passed, with Bobby's legs screaming for relief as he struggled to stay afloat. His shoulders joined in shortly after, crying with the ache of over-exertion. Even as his survival instinct kept him in the present, Lingya's presence called to him to join her in the past.

In the background, the echoes of other spirits joined in. "Come to us," they said. "Come down." He pushed them away as best he could but in the back of his mind, he knew they would soon get their wish.

As water clogged his throat, Bobby thought of all that had brought him to this point: his time at the academy and his incredible adventures with Jinx. He thought of all he had learned and grown to believe since that fateful earthquake over a year ago. Mostly he thought of his parents and the friends he would never see again.

Bobby clawed to the surface and took a final gulp of air. Then he slipped into the darkness, drifting toward the bottom of the well.

***

Down and down, Bobby fell. At first there was only darkness. Then a faint light appeared: a pinprick of hope. At first, he thought it was a trick. But the light grew stronger the further he sank. With the last of his strength, Bobby inverted and kicked. Maybe it was just hypoxia, but if he died before reaching the bottom, he would never know.

He passed a dark side tunnel, but the light wasn't coming from there. He continued falling, drawn by the light and a sort of hymn that he recognized as the spirits' voices calling to him in unison. They were loud now, a chorus of wails and pleas that rang in his ears like a storm bell.

At last he reached the bottom. A pile of gray bones lay on the stones beneath him—dozens of human remains glowing with an intense inner light. Bobby thought of the murals in the Eagle's Nest and recalled Chief's explanation: *intense spiritual energy can be seen, but only by the extremely gifted.*

For whatever reason, there was tremendous spiritual energy trapped in these bones. He swam closer, laying a hand on a skull perched atop the pile. Anguish beyond measure resonated in Bobby's head. The pain was so overwhelming he barely recognized Lingya's voice.

"You have come at last," she said.

"I … I don't understand," replied Bobby. "How did you come to be here?"

"Save me," said Lingya. But the oxygen in his lungs was gone. His mind cried in panic, his body screamed in pain.

"Save me," echoed Bobby.

For a moment there was silence. Bobby hovered over the bones, on the verge of death. Then Lingya came to him once again, barely more than a whisper in his mind.

"Come," she said, caressing his mind. "It is time you knew the rest of my story."

***

She'd been such a fool. After seeing him with the pale man, Lingya knew Ek Chuaj was up to something. She also knew that figuring it out was the only chance she had of freeing herself from his demands and getting her son back.

The plan had been simple. She returned to the village where they had grown up and sought the answers about the night it was destroyed, and how Ek Chuaj had walked away when everyone else had perished.

After taking only two nights to travel a distance best covered in four, Lingya was exhausted by the time she reached the village. Falling to her knees, she wiped away tears as she surveyed the carnage. The huts had been torn apart; peoples' belongings strewn across the ground like garbage. Thankfully, there were no bodies. Whether they had been buried by the invaders or carried off into the jungle by predators, she didn't know.

Making her way to her family's home, Lingya rummaged through the ransacked storage room in the back until she found what she was looking for. Below the broken shelves, half hidden under piles of rotting herbs, lay the same idol of Hunhau that Bobby now possessed.

Moving to the center of the village, Lingya set the talisman on the ground in front of her and chanted the song of the dead taught to her by her mother from an early age. At first, nothing happened. Despite the violence that had claimed the lives of all its inhabitants, the villagers had lived in peace, allowing most of them to move into the afterlife when their time ended.

"I know you are still here," she whispered into the breeze. "Please, speak to me."

With agonizing slowness, the spirit of Nohchil materialized before her. "I do not wish to be here," said the dead leader of her village. "Let me go."

"Please," said Lingya. "I need to know what happened here."

The ghost laughed, a haunting echo that made her bones ache. "Pain and betrayal happened. Just as it will for you."

"Please, I need details. How did Ek Chuaj escape? How did he come by the foreigners' weapons and armor? Did he defeat them in battle?"

At the mention of his son's name, Nohchil flew into a rage. Storming around the clearing, he waved his arms, yelling at unseen enemies. The force of his anger made Lingya shudder and cry out as waves of dark energy bombarded her senses. Her first reaction was to drop the link and sever the connection to the spirit world. But she needed answers. Gritting her teeth, she held tight as the spirit wailed on.

Gradually, Nohchil's actions grew less violent, until he paced about the clearing mumbling to himself. Lingya scooped up the Hunhau idol and went to him. Stopping directly in his path, she extended her arms. "Share with me your story," she said.

With a grim stare, Nohchil placed his spectral hands in hers and revealed to her what had transpired the night their village was destroyed. When he was done, Lingya tucked the Hunhau idol into her travel sack and took her leave.

***

Armed with the truth, Lingya felt invincible as she raced back to the temple. She stopped by the hut briefly to see Maximon before heading to the temple. For the second time in a week, she stormed through the halls, looking for Ek Chuaj. A maid said he'd been last seen heading for the fountain room. *Perfect. I will corner him there just as he did to me.*

As Lingya approached the chamber, she thought she heard voices. *Strange.* It was after visiting hours and the priests were all at prayer session. *Who could be with him?*

She came around the final bend and caught a flicker of movement that looked like two people. Yet when she entered the room, Ek Chuaj was alone, crouched awkwardly near one of the stone benches in the far corner.

Ek Chuaj straightened and tucked something into his tunic. "Ah, my betrothed!" he said, throwing his arms out wide. "I was beginning to wonder where you went. No doubt having one last tryst with my fool cousin." He waved dismissively. "Have your fun, fleeting as it is. You will be mine forever once we are wed."

"Which will be never."

Storms brewed in Ek Chuaj's eyes. "What did you say?"

"You heard me," said Lingya, mimicking his gesture. "I will not marry you. Not now, not ever."

The storm clouds darkened, contorted Ek Chuaj's face into a tapestry of anger and confusion. "Need I remind you that, not only could I have Maximon executed for his crimes, but I also have your infant son in my care?"

"About that," said Lingya. "You will release my son. Max, Bahlam, and I will be leaving this town." Emboldened, Lingya threw back her head. "Actually, you know what? We aren't going to leave. You will. Leave this city and never return!"

Thunderous rage burst forth as Ek Chuaj rushed toward her. Grasping her by the shoulders, he lifted Lingya until her feet barely touched the ground. Bringing his face within inches of hers, he said, "And why would I do such a ridiculous thing?"

Trembling in his grasp, Lingya swallowed hard. "Because I have been to our village. I know your secret. Go on, tell the priests about Maximon. I will tell them what your father's spirit revealed to me."

The storm erupted as Ek Chuaj flung Lingya against the wall. She hit with a thud, sliding to the ground, where she lay cradling her arm.

"You stupid girl!" shouted Ek Chuaj. "You stupid, stupid girl!" He rushed at her, kicking her hard in the gut. Lingya doubled over, clutching her chest as EK Chuaj's fury rained down upon her. He kicked her three more times before stepping back. He tilted his head, combing his hands through his hair. "What have you done? Do you have any idea?"

Lingya pulled herself into a ball. She'd seen Ek Chuaj's rage directed at other people before, but never at her. Instinct screamed at her to do something, to run, or at least say something to make him stop, but all she could think about was the pain.

"Look at me. Look at me!" he yelled. "You have done this, not me!"

Struggling to see through puddles of tears, Lingya gazed into the face of Ek Chuaj and saw something she hadn't seen since they were children: not hatred or anger, lust or conceit, but something far more dangerous…fear.

"I am sorry for this," said Ek Chuaj, "but you leave me no choice." Pulling his hand back, he made a fist. With a disappointed frown, he struck her with such force it knocked her senseless.

***

Lingya awoke to a rhythmic bouncing sensation that made her wish she was still unconscious. Her ribs ached, her head pounded. She cracked open one eye to find herself on Ek Chuaj's broad shoulder. He took a step and the bouncing motion became clear. He was carrying her down a flight of stairs.

Lingya struggled to think straight as Ek Chuaj set her down and lit a brazier. The space around her sprang to life. Lingya thought she knew every room in the temple, but this one was new to her: earthen and raw with a stone well in the middle.

Lingya screamed as Ek Chuaj grabbed her wrist and dragged her toward the well. "What are you doing?" screamed Lingya. Rolling onto her back, she clawed at his arm with her free hand.

Ek Chuaj stared down at her. "You brought this upon yourself."

"Stop!" she yelled. "Let me go or I will tell everyone your secret!"

Ek Chuaj sighed and set her down at the lip of the well. "I'm afraid the time for secrets has passed," he said.

Dropping her arm, he hoisted her onto her feet. Terror paralyzed Lingya as she realized what Ek Chuaj was about to do. She couldn't move. She could barely speak.

"Please, no," she cried.

Dropping one shoulder, Ek Chuaj hooked an arm behind her legs. With one fluid motion, he lifted Lingya off her feet and tossed her into the well.

***

As Lingya's body drifted toward the bottom of the well, the vision of her final moments began to fade, threatening to return Bobby to the real world.

"Avenge me," whispered Lingya's spirit.

"How can I avenge you?" asked Bobby. "The instant you leave my mind, I'm going to drown right alongside you."

"You are the Holcan. You will find the way."

Lingya's words rang in his mind. He'd been thrice drawn into the spirit world, each time witnessing long stretches of time. Holcan: the Chosen One, with the ability to enter the spirit world, a plane of existence where time had no meaning...

Suddenly, the trials from the prophecy made sense. They weren't random acts declaring him the Holcan, they were lessons, teaching him how to enter the spirit world.

He was weightless in the water. *Just like floating over the electric fence...*

Every instinct in his body urged him to fight, to swim for the surface. *Remain perfectly motionlessness,* he told himself. *Just like riding on the back of the anaconda.*

He felt the ache in his limbs. *Ignore the pain. Clear your mind.*

His lungs were on fire. *Don't think about the danger. Focus on the void.*

There was one last trial remaining: live forever without aging a day. *Here goes nothingness.*

Bobby gave in to freedom. He gave in to motionlessness, to emptiness. He gave in to death.

***

Bobby woke in darkness. A faint glow cast shadows on a sandalwood bridge a few feet away. He stood, realizing as he did so, that the light was radiating from him. *I'm in the spirit world*, thought Bobby, remembering how he'd glowed during his journey to the core of the earth to delay the collapse of the Jade Academy.

A light in the distance shined much brighter. Bobby moved toward it, spotting bonsai trees and rock sculptures along the path. *I'm in my Zen garden*, he thought. The light emanated from the central dais. As he drew closer, he discovered that the pedestal with the lotus flower was not there. Instead, a fountain stood in its place. Walking up the steps, he discovered that the fountain was an exact replica of the one inside the temple.

Gems embedded in the base twinkled like stars in the night sky, but that wasn't where the light was coming from. The water pouring from the fountain possessed an intense white luminesce that reminded Bobby of the pond inside the Nexus. He stood gazing into the glowing depths, mesmerized by the shimmering eddies that swirled within.

"What is this place?" he asked.

"A place of your own design," said a voice from behind him.

Bobby turned to see Lingya shimmering with the same gossamer glow he possessed.

"Don't you mean the Fountain of Youth?" he asked. "That is what this place is, isn't it?"

"Just like the trials in the Holcan prophecy, the fountain is just a test," said Lingya. "It shows the way for those who are ready. Those who solve the riddle and find the secret passage gain entrance to the true source of power—The Well of Eternity. Once inside the well, they must master themselves or die."

Bobby thought about drowning in the well. "Literally sink or swim," he said dryly. "Does this mean…am I dead?"

"You are in the in-between," said Lingya. "The void; purgatory; the endless nothingness between life and death."

"The spirit world," said Bobby with awe. "That means I did it, right? I passed the final test."

"Within this place, a single moment can stretch into eternity," said Lingya. "What you choose to do with it is up to you." As she spoke, other spirits began to appear. Ancient Mayans dressed in eclectic garb stepped out from the conifer forest surrounding the fountain. Others made their way through the garden, joining them at the base.

"Who are all these people?" asked Bobby.

"Supplicants and others like me," said Lingya, "people who died at the bottom of the well without mastering its power."

"The spirits are the other voices I heard in the temple?" asked Bobby. "The bones at the bottom of the well?"

Lingya nodded.

"And they all have a story to tell, don't they?" asked Bobby. "A tragedy like yours?"

Lingya nodded again. "You can set them free. You are the Holcan."

Bobby turned to the nearest spirit, a young man with dark skin and sad eyes. "Come. Tell me your story," said Bobby, extending both hands. "And go slow," he added. "We have all the time in the world."

***

When the last spirit had replayed its final moments, Bobby returned to the fountain. He had no idea how long he'd been in the Well of Eternity. It might have been hours, perhaps days, or even years. He felt neither hunger, thirst, nor exhaustion.

"Wow," he told Lingya, shaking his head. "That was amazing."

Indeed, experiencing other people's lives had been unimaginable. In the blink of an eye, he'd witnessed birth, childhood, adolescence, and maturity. He'd felt love and hate, joy and sorrow, ugliness and beauty, along with countless other sensations so vivid they set his mind afire.

"Thank you for freeing us," said Lingya. "Because of you, we can finally be at peace."

Bobby clasped his hands together. "It was my honor. But now I think it's time for me to go."

Lingya took Bobby by the hand and led him to the steps of the fountain. "Drink from the waters and you will return to your time," she said. Taking from him the idol of Hunhau, she brought it close to her lips. With a whisper, the talisman began to glow. "Your grasp on the void will fade once you leave this place. Time will return to normal. I've imbued the idol with anima to buy you some time, but you must hurry. Find a way out before it's gone, or you will join us here forever."

***

At first, Bobby felt perfectly fresh as he regained his body and searched for an escape. Renewed by his time in the spirit world, he swam back to the dark side tunnel he'd noticed during his descent. Holding the talisman in front of him like a fog lamp, he followed the tunnel outward until it led up.

Bathed in the anima from the Hunhau talisman, he could have followed the tunnel blindfolded. As he swam farther, the idol dimmed and his strength waned.

Gradually, his arms and legs began to ache, and he knew that time marched onward once again. The burning in his lungs soon returned. It grew and grew until he thought he might burst. Then he saw true light up ahead. The anima in the idol sustained him, giving him the strength he needed to ascend the last few yards.

When he broke the surface, it was to the realization that he recognized his surroundings. A blossoming red fig tree stood nearby, as did a familiar apple tree. Bobby climbed out of the pond inside the garden where the Scarlet Seer had revealed herself to him. The solarium lay in shadows, with the intense jungle sun low over the west roof.

Bobby took a moment and wrung out his clothes. He was returning the Hunhau idol to his pocket when the ground trembled. The slight tremor knocked him back to his surroundings. *Apparently, the destruction caused by Jinx has unsettled the pyramid.*

Still dripping wet, Bobby headed to the far exit. He needed to find his friends and fast. Something told him the worst of their adventure wasn't over yet.

CHAPTER TWENTY-EIGHT

T he sun had just abandoned the forest, turning the tops of the trees into a jigsaw of slate gray, as the last of the refugees made their way out of the main chamber and onto the open terrace surrounding the temple. High above, pregnant storm clouds threatened to unleash their wrath upon anything unfortunate enough to lie below.

Jinx helped direct a young Latina girl to a crumbled structure that might have once been a granary or pottery. Clay vessels of every size and shape lay in the dirt, their broken shards decorating the ground like seashells on a storm-wrecked shore. A giant slab occupied the center of the space. Probably a worktable, the long, flat block of limestone now served as a bench on which the young children sat.

Lily propped against the far pillar while Trevor inspected her sore knee. Ana cuddled at Lily's side, her dolly hugged tight to her chest. Nearby, Jacob talked excitedly with Mikey Blanchert, reenacting scenes from their conflict with the Core guards. Jinx moved to join them, then stopped as Mikey shot him a glance.

Jinx retreated to stand close to Willy, who lay next to Lily, across from Ana. The pale slender boy was still unconscious. No one had seen Mercy or Ashley since they'd evacuated the temple.

"Good gracious, Jinxy," gasped Lily. "How hard did you hit him?" She lifted one of Willy's eyelids to check his pupils.

"Not nearly as hard as he deserved," said Jinx. "Having him inside my head…making me do all those things…it was worse than a nightmare."

Mikey shot him another nervous glance. Jinx scowled and kicked at a dilapidated wall, breaking off a chunk of gray limestone. "Has anyone seen Bobby?"

Lily lifted her head, still cradling Ana under her right arm. "I told your grandma how to find the back entrance to the grotto. She and Slab went to see if he's there."

"Maybe we should go back to the fountain room and check the trap door?" said Jinx.

Trevor looked up from examining Lily's knee. "Dude, I gotta take care of beau. Besides, those quakes are no joke."

The temple had shaken several times during their evacuation. Now it gave another ominous moan. The ground beneath their feet trembled as if some massive god were stomping through the rainforest.

Slab and Melody showed up as the tremors died down. Melody looked dog-eared, with mud in her hair and a trickle of blood running down her nose.

"Oh dear, are you okay?" asked Lily.

"It's nothing." Melody wiped the blood away with a grimace. "We found the mossy boulder right where you told us to look. We went in, but the grotto was empty. We checked the stairs, the well, everything. There was no sign of either Bobby or Ashley."

"So, what now?" asked Jinx.

"I need to go back inside. There are still children trapped in the lab."

"I'll come with you," said Jacob. "In case the goon squad shows up."

Melody shook her head. "I can handle myself. Besides, I'm the only one who can wake them up."

"What about us? What do we do if the guards show up again?" asked Jinx.

"Slab will stay here and look after you until I get back," she said. "If Bobby is in there, I'll find him."

She hurried off, heading for the tiny service entrance Bobby and Jinx had used when they first arrived. Jinx slumped down next to Lily.

Less than a minute later, a platoon of Core guards poured out of the pyramid. Some were dressed in their standard black uniforms. Others wore jungle fatigues. All of them carried assault rifles.

"Holy hell," said Jacob, as nearly two dozen armed soldiers came rushing toward them. "We're screwed."

As he spoke, the heavens cracked open and let loose a deluge. The heavy rain quickly soaked through their clothes and turned the barren fields into a marshland.

Jacob took three steps towards the oncoming guards before Trevor caught him by the arm and whirled him around. "Bro, those aren't Taser guns they're carrying," he said. "Remember what Ashley said? We're expendable now."

Jacob gave no reply as heavy rain pounded the earth. Then shots rang out and everyone was on their feet and moving. Children screamed and bolted for the jungle. Jinx and his friends tried to herd them up the terrace, away from the temple.

The guards formed into a line, advancing up the terrace in an orderly march. Core agents dressed in suits stood among the soldiers, ready to neutralize any arcane assault.

Trevor picked up Ana and carried her. "We stay together," he said, heading for the jungle. Lily nodded and followed, leaning heavily on Jinx for support.

Slab was the only one who did not flee. Over his shoulder he said to them, "You go. I fight." The kindhearted giant stepped over to the crumbling wall of the ruined building. With a mighty groan, he tore off a huge chunk of stone.

Slab hoisted a four feet wide mass of limestone in front of him like a shield. Then he crouched down and advanced toward the oncoming soldiers.

Meanwhile, Jinx and Lily climbed the stairs to the second terrace, right behind Trevor and Ana. A peel of thunder matched another deep rumble from the temple, shaking Jinx's bones as well as the ground beneath him. More shots rang out. Trevor stumbled in the mud and dropped Ana. Jacob helped lift her back up. Behind them, Slab let out a furious bellow.

"I've gotta help the big oaf," said Jacob.

Lily grabbed Jacob's wrist. "For heaven's sake, you'll be killed!"

Jacob pried his arm free. "Better to die a hero than live as a coward." Before anyone had a chance to protest, he turned and raced after Slab.

The ground shook again, opening a fissure less than ten yards away. The guards were upon them now. Jinx spotted Sandman, flanked by Parker and Franklin in the vanguard. The stone-faced soldiers advanced methodically up the terrace. Between Lily's bad knee and the trembling ground, it wouldn't be long before they caught up.

Then the guards caught sight of Slab and his limestone shield. Jacob crouched behind him. When they got close, Jacob dashed from behind Slab and disarmed a mercenary with two quick punches and a kick to the groin. The man fell over, writhing and groaning. Jacob ducked behind Slab, who advanced on the next guard.

Jinx and Lily scrambled up the remaining two terraces right behind Trevor, who did his best to help the other children while carrying Ana. Meanwhile, Sandman ducked behind a pile of ruins, circumventing Slab and Jacob. The guard captain sprinted across the open field, his eyes set on Jinx and company.

By now, the fastest, most athletic kids had already reached the jungle's edge. Most of the children, however, struggled to make their way up the second and third terraces. Jinx looked over his shoulder. Sandman was less than fifty yards away.

Jinx turned back to the forest. It was over twice that distance. All around them, children collapsed to the ground as Sandman put them to sleep. A wicked grin on the guard captain's face told Jinx that he was saving the best for last.

Trevor threw Ana on his back and swept Lily into his arms. "Run for it!" he said. The trembling earth roiled beneath his feet as Jinx huffed to keep pace with his lanky friend. Sandman followed, with

Franklin and Parker close behind. "Run all you want, cadets," called the guard captain. "There is no escape."

Jinx and his friends hit the edge of the clearing and plunged into the jungle. Sandman stopped at the tree line, his massive frame a solid gray against the shifting static of the storm. "You think you can hide in the jungle? Silly children, my soldiers will hunt you down."

In the monochrome shadows of the undergrowth, Trevor's foot caught on an unseen root. He went sprawling. Lily tumbled out of his arms and into the mud. Ana flew off his back and into a giant fern.

Sandman strolled up to them casually. Beside him, Parker raised his assault rifle, the eagle tattoo on his bicep bulging as he targeted Jinx. "End of the line, little boy."

Then a thunderous boom rocked the rainforest. The ground heaved. Parker stumbled, firing harmlessly into the air. Jinx thought at first it had been another earthquake. Then he saw smoke billowing from a black box back near the edge of the jungle.

"Someone blew up the power generators!" cried Lily.

Lightning flashed and the jungle lit up again. Jinx caught movement in the shadows. Then a team of soldiers in olive-green fatigues burst into the clearing.

"Nobody move. We have you surrounded."

* * *

Within the secret lab at the top of the pyramid, Melody braced herself against the wall and took a deep breath. She'd managed to set a quarter of the children free so far, but the price was severe. With each child she freed, it became harder to focus, a floodwater rising in her brain, trying to drown her.

Pushing off from the wall, Melody staggered to the next table, a steel gurney holding a slender Asian boy with dimpled cheeks rosy with acne. She leaned over, placing a hand on the boy's forehead. His eyes fluttered open.

"No! The prisoner must not be released!"

Melody spun at the sound of the voice but there was no one there. *Who's there? Get out of my head.*

The Asian boy looked up from the gurney. "What's going on? Where am I?"

Melody pointed to the opening in the wall that served as a window. "They've been experimenting on you, but you're free now," she panted as she pulled out the needle in his arm and untied his restraints. "Go now. Follow the others."

Outside, the steady downpour played pitter-patter against the hard stone. The boy slid off the table and went to the open window and the procession of children she'd woken before him.

From far below came the sharp retort of gunfire echoing over the sound of the rain and thunder. Clearly the Core's mercenaries were attempting to recapture the escaped children.

Melody stumbled to the next table. She set her hand on the child's forehead—a skinny pre-teen girl with almond skin and chestnut hair. With her other hand, Melody pulled out the needles and tubes. The floodwater in Melody's head rose again.

"The prisoner must not go free!" The voice was getting louder, making it nearly impossible to concentrate.

Melody put her hands on her temples, screaming, "Leave me alone!"

"The prisoner must not be released!" shouted the voice.

Melody squeezed her head. *Ignore the voice.* Glancing to her right, she counted three full rows of children still unconscious and restrained. *Just keep going.*

Beneath her fingertips, the girl's eyes popped open. "Go. Follow the others," said Melody, feebly pointing toward opening.

The girl got up and made for the window. As soon as she'd disappeared over the edge, Melody fell to her knees. She drew a series of long, ragged breaths. Finally, she straightened up. Holding on to the wall for support, she made her way to the next table.

* * *

In the gray void of the afterlife, the spirit of Ek Chuaj raged like a tempest. He stormed through the darkness, searching for someone or something to listen to him; to know his story; to share his pain. He wanted to find the Holcan, desperate to convince the boy that he was the victim, not the villain. He wandered downward, hoping to find the Holcan by the well, but the grotto stood silent and empty. He left, passing through the trap door into the fountain room as easily as a jungle cat slips through shadows.

He strode toward the main chamber, his temper a palpable force in need of a target. The passages were full of foreigners. How long had it been since anyone had inhabited the temple before this? Time held no meaning in the void. It felt like he'd been alone forever.

He stopped to yell at the first people he saw, but they were as blind to his presence as Lingya had been to his schemes. Ek Chuaj moved on, his mood growing blacker by the moment as he ascended higher in the ziggurat.

He was near the summit when he spotted her. The foreign woman had hair like sunlight and clothes the color of blood. Her face wore ritual paint, though he had no idea what her faux smile symbolized. Ek Chuaj assumed she was a warrior of some kind. Rare in his culture, but not impossible.

She leaned over a table, attending to a young child whose soul appeared ready to pass over to the other side. She lay a hand on his head and the boy's spirit grew stronger, nestling back into his frail body. Whatever the red woman was doing, it was draining her strength. She dropped to a knee, drawing several deep breaths before rising shakily to her feet. As she rose, Ek Chuaj caught a glimpse of light within her; a brief flash of pale white against the backdrop of perpetual shadows.

He drifted closer and confirmed what he'd sensed from distance. There was a crack in her mind; a tiny doorway that had been pried open by some form of mental manipulation. Normally, Ek Chuaj could not enter the mind of another without their permission, but this one was different. Willing or not, he could pry at the opening and force his way in.

The red woman lifted a hand to her head, then froze. Did she feel his presence? Ek Chuaj remained motionless, fearful that she might sense him and shield herself. She scanned the room. Her eyes probed every shadow, but his shadows lay beyond her sight. A long silence fell.

Finally, Ek Chuaj's patience paid off. The red woman turned away, staggering toward the stairs that led down the side of the pyramid. Ek Chuaj closed the distance between them. Extending both arms, he grabbed the red woman by the neck.

"Time for my revenge," he whispered, and forced himself into her mind.

CHAPTER TWENTY-NINE

It took Jinx almost a full five seconds to realize the soldiers who'd burst from the jungle weren't pointing their guns at him. Instead, they were leveled at Sandman and his guards. Jinx was still struggling to make sense of this when Chief broke into the clearing.

"Hell yeah!" exclaimed Jinx. Trevor and Lily stared, baffled.

"Really?" said Sandman, eyeing the weapons pointed at his chest. His eyes narrowed. Chief's commandos swayed on their feet. Their grips relaxed, and their guns fell to the mud with a splash.

"So, you're the disturbance in the forest my scouts detected," said Sandman. "I'll admit you're good. Three patrols went missing since I got word of an armed party entering La Muerte Verde. It takes skills to mask your location the way you did. Too bad you aren't as skilled at combat."

Sandman returned his gaze to Chief's commandoes. One by one, they dropped to the ground, fast asleep. Sandman turned to Parker, who still had his assault rifle trained on the kids. "Shoot these men first, then the cadets."

"I wouldn't do that if I were you," said a voice from the forest. It was Ana, all but forgotten behind the fern where she'd fallen. Rising to her feet, she came to stand next to Jinx.

"Your guns might backfire," she said. "You wouldn't want them to explode in your hands."

Parker and Franklin exchanges worried glances. "Stand fast. That's an order!" shouted Sandman. "She's trying to get inside your heads."

"A gesture I appreciate, but is unnecessary," said Chief. "I believe they'll find their weapons quite useless."

A hollow click proved Chief's point as Franklin pulled the trigger to no avail.

"I've disabled the firing pin in each of your rifles," said Chief. "An easy trick really. Guns are simple mechanical devices, after all."

"That still leaves us three on one, old man. These kids are of no use and your men are passed out cold," said Parker. He pulled a tactical knife from his belt.

"On the contrary," said Chief, "I only needed to know the game in order to play it." As he spoke, the commandoes on the ground began to stir. Sloughing off the effects of Sandman's persuasion, Chief's soldiers reclaimed their weapons and rose to their feet.

"Putting people to sleep is a parlor trick," said Chief. "One easily countered, I might add, so long as you are connected to enough anima. Now, I suggest you surrender before we're forced to harm any of you."

Parker and Franklin laid down their weapons and raised their hands. Then the earth gave a mighty heave. The trees around them swayed. A young cecropia tore from the moist earth. With a loud crack, the tree toppled into the clearing. Chief and his commandos dove for cover. When they got up, Sandman and his guards were gone.

"What the heck was that?" asked Jinx. "We aren't even close to the temple."

"Must be tunnels that extend under the jungle," said Trevor.

Chief picked himself up, wiping the mud from his camouflage pants and jacket. "You kids are going have to repair the damage to the temple," he said. "My team and I need to go after those mercenaries and round them up before they hurt someone."

"But none of us have the ability to fix the damage," said Jinx.

"Remember how you helped me keep the Jade Academy from collapsing? It's the same thing. Just combine your energy to repair whatever's broken."

"But I'm the one who broke it in the first place," whimpered Jinx.

Chief strode over, put both hands on Jinx's shoulders, and looked him deep in the eyes. "Then you have the power to fix it. Trust your friends to help you, but most importantly, trust yourself."

Jinx gave a nod and went to stand by Trevor, Lily and Ana. "Honest to goodness, we'll do our best," said Lily.

"That's all anyone can ever ask for," said Chief. Then he and his commandos turned and disappeared into the forest.

* * *

Willy awoke to an oppressive weight upon his chest and the distant sensation of something coarse slapping him across the face. He opened his eyes and discovered Mercy, sitting atop him. The albino simian swung her arms back and forth, smacking him on the cheek with each pass. When she saw him stir, Willy's pet pulled back her gums, revealing crooked yellow teeth.

Willy shoved her off, pushing himself up with one elbow. The other hand went to his head where a punk metal band had taken up residence. His heavy white robe was soaked with mud, turning the bone-colored fabric into a collage of brown, green, and gray filth.

He stared at his surroundings, trying to remember how it had happened. He lay in the corner of one of the ruined buildings outside the temple. A giant slab of limestone stood nearby, encircled by half-a-dozen crumbling pillars.

The last thing he recalled was seeing Ashley flee. He'd been too busy manipulating her brother to realize she'd abandoned him until it was too late. When his concentration broke, the brat knocked him out. Someone must have dragged him here after that.

The ground gave a low rumble; proof that the damage he'd caused while controlling Jinx still endured. He cocked his head to the side, listening for others. Through the clatter of pouring rain, he heard a piercing wail.

Like a hyena tracking an injured gazelle, Willy walked to the corner of the ruins. High atop the pyramid, a solidary figure stumbled down the broad, slippery steps. Even through the dense torrent, Willy recognized the crimson outfit of the Scarlet Seer. She staggered and lurched, half sliding, half falling down the tall limestone blocks.

It wasn't just the stairs or the rain that gave her trouble. She seemed to be struggling with some kind of inner conflict, reflected in her bizarre, drunken behavior. Willy probed her aura, read her emotions, and drew back in shock. There were two personalities within her.

One he recognized as the tightly controlled mind of the woman who had run the temple. The other entity was foreign and strange, some sort of evil spirit. It was exactly the sort of mind Willy craved. The balance between the two minds was precarious. It wouldn't take much to tip the scales and push her over the brink.

Willy bristled as he recalled how the woman had kept her real identity a secret. He wanted revenge for that deceit. All he needed was a target, something to catalyze the strange entity inside her.

Sounds of shouting and fighting in the distance told him the other students were close by. He would give the entity inside the Scarlet Seer the push it needed, but how?

Mercy jumped onto his shoulder. Through their psychic link, Willy saw images of Trevor, Lily, and Jinx talking with an old man with long black hair. Then the kids sat down in a circle and joined hands, preparing for some kind of séance. Mercy shrieked in jubilation. It would be the perfect opportunity to strike.

He liked Mercy's idea, except that it meant leaving the Scarlet Seer to potentially regain control. The presence inside her thrashed once again, struggling. Willy salivated. The spirit possessed such wonderfully vile emotions…

Then someone appeared at the service entrance at the base of the pyramid. Willy recognized the person immediately. Mercy leapt up and down, pounding the ground with excitement. Indeed, he couldn't have asked for a better target.

Sending images through the link, Willy gave Mercy free rein to go after Trevor, Lily, and Jinx. Meanwhile, he would stay here and feast upon the dark emotions of the spirit, right after he unleashed it upon Bobby Ether.

* * *

Despite the downpour, Bobby was glad to be outside, free from the trembling temple and out in the open. Outside there wasn't a ceiling threatening to crash down on his head.

From somewhere above came the grating sound of tumbling stone. Stumbling down the steps of the pyramid, Melody tripped and fell down a rung before regaining her footing.

He started to rush to her aid, but she held up a hand. "Stay back," she said. "Do not come any closer." The sky crackled as a bolt of lightning split the sallow dusk in two.

"What's the matter?" asked Bobby. "Are you hurt?"

"All of the children from the lab are freed," said his grandmother. "The temple is vacant, but it has cost me dearly. There's something inside me, a voice ... I don't know how much longer I can fight it."

Bobby narrowed his eyes. There was something strange, yet familiar about the aura around her, an apparition he almost recognized...

Melody's eyes flashed to a crumbled building with a chunk of the wall torn off. Bobby traced her gaze and caught a glimpse of someone spying on them from behind the rubble. Bobby instantly recognized the bald head of Willy the Creep. Melody's gaze shifted to him. Bobby felt uncomfortable warmth ignite in his brain.

"What are you doing?" he asked.

His grandmother stared at him, a tortured expression on her face. Bobby gripped the sides of his head as the heat intensified. It spread to his chest, then to his arms and legs, as if his blood had been saturated with gasoline and set on fire. Fiery pressure throbbed inside his veins. He looked at his arms and saw raw purple lesions. Red rashes sprouted on his neck. He scratched at the inflamed sores, tearing through the tender flesh. His hands came away slick with blood.

This can't be happening, he told himself. He closed his eyes and tried to block out the pain, but his head pounded with the sound of his own heartbeat. *You're hallucinating, Bobby. The things you're seeing aren't real. Focus your mind. Think cheerful thoughts.*

He thought about his parents, then of Jinx and how proud he was of his little cousin. The two of them had been through so much together. Bobby glanced at his arms and saw tan, unblemished skin. His hands were clean. His neck held no gaping wounds.

Melody's face contorted in a mixture of anguish and rage. Her eyes were not those of his grandmother. Bobby's throat went dry. He recognized that callous gaze.

"Ek Chuaj," whispered Bobby.

"You have freed Lingya," said the Mayan inhabiting his grandmother. "Now you will witness my story and share my pain!"

***

The scene before Bobby was the same and yet different. The temple stood as it did now, with people fleeing for their lives before an army. Except the people fleeing weren't the kids from the academy, and the pursuing army wasn't the Core and its mercenary soldiers.

No, the people running for their lives in Ek Chuaj's vision were Mayans: the ancient Mayans of his era. The army chasing them were the Spanish Conquistadors: the invaders bent on destroying the Mayan culture.

"How did this happen?" said Bobby.

"I'm glad you asked," said Ek Chuaj.

Suddenly the scene shifted. Ek Chuaj was in the fountain room inside the temple. Bobby saw the scrawny pale man, the same man Lingya had seen whispering with Ek Chuaj in the garden.

"Here. Give this to Tonatiuh," said Ek Chuaj. "It shows the location of all our lookouts, with routes through the jungle to avoid detection." Opening the secret passage, he ushered the spy into the stairwell. "And remember," he said, grabbing the spy's arm, "tell him to attack only if he sees the bonfire. If my plan works, the city will be his without a fight. Now go. Once you've delivered the message, return and take your place."

Footsteps echoed in the hall. "You must go!" barked Ek Chuaj. Pushing the spy into the tunnel, he closed the trapdoor as Lingya entered the room.

"I know what happens next," interrupted Bobby.

"What you don't know is the pain it caused me," said Ek Chuaj.

"Yeah, I am sure you were real torn up about murdering Lingya and tossing her into the well," scoffed Bobby.

"See for yourself," said Ek Chuaj. The scene shifted, jumping past Lingya's final moments to what came after.

With cold hands and sweaty brow, Ek Chuaj returned to the main chamber where High Priest Kukulkan spotted him.

"I have been meaning to commend you," said the high priest. "Reports come in daily from other cities under attack, and yet even our farms and outlying regions remain safe. Your security measures have been exceptional! Truly, you were sent by the gods."

Ek Chuaj ducked his head to hide the flush in his cheeks, caused not by modesty but the fire that still burned in his veins over the altercation in the well.

"I am sorry to say our perimeter may not be as secure as we had hoped," replied Ek Chuaj. "I just uncovered a plot to infiltrate our defenses."

High Priest Kukulkan set both hands on his cheeks, his mouth hanging open. "Whatever do you mean? Surely you have not found another spy!"

Ek Chuaj shook his head with all the despair of a convict being led to the gallows. "The man I told you about before, Maximon. He has been spotted passing information to the invaders."

Kukulkan let out a groan that was so high pitched it was almost a squeal. "But didn't we let him go? I thought you said he was innocent!"

Clasping his hands before him, Ek Chuaj put on his most modest face. "This is all my fault. He was from my village. I thought we could trust him. Now I fear he plans to betray us and Lingya has gone to join him."

"Lingya is missing?" asked the high priest in shock. "She is one of my most loyal servants."

"Not all servants are as trustworthy as they appear," said Ek Chuaj. "I am confident she is gone, but fear not, I know another way to get the traitor to reveal himself."

"You have a plan?" asked High Priest Kukulkan.

Ek Chuaj nodded. "Meet me at the altar," he said. "With your blessing, we will not only expose the traitor, but petition the gods to lift the plague as well."

The high priest beamed as he hurried down the hall. "Yes, a sacrifice to please the gods, who will then thwart the invaders and lift the curse!" He rubbed his hands together in satisfaction. "What a truly wonderful idea!"

***

Like palpable ghosts, Trevor's and Lily's presence hovered around Jinx. Their bodies sat in the clearing just inside the jungle's grip, where Chief and his men had come through. Their spirits, however, floated beyond, to the temple and its dying heart.

Through the void, Jinx felt his friends' anima channel into him. He knew the temple as never before, felt it tremble and recognized its pain. Its sick heart sent ripples that disturbed the forest. Its back was broken, the pillar in the main chamber cracked from Jinx's earlier tantrum.

Broken but not shattered. Not if Jinx had anything to say about it.

He set his mind to the task at hand and probed the wound, exploring the hollows in the stone in an effort to discover the full extent of the damage. Whenever his twisted genes threatened to send him spinning off course, Trevor and Lily nudged him like bumpers on a bowling lane. With their help, he rewove the structural fabric of the pyramid, knitting the stony flesh back together, stitch by limestone stitch.

If it had only been the central column, they might have already prevailed. Instead, the weakened pillar gave other areas permission to fail. Neighboring blocks bore deep cracks from the increased pressure. Walls on lower levels buckled from the compromise to their structural integrity.

Through the link, Jinx shared his thoughts. "We can do it. It's just going to take a lot of time and a tremendous amount of anima."

The link glowed with Lily's positivity and encouragement. Trevor's presence was a rock of confidence as strong as that which he sought to recreate. "You can do it, little buddy."

With the two of them, Jinx tackled the outlying regions, getting a sense of how to knit the stone back together in a way that held fast.

An infection lay within the walls where Jinx's anima had been used to damage the temple. Jinx opened himself to this infection, re-absorbing the energy back into his being. The stone welcomed the change, the rightness of healing a festering wound.

Something rattled his consciousness. Had it not been for Lily's spirit beside him, his chi would have swerved wildly, causing incal-culable damage and likely rupturing the temple beyond repair. He probed for the source. Something was happening on the surface, something that dimmed the causeway of his consciousness, making the path flicker and fade in and out.

"I need to withdraw," he told the others. "Something is happening to my body."

Trevor and Lily guided him out. "Don't worry, lil' dude. We'll hold it down until you get back," said Trevor.

"Hurry back, dear," said Lily. With a final affirmation, Jinx float-ed to the surface to reclaim his body.

CHAPTER THIRTY

It was a vision, Bobby knew that, and yet it was also real. Everything he saw had actually occurred in the past. That knowledge made it all the more terrifying, for this was Ek Chuaj's nightmare: the events that had turned him into the monster he was now.

After telling Kukulkan to meet him at the altar, Ek Chuaj made his way to the servant quarters where Lingya's child, Bahlam, was being held. The attending maid protested as he went for the baby. Ek Chuaj shoved her out of the way with one hand. The old women slammed against the far wall, smacking her head with a loud crack. Without a glance at the maid, Ek Chuaj tucked the swaddled bundle under his arm and left.

Outside on the lower terrace, twilight had turned the sky ashen grey. A crescent moon offered little aid as he picked his way across the terrace to the amphitheater at the base of the temple. Pushing through the gathering crowd, he spotted the high priest waiting on the main stage.

"This child belongs to Lingya and Maximon," said Ek Chuaj, handing the child to High Priest Kukulkan. "I expect Maximon will come forth once we begin. If not, we shall sacrifice his son to the gods. Either way, the traitor will be punished and the gods shall be appeased."

"A clever plan," said High Priest Kukulkan, nodding his approval. "Build the bonfire," he commanded his servants. "We will light the sky as a signal to the gods to witness our faith and accept our humble offering."

Ek Chuaj scanned the crowd as he took his place beside the priest. In truth, he did have a clever plan, just not the one the priest expected.

There, in the back was the person he was looking for. He gave the pale man a barely perceptible nod. The spy nodded back. *Good, everything is in order.*

With preparations complete, High Priest Kukulkan came forth and addressed the audience. Donning an ornate staff and a gaudy gold crown mashed down on his bulbous forehead, the ruler of the city lumbered about the stage. Passing off the ceremony as his idea, he talked about the exalted nature of the gods, their divine power, and how they would deliver salvation because of his supreme faith and devotion.

Ek Chuaj let the blathering fool drone on for a good ten minutes. When the fat priest started to wind down and drift towards the unlit pyre, Ek Chuaj nodded to his spy.

From out of the crowd, the pale man came forward. "Your high holiness!" he said, pushing his way to the front of the gathered throng. "I bring news! The invaders are amassing an army outside the city limits!"

A chorus of screams and shouts rang out. High Priest Kukulkan glared at Ek Chuaj. "You said we were safe—that you knew their ways! How did their army get so close?"

Ek Chuaj shrugged. "I meant to tell you about their movements. I must have gotten distracted."

From the folds of his cloak, the pale man produced a note and handed it to the ruler. Kukulkan read it. His face grew redder and redder as he absorbed the contents.

"This is preposterous! You can't be serious," he said, turning to Ek Chuaj.

Ek Chuaj shrugged again. "What is it?"

"This note is from the leader of the invaders: Tonatiuh, the Red Sun. It says he will broker a peace to avoid bloodshed, but only with the military leader of the city. It says that all members of the clergy, including the high priest, must step down. They will spare all our lives, but only if we do not invoke the gods."

Ek Chuaj did his best to look surprised. Placing a palm on his forehead, he said, "You're telling me the Spaniards won't attack if I am in charge? It is a heavy burden for certain, but surely the right decision to save so many lives."

High Priest Kukulkan's mouth flopped open like a fish out of water. Grabbing a torch from a nearby acolyte, he stepped to the pyre. "We must perform the ceremony at once. We shall beg the gods for protection. Surely they will save us!"

Ek Chuaj stepped in front of him, barring Kukulkan from lighting the fire. "Think about what you're doing. The gods did not save my village, or any of the other cities the Spaniards have destroyed. Besides, what if they see the fire and think we are preparing for war? They might attack before we have a chance to broker peace."

The high priest raised his free hand to his brow. "That would mean turning over control of the city."

Ek Chuaj put a hand over his heart. "I swear I would remain loyal to you. We need only pretend that you have given me control."

The high priest's eyes brightened at this. "A clever ruse," he said as a smile crept across his face. "Meanwhile, the other priests and I could secretly pray to Buluc Chabtan to curse the invaders and send them to the underworld!"

"Yes!" Ek Chuaj agreed. "With the god of war on our side, my hunters and I will rise up and slay the Spaniards. We will destroy their army without a fight!"

Kukulkan's smile broadened as the idea swirled in his head. "I shall be the ruler who vanquished the invaders!" he declared.

"But first you must step down and make me high chief," reminded Ek Chuaj.

Kukulkan's face burned bright red as he extended the ceremonial staff. Then he pried the crown off his head.

"Stop!" said a voice in the crowd. "You are being deceived." All eyes turned as Maximon made his way to the front.

"What is the meaning of this?" asked Kukulkan.

"This man is a fraud," said Maximon.

"That man is the traitor!" said Ek Chuaj. "Soldiers, arrest him!" Guards moved to intercept Maximon, but Kukulkan waved them off.

"I am no traitor," said Maximon. "Ek Chuaj has made a deal with the invaders to take over the city. When Lingya returned from our village, she told me about the deal he made with Tonatiuh to appoint himself High Chief. Lingya confronted him and he killed her!"

High Priest Kukulkan turned from Maximon to Ek Chuaj. "You said Lingya ran away."

"I have done nothing," said Ek Chuaj. "Lingya is probably hiding in the forest somewhere, waiting for the Spaniards to attack." He snatched at the crown but Kukulkan pulled it out of reach.

"You really expect us to believe that Lingya wouldn't show up with you about to sacrifice her child?" asked Maximon.

High Priest Kukulkan turned to Ek Chuaj. "Is what he says true? Did you do something to Lingya?"

"It's all lies to save himself," said Ek Chuaj. "Where is your proof of anything?"

"She is gone," said Maximon softly. "I can feel it in my bones."

Kukulkan paced back and forth as Maximon was brought up onto the platform by the guards. "If Ek Chuaj is telling the truth," said the high priest, "then you and Lingya are in league with the invaders. In that case, I should sacrifice you and your son." Turning to Ek Chuaj he said, "But if Maximon is telling the truth, then you are the traitor and murdered Lingya to hide your secret."

He continued to pace, the heavy thud of the staff echoing over the murmurs of the crowd as the high priest contemplated what to do. As the seconds stretched out, the pale man slipped into the audience. Moments later, a chant broke out from the masses. "Blood pit! Blood pit!"

Ek Chuaj raised a hand to his face to hide his grin. Even Kukulkan was not stupid enough to deny the crowd's demand.

Kukulkan stopped. Lifting the staff over his head, he waved it back and forth. "There is only one way to know the truth—one way to reveal who is the traitor."

"Blood pit! Blood pit!" chanted the crowd.

"These two men have accused each other of conspiracy and lies." Thrusting the staff high above his head, Kukulkan yelled, "Let their dispute be settled by a fight to the death in the blood pit!"

The crowd roared. Kukulkan gestured to quiet the crowd. "If Ek Chuaj wins, Maximon is the traitor. Upon his defeat, his son, Bahlam, will be sacrificed to atone for the sins of not just his father, but his mother as well. If Maximon wins, Ek Chuaj's blood will sate the gods' demand for justice."

Cheers from the spectators rose to a fervent pitch. Kukulkan waited for them to quiet before continuing. "One way or the other, the gods will have their vengeance…with blood." He signaled the guards, and both men were escorted to the fighting pit dug into the ground beside the stage.

Maximon tried to resist and was pushed from behind, landing face down in the mud. A chorus of laughter went up as the crowd shifted to the pit to witness the fight. Ek Chuaj jumped in by himself. Shouts and boos rained down upon them both.

Kukulkan leaned over the side. "Pray for your lives. One of you will walk out of here a free man. The other will meet the god of death."

***

Jinx woke to the vice grip of strong hands around his neck. Rough and calloused as they were, it took a moment to realize they weren't human. He glanced over his shoulder and discovered Mercy mounted on his back. The albino monkey grasped his neck, throttling him with both hands. Jinx bucked, flinging himself backward in an effort to flatten the primate against the ground. Instead, Mercy hopped nimbly up to his head and clawed at his face.

Trevor opened his eyes. "Hey lil' dude, is everything—" Leaping to his feet, Trevor swung at the top of Jinx's head. Mercy jumped lightly from Jinx to Lily, who remained deep in meditation.

"Oh, no you don't," said Trevor, diving at Mercy. Instead, Trevor plowed straight into Lily, knocking her into the mud. She opened her eyes, took one look at the simian sprawled next to her and let out an ear-piercing scream. Trevor covered his ears as he rose into a crouch. "Chill beau, I got this."

"Hurry babe. We've gotta fix the temple," said Lily.

"Yo, I gotta catch the pyscho beast first," said Trevor. He dove at Mercy. The agile primate danced out of reach to a low tree branch. Mercy barred her fangs and hissed at the three kids. Plucking a hard, spiky seed the size of a walnut, Mercy flung it at Trevor's head.

"Oh, it's like that?" yelled Trevor. "Come on then, you pyscho simian. I'll smack you so hard you'll fly back to the Land of Oz where you belong."

Sprinting to the tree, Lily jumped and snatched at the primate's tail. With casual ease, Mercy sidestepped Lily's hand and tossed a seed in her face. These antics continued for several minutes as Jinx and his friends tried to figure out a way to rid themselves of the infuriating pest.

"We can't meditate like this," said Jinx, as a barrage of seeds, sticks and leaves rained down on them.

"Not to mention she'll try to strangle you again the instant we close our eyes," said Trevor.

"Sounds like you guys could use some help," called a voice from the forest. Jacob detached from the trees and strode into the clearing. Behind him, Slab cradled his right arm, where a deep gash spilled crimson blood down the tattered remains of his obsidian soldier uniform.

"We need the monkey off our back...literally," said Jinx, as Mercy launched another pod at him. Slab stepped forward and caught the projectile in a massive mitt. Making a fist, he crushed the pod to pieces.

"Consider it done," said Jacob.

Crossing to the sweetgum tree that housed the monkey, Slab wrapped his thick arms around the trunk and shook. The sturdy tree swayed. The branch holding the monkey bounced. Unable to keep her balance, Mercy raced along the slender limb toward a neighboring fig tree. Like a spring, she bunched up and launched herself into the air.

From the depths of the tree on the other side, a shadow uncoiled itself and pounced. It wasn't until its claws glinted in the dim light that Jinx recognized the jaguar.

Like a missile made of night, the panther tore through the air. Colliding with Mercy midflight, the panther's powerful jaws crunched down on the monkey's throat. The jaguar landed on the same branch Mercy had fled from, with the albino primate held tightly in its maw.

Mercy flailed wildly, trying to free herself from the predator. The panther tightened its grip. With a sickening pop, a spray of blood rained down from the tree. The jaguar took its prize and ascended until it was high above, beyond where Chief and his team had disabled the fence's electrical current. Then the panther flung Mercy out into the void. The ghostly creature floated through open space, its pale, colorless eyes unfocused in fear, its simian face twisted into a haunting visage of hatred.

Mercy hit the fence square with her back. Instantly, fifteen thousand watts shot through her wiry frame. The damp air filled with the putrid stench of burning fur and charred flesh. Mercy's eyes liquefied in their sockets, her flesh melting into the metal links of the fence, suspending her high overhead. Then gravity took over, peeling her off the electric rack to plummet to the earth. Her carcass landed in a puddle, sending up a hiss of steam as her fried remains congealed almost instantly.

The jaguar sat on the now sturdy branch, licking its forepaw, where a dollop of blood had spoiled its otherwise pristine ebony coat.

Jacob spat on the ground. "Good riddance."

"My goodness," gasped Lily. "I used to think monkeys were cute!"

"Guys, this is no time for Animal Planet," said Trevor. "We need to get back to the temple and finish reversing the damage." Pale to the point of anemia, Jinx rocked forward, nearly flopping face first into the mud.

"Heavens, Jinxy, you're exhausted," said Lily, placing a hand on her friend's forehead. "And you're burning up. You need to rest."

"We need to take care of the temple first," replied Jinx.

"Tell me what to do," said Jacob, taking a seat in between Trevor and Jinx, and gesturing for Slab to join them. "You too, you big oaf."

Slab detached himself from the tree where he'd dislodged Mercy and came to stand over the band of friends. "Slab no help," he said. "Slab no have power."

"I think you've already proved everyone wrong on that front," said Jinx, his eyes drifting towards the dead monkey.

Slab took a seat between Lily and Trevor, nearly squashing them as he plopped to the ground. His long legs splayed out to either side.

"Follow my lead," ordered Jinx. A resurgence of color painted his cheeks. He took Jacob's and Lily's hands in his own. "We're going to fix the temple together."

CHAPTER THIRTY-ONE

Unease crept over Bobby like a swarm of fire ants as he witnessed Ek Chuaj and Maximon enter the blood pit. Even from a young age, Ek Chuaj had always been much bigger and stronger than Maximon. Now, after hours of training with his soldiers, Ek Chuaj was tougher and stronger than ever before.

Weapons were tossed into the ring: a spear and a short sword. Maximon barely managed to grab the spear before Ek Chuaj cut him off. His older cousin stepped on the shaft as Maximon pulled back. The spear broke midway, leaving Maximon with nothing but a bronze blade and a handle the length of his forearm. He scurried to the far side of the pit as Ek Chuaj picked up the other half of the spear then retrieved the short sword.

Maximon huddled in the far corner as Ek Chuaj examined the broken handle. With a few flicks of the sword, Ek Chuaj whittled the broken end into a makeshift dagger. He thrust the weapon a few times, testing the grip.

With a smile, Ek Chuaj turned to Maximon. "Shall we?"

"Please, cousin," said Maximon, "you don't have to do this!"

"Oh, but I want to do this," said Ek Chuaj.

"Why do you hate me so?" asked Maximon. "What have I ever done to you?"

Ek Chuaj let out a bark. "You stole Lingya!" he bellowed. "You ruined my life!"

"I was protecting her," said Maximon. "You nearly killed her."

"She was mine!" shouted Ek Chuaj. "You had no right to interfere."

244 • R. SCOTT BOYER

"And now you really have killed her," said Maximon. "In front of the priests, in front of the gods, I beseech you, admit your crimes!"

Ek Chuaj stalked across the clearing toward Maximon, who scurried along the wall until Ek Chuaj pinned him in a corner.

"You are the villain of this story, not me," said Ek Chuaj. "Come, let me prove my innocence before the gods."

Ek Chuaj took a step closer. Maximon swung the spear in a feeble attempt to ward him off. Ek Chuaj knocked the spear away with a casual flick of the sword. He paused, as if insulted by Maximon's lack of fighting prowess. Maximon used the opening to slip past Ek Chuaj and out into the middle of the pit again. The din of the crowd rose to a fever pitch.

"Face your fate like a man," said Ek Chuaj.

"I'll face my fate just as soon as you admit your crimes," replied Maximon. His dark cheeks were flush. "You killed her. You killed my love!"

With a sigh, Ek Chuaj ducked his head and stalked his prey once more. Dashing forward, Maximon swung the half spear at his cousin's head. Caught off guard, Ek Chuaj dove to the ground. Once again, the crowd went wild.

Rolling with his momentum, Ek Chuaj sprang to his feet to face his rival.

"What if I did kill Lingya?" asked Ek Chuaj as he circled Maximon. "Would you want me to tell you how much I enjoyed it? How I beat her unconscious first? Or would you prefer I claim it was an accident, that she left me no choice? Tell me Maximon, do you want to know what her final moments were like?"

Rage contorted Maximon's face. With an inhuman roar, he rushed at Ek Chuaj. This time Ek Chuaj held his ground. Bringing the sword up to his right shoulder, he dropped his left hand to his waist. When Maximon thrust the spear, Ek Chuaj pivoted to his right. Deflecting the blow with the sword, he drove the makeshift dagger into Maximon's gut.

Instantly, the din of the audience ceased. With a heavy grunt, Maximon dropped the spear and fell to his knees. A chorus of awed murmurs spread. Maximon grabbed at his abdomen where blood rushed from a gaping wound. He coughed and a stream of blood flew from his mouth.

Maximon fell to the dirt. Ek Chuaj threw down his weapons and turned to Kukulkan. "I have proven my innocence. Free me and accept the invaders' demands or fiery vengeance shall rain down upon you for defying the judgement of the gods!"

Visibly pale, Kukulkan nodded. A rope was tossed into the pit for Ek Chuaj to pull himself out. The high priest waited until Ek Chuaj had regained his feet on the stage. "You are innocent according to our law," intoned Kukulkan in a voice devoid of any emotion save shock.

Ek Chuaj extended his arm. "Now give me the crown."

Kukulkan didn't move. Ek Chuaj reached for his staff. Kukulkan stepped back.

"You have taken the life of one of the traitors, but the other, Lingya, is still at large," said the priest. "To truly satisfy Buluc Chabtan, you must sacrifice her child." Pulling a small gold dagger from his belt, Kukulkan tossed it at Ek Chuaj's feet.

"I won the challenge," said Ek Chuaj. "Give me the crown."

"Only the blood of both traitors will save us from the invaders. Since you are the victor, the honor is yours." Kukulkan gestured to an acolyte by the pyre and the bonfire was lit. With a crackle of heat, the smoke curled its way skyward.

"What have you done?" yelled Ek Chuaj. "You will destroy us all!"

"We finish what you started," said Kukulkan. "Or do you disdain the blessings of the gods?"

With solemn resolve, Ek Chuaj kicked the dagger aside. "Not even the gods can save us now."

"Guards, arrest him!" shouted Kukulkan. Four soldiers came forth. High Priest Kukulkan leaned in close and whispered, "Do you really think I trust you just because you won in the blood pit? You may have taken me for a fool, but I shall not play the role a second time. Prove your honor. Prove your loyalty to me and to the gods. Sacrifice the child!"

Ek Chuaj turned a deadpan stare upon the priest before letting his eyes drift to the bonfire. With true night fallen, the huge blaze lit up the sky like a beacon to the heavens.

"You have doomed us all," he said to the priest.

A servant retrieved the dagger and handed it to Kukulkan. The priest pressed the dagger into Ek Chuaj's hand. "Perform the ritual or die."

With measured steps, Ek Chuaj approached the altar. A priest brought forth the baby, still swaddled in cloth from head to toe, and set it upon the stone slab. Gripping the gold dagger with his left hand, Ek Chuaj peeled back the cloth with his right.

The hundreds of spectators grew silent. The infant boy lay naked on the stone. The crowd murmured as the baby began to cry. Ek Chuaj stood there, the dagger poised in his hand.

Seconds dragged on. The baby's cries escalated into protest against the cool night air. Ek Chuaj remained motionless. Slowly, the slender dagger slipped from his grasp and fell to the floor. An acolyte retrieved the blade, returning it to Ek Chuaj yet again.

Still Ek Chuaj remained motionless. People in the audience started to grumble and shout for the sacrifice to be fulfilled. Kukulkan came up behind Ek Chuaj. "If Maximon truly was the traitor, then destroying his bloodline will please the gods. But if you really have been playing me for a fool, then this child's blood shall be on your hands. One way or the other, I win."

Still Ek Chuaj remained motionless.

"What are you waiting for?" High Priest Kukulkan glanced from Ek Chuaj to the infant. Bahlam's hair and skin were those of his mother: Lingya's dark chestnut curls and beautiful almond complexion, but Bahlam's eyes...

Kukulkan glanced from the child to the man in the pit.

"The cheeks, the nose, the eyes...none of them match Maximon," said Kukulkan. "They match—"

"Mine," whispered Ek Chuaj. "I took what was mine. The child is mine."

A broad smile spread across Kukulkan's face. "Such fitting justice for a traitor," said the priest. "You have ten seconds to slay your son, or I will have the guards cover the altar with your blood instead."

Off in the distance, a bolt of lightning blew up the sky. Seconds later, a thunderous boom heralded a mighty rainstorm. Bahlam screamed as fat raindrops struck his naked body. Ek Chuaj turned his face to the heavens and stared into the heart of the storm. One of the guards poked him in the ribs with a spear.

"The gods are angry!" said the guard. "Perform the ritual!"

Ek Chuaj brought the dagger up over his head. Another shaft of lightning ripped the sky. Thunder followed sooner this time, matched in intensity by Bahlam's shrieks.

"The gods demand blood!" said Kukulkan. "You must perform the ritual!"

"I can't," said Ek Chuaj, staring into the face of his son.

The guard dug a spear into Ek Chuaj until a trickle of blood ran down his leg.

"It is your life or the child's," said the priest. "Decide."

Ek Chuaj lifted the blade once again. "I never believed in the gods," he said, shaking his head. "And this is their revenge."

High Priest Kukulkan lowered his voice against the crowd. "If I hear another peel of thunder before you sacrifice the child," he whispered, "it's going to be your blood and your son's on the altar."

Ek Chuaj's arms trembled. The tip of the dagger wavered as thick tears rolled down his cheeks. "May the gods have mercy on me!" he cried.

Lightning flashed in the sky. With a scream, Ek Chuaj plunged the dagger downward. A split second later, a thunderous boom rang out.

Ek Chuaj froze. The dagger hung millimeters from Bahlam's chest. The irate baby kicked and wailed as cold rain pelted him.

Ek Chuaj closed his eyes, bracing for the guard to end his life. Instead, the tip of the spear fell away. The guard hit the ground with a heavy thud. Ek Chuaj turned and saw Pedro de Alvarado and his army of conquistadors boarding the stage.

The red-headed Spaniard known as Tonatiuh to the natives had his pistol out, smoke curling from the barrel. Ek Chuaj glanced at the dead guard and discovered a gaping hole in his chest.

"You're welcome," said Tonatiuh. The Spaniard returned his harquebus to its holster. Behind him stood a small army of soldiers, their metal armor and crested helmets gleaming in the firelight. Several of the acolytes and priests dropped to the ground. Others gripped their weapons, ready to resist.

"Order them to stand down," said Tonatiuh. "No one else needs to die."

"Oh, thank the gods," said Ek Chuaj, and flung his dagger into the pit. "Do as he says!" he shouted to the other Mayans.

"What is happening?" asked High Priest Kukulkan. "How did these invaders breach our perimeter?" Turning from Tonatiuh, he stared at Ek Chuaj.

"I could ask the same thing," said Tonatiuh, glaring at Ek Chuaj. "You weren't supposed to light the signal fire until after the city was secure. Instead, we came through the secret passage and discovered the temple still guarded. We had to kill twelve able-bodied men. You promised me the city without a fight!"

"Have mercy!" Ek Chuaj threw himself to the ground. "The priest gave me no choice. I spread out the perimeter defenses just as I promised so that your men could slip through the jungle and into the temple undetected. Certainly, that proves my loyalty!"

"You were only ever loyal to yourself," said Tonatiuh. "When I found you in your tiny mud village, you bargained for your life, but only after you watched your father die trying to protect you. Only after you knew the battle was lost—only then did you emerge from your hiding place and beg for your life."

"I serve you now!" said Ek Chuaj, clasping his hands together. "I will be your humble and loyal servant, I swear it!"

The red-haired Spaniard set the tip of his blade at Ek Chuaj's throat. "What need do I have for your loyalty now? You failed to take the city. Now we must fight those who resist."

"Please, it's not too late," said Ek Chuaj, groveling on his knees. "The soldiers are loyal to me. Execute the priests! Prove to the people that their gods will not protect them. Then they will fall in line. I swear it!"

"Betrayer!" yelled Kukulkan. "May Buluc Chabtan devour your soul!" His eyes darted to the spear lying on the ground beside the guard that Tonatiuh had shot.

"Don't do it," warned Tonatiuh.

Diving for the spear, Kukulkan called to his people, "Rise up! The gods will protect the brave and punish the—"

Pedro de Alvarado took a step towards Kukulkan. As the priest stood up, Alvarado drove his sword through the priest's prodigious belly. Kukulkan's beady eyes went wide, blood spurting from the mortal wound.

"There is your sacrifice," said Ek Chuaj, and spat on the priest's lifeless face.

A pregnant pause ensued in which no one moved. Then one of the guards in the back took up a battle cry. "For the glory of the Mayan empire!" he shouted and lunged at the nearest Spaniard.

"For the empire!" shouted dozens of other warriors around the clearing. The air filled with the clatter of spears striking swords.

Lifting his foot to the priest's chest, Tonatiuh nonchalantly pried his sword free. Turning to Ek Chuaj, he said, "This is exactly what I did not want to happen!"

Ek Chuaj groveled in the mud, hands clasped before him. "Spare me," he pleaded. "Please, I beg you."

Tonatiuh extended his sword, resting the tip at the base of Ek Chuaj's throat. "Unlike you, I am a man of honor. I gave you my word you would not be harmed if you helped us take the city. You have not delivered as promised, but you at least got us this far."

Ek Chuaj let out an audible sigh.

"Go," said Tonatiuh. "Run and hide somewhere like the coward you are until the fighting is over. If I see you again, I will kill you myself."

Without a thought for his son or his fellow Mayans, Ek Chuaj took off, running past natives and invaders alike. His worst nightmare had come to pass. He'd lost Lingya, he'd failed to take the city, and both Mayans and Spaniards would kill him on sight.

With nowhere else to run, he headed for the rainforest.

CHAPTER THIRTY-TWO

Bobby sat up and rubbed his eyes, wiping away rain but not the haunting imprint of Ek Chuaj's memories. He lay near the base of the temple, close to the amphitheater from Ek Chuaj's visions. The storm had receded to a steady drizzle that tickled his cheeks and bogged down his hair.

Meanwhile, the images in his head would not let him be. Bobby shook his head and tried to focus on the present. His grandmother stood a few feet away. She wore a dazed expression, as if someone had struck her over the head with a Louisville slugger. By the crumbled ruins, Willy writhed on the ground much as Bobby imagined himself doing just moments before.

The Creep screamed Mercy's name over and over again. Bobby recognized the reaction. Something had happened to Willy's pet. Melody went to the bald boy, her eyes wild with rage. Willy rose up onto hands and knees, watching her. She gave him a vicious, almost feral snarl that belonged not to Bobby's grandmother, but the demon within. Gripping the nearest pillar, Willy hoisted himself up and ran for the jungle.

Pushing himself up onto his feet, Bobby staggered after the smaller boy. Electric pain shot through his legs. He took two steps and pitched forward into the mud. His grandmother turned to face him, her eyes burning with the fiery hatred of Ek Chuaj.

When she spoke, her voice was deep and alien. "Such hatred. Such anger. That one sought to feed off of me," she hissed, with a nod toward the fleeing Willy. "Using me for his own purposes, that I can understand. But you would sacrifice me for this vessel."

The spirit of Ek Chuaj gestured at Melody's body. "You have witnessed my nightmare, seen the injustices thrust upon me, and still you seek to destroy me." From her hairline, red paint dripped down Melody's face, streaking scarlet down her cheek.

"Let my grandmother go, you monster," said Bobby.

Ek Chuaj snarled like a hyena. The weeping face paint twisted the expression into a hideous smile. "When I found her, I knew this host was powerful," he said. "I did not realize she was precious to you."

"Let her go. I will help you," said Bobby. "I can free you as I freed the others."

"You were given the chance to help me!" shouted Ek Chuaj. "Given the chance to stop Maximon and the Spaniards from ruining my plans."

"What are you talking about?" said Bobby. "I can't change the past. All I can do is help you come to terms with what transpired."

"Lies!" yelled Ek Chuaj. "You are the Holcan: the Chosen One. You could have stopped Maximon from revealing my plan; stopped Kukulkan from ordering me to sacrifice my own child; stopped Tonatiuh from betraying me after I risked everything to help him! Instead you allowed them to take everything that I loved. Now I will take from this host everything that she loves. After that, we will be bonded in agony. We will be together, forever."

Ek Chuaj thrust himself into Bobby's mind. Against his will, Bobby's legs began to move. Rising to his feet, he followed his grandmother to the crumbled remains of the stadium. Forcing him to take a seat on the limestone altar, she swung Bobby's legs up and forced his head back, so he lay flat.

"Tell me, Holcan, did you know Mayans rarely sacrificed their own people? Unlike the Aztecs, the Maya people offered up food, animals, and idols smeared with their own blood."

Bending down, Melody picked up a long, jagged shard of what had once been a clay pot. Turning it over in her hands, the spirit within tested the edge with her thumb.

"It was only in times of true distress, plague or famine or war, that my people would sacrifice one of their own. The stronger the family tie, the greater the honor to the gods," said Ek Chuaj. "That is why Kukulkan demanded that I complete the ritual: not because he wanted the blood of a traitor, but because he wanted me to sacrifice my own child—the strongest bond there is." The spirit laughed. "Of course, the bond of grandmother and grandson isn't as powerful as father and son, but it is close enough."

Bobby's eyes went wide as Ek Chuaj lifted the dagger and placed it over Bobby's abdomen. Tears swelled in Bobby's eyes, not for himself but for his enemy. "You don't have to do this," he said. "You didn't kill your son. You don't have to kill me."

"I would have! Don't you see?" said Ek Chuaj. "That is my crime. I was willing to sacrifice my own son to save myself."

Melody's hand drew the jagged shard down Bobby's stomach, opening up a thin crimson line that pooled at his navel before trickling off his abdomen and onto the altar. She drew another slash across his forehead. His cool skin turned warm as thick blood ran into his eyes, turning his already blurry vision watery pink.

Melody stood over him now, her bewitched eyes sparkling azure with madness. For a moment, a bemused expression painted her face. Then she shifted the makeshift dagger to his chest, centering the tip directly above his heart. Bobby's body went rigid, his muscles tightening into knots as he tracked the tip of the crude blade.

"All who betrayed me shall die," she said, and raised the shard high above her head. Fat droplets of blood dripped from the tip, falling in his face to punctuate the spatter of rain.

The muscles of her arms went taut. Unable to move, Bobby used all his strength to avert his eyes. A blurry shadow beyond Melody's right shoulder moved towards them.

"Stop," said a commanding voice.

The pressure holding Bobby in place decreased ever so slightly. Tipping his head up, he saw two figures emerge from the gloom.

Jeremiah bore an expression of grim determination, as if someone had asked him to complete a task both impossible yet vital at the same time. Behind him, Cassandra held both hands to her mouth, eyes wide, as if unable to comprehend what lay before her.

"What are you doing?" asked Jeremiah, his voice laced with disbelief.

Melody blinked several times, but the pressure binding Bobby to the altar did not relinquish. "All who oppose me must be vanquished," she said.

"Melody, sweetie," Jeremiah's voice was imploring. "I know you're in there. I know you can hear me. You've got to fight it."

"Melody is not here anymore." It was her voice, but the smug tone belonged to Ek Chuaj.

"I don't believe that," said Jeremiah, taking a small step toward the altar.

The spirit's eyes narrowed. Its lip curled into a vicious snarl. With a scream, Jeremiah dropped to his knees, clawing at his head. Cassandra moved to help him and fell too, gripping her head as though it might explode.

"You cannot stop me," said Ek Chuaj. "I shall use this body to reclaim the temple. All of its inhabitants will serve me and obey my will."

Jeremiah lifted his head, crawling on hands and knees through the mud. He screamed again. The veins on his forehead bulged, and the tendons of his neck strained with effort. And yet, he kept coming. The spirit stepped to the other side of the altar, still holding the jagged shard poised over Bobby's heart. Jeremiah inched closer, drawing even with the nearest pillar.

The spirit's eyes were glued on Jeremiah. "Come another step closer and I will kill your grandson."

With Ek Chuaj's attention divided, the bonds holding Bobby lessened. Gritting his teeth, Bobby extended his arm toward his grandfather. *Lend me your strength*, he pleaded.

Two yards away, Jeremiah raised his hands in surrender. At the same time, he rose into a crouch. Bobby locked eyes with his grandfather and gave him an imperceptible nod. Behind him, Cassandra stretched out and grasped hold of Jeremiah's ankle.

Jeremiah lunged, stretching out for his grandson's hand. Bobby leaned toward him with all his might. An instant later, Melody dropped her arms, plunging the makeshift dagger toward Bobby's chest.

Bobby's fingertip grazed his grandfather's outstretched hand. The invisible bond shattered. Bobby flung up his left arm, deflecting the blow with his forearm. The spirit stepped back. Bobby grabbed Melody's wrist. The same power that had freed him a split second earlier flowed through him into her.

The bond of love that had forced his grandparents apart for so many years coursed through Bobby's veins, scorching the spirit inside Melody. Ek Chuaj thrashed madly, trying to break free. Bobby held tight. Melody's eyes rolled in their sockets. Her jaw jackhammered up and down. With her free hand, she clawed savagely at Bobby's forearm, trying to tear her arm free.

Melody's nails dug into his flesh, scoring deep gouges that spurted blood in hot gushes. Still he refused to let go. Slowly, her spasms began to subside. Her mouth snapped shut, drawn into a pencil-thin line. Her eyes stopped rolling, the fair blue pupils expanded as the giant black irises shrank and focused.

Bobby released his grandmother's wrist as she withdrew her nails and slumped to the ground. She lay on her side, head leaning against the altar, a dazed expression on her face. "Where am I?"

Jeremiah made his way over to his wife. Kneeling at her side, he put an arm around her and brushed a tangled mass of yellow hair out of her face. "Everything is going to be okay," he said in a hushed tone.

* * *

Bobby was helping Jeremiah get Melody upright and sit her on the altar when his friends arrived. Trevor led a small pack of kids. Lily and Jacob followed closely behind. Lily was soaked to the bone but seemed in high spirits, with a huge hug for Bobby and a bright smile for everyone else.

In the rear of their little party trudged Slab and Jinx. Both looked thoroughly exhausted. Still, Jinx wore a grin of sheer elation, swinging his arms eagerly when he saw Bobby and Jeremiah.

"We did it!" he yelled as he ran up and hugged Bobby, who seemed to be gathering embraces in bunches. "We fixed the damage to the temple and made it safe again."

It took Bobby a moment to realize that the ground had stopped heaving. He'd been so preoccupied with Ek Chuaj's efforts to eviscerate him that he hadn't noticed.

Bobby put his hands on his cousin's shoulders to settle him down. "I want you to meet someone," said Bobby, stepping aside to provide a clear view of the person sitting on the altar. "Jinx, this is your grandmother, Melody Ether."

Melody's head stayed down, her eyes closed. "She's still very weak," said Jeremiah. "After what that spirit did to her, I have no idea if she can even hear us, let alone understand what's going on."

As if in response, Melody's eyes flickered, and her head came up. She shook her head and rubbed at her brow, as if waking from a terrible nightmare. "Jeremiah, is that you?"

"I'm here, my love." Jeremiah knelt beside her and took her hand in his own. "I found the clue you left for me at the bank and followed it to the surgical center. Once I realized you'd changed your features, it wasn't hard to put the pieces together."

Melody flushed with color. She lifted a hand to her cheeks. "I never meant to deceive you. I just wanted to get our grandson back and needed to make sure no one would recognize me."

Jeremiah reached up and pried his wife's hand away from her face. "I understand why you did what you did. You're safe now, that's all that matters."

"You don't mind?" said Melody, an edge of fear in her voice. "I can have the surgery again to change me back if you'd like…"

Jeremiah raised her hand to his lips and kissed it gently. "I'll admit the new you will take some getting used to, but I do like the tight leather pants. Any chance you've got another pair? These look like they've seen better days."

Melody feigned indignation, chiding him, "Why, Jeremiah Ether, I never!"

Bobby and the others broke into fits of giggles. Even Slab chuckled.

Still bouncing with excitement, Jinx told everyone how Slab tore a tree from the ground to dislodge Mercy and how a jaguar had ripped the albino monkey to pieces.

"So now we can go back inside, study both the fountain and the well, and finally solve the mystery of the Fountain of Youth," said Jinx.

"No need," said Bobby, pulling the Hunhau talisman from his pocket. "I already solved it," he said with a wink. He went on to tell them all about his experience after he chased Ashley: about being knocked into the water, and his time spent in the Well of Eternity. He finished by telling them about the souls trapped at the bottom of the well and how he'd listened to their stories and set them free.

As Bobby finished, Chief and a team of commandos arrived, escorting a small group of children along with a handful of captured Core soldiers. Bobby recognized Franklin and Parker, the two guards Ana had disabled.

"Where's Sandman?" asked Jinx. "Did you guys catch him?"

Chief prodded the mercenary in front of him with a stick, motioning for him to take a seat in the dirt, hands behind his head. The others followed suit.

"Their leader fled into the jungle," said Chief. "We can track him later. For now, we want to make sure all of the children are safe, which means apprehending as many of the Core's agents and mercenaries as we can find."

"What about Ashley and Willy?" asked Bobby.

258 • R. SCOTT BOYER

"These are all the kids we've come across so far," replied Chief. "It will take time to find the others, assuming they want to be found. If the two you speak of wish to evade us..." He shrugged, letting the thought trail away.

"The sooner we get to it, the sooner we all get to go home," said Melody. Already, color was starting to return to her face. She sat upright on her own, without leaning on Jeremiah for support.

"That sounds like an excellent idea," said Jeremiah. "I just got here, and I'm already itching to leave."

"There's one thing I need to do first," said Bobby. Promising to meet them again shortly, Bobby headed across the plateau to the stone ruins where he'd first encountered Maximon's ghost. Entering the remains of the hut, he went to the back room where the Mayan's skeleton lay half buried in the earth. Setting his hand atop the skull, Bobby communed with Maximon, sharing with him the news that Ek Chuaj was gone and Lingya was now at peace.

"Thank you, Holcan," said the fisherman. "I too shall be at rest soon. But first, I must share with you the last of my story."

***

With all the chaos and clamor of battle, no one noticed Maximon as he climbed from the blood pit and limped to the altar. Gripping his side to stem the blood flow, he covered Bahlam with a blanket and tucked him under his arm.

It was a slow, arduous trek back to their house with Bahlam crying the entire time. They encountered Spanish soldiers, but he carried no weapon and offered no opposition, so they let him be, as they engaged others who sought to strike them down.

For the next three days, Maximon hid with Bahlam in the tiny hut he'd shared with Lingya. He bandaged his wound using strips of bed linen bound around his waist.

When the fighting died down, the Conquistadors combed through the houses, looking for survivors to take as slaves. When he heard the clank of armor, Maximon tucked Bahlam under the bedsheets and placed a hand over his mouth to keep him from crying out. Then he unwrapped his bandages to expose his wound and lay perfectly still. Thankfully, the soldier who appeared in the doorway gave the bedroom only a cursory glance. Seeing what appeared to be a dead man and with nothing of value in sight, the soldier moved on to the next house.

***

What little food and water they had ran out quickly. Bahlam cried nonstop, making Maximon fearful that another soldier would hear his son and return to investigate. Incapable of walking all the way to the river, Maximon waited until nightfall to scavenge the surrounding cottages.

A moonless, overcast night greeted him as Maximon left Bahlam by the bed and went looking for food and water. Unable to see beyond his hands, he searched each room by touch, hoping for some scrap of dried meat or flask of water. Three houses down, he found a half jug of water and enough maize to last a few days. Stumbling home, with one hand still clutching his side, he tripped over something and fell.

He gasped as his wound tore open, pouring blood once again. The water jug smashed on the ground. The maize flew from his hand.

Maximon lay in the dirt for a long time before he found the strength to roll onto his side. Groping in the pitch black for the corn, he found a body instead. He felt the cold, hard metal of the man's armor and knew it had to be one of the invaders. Hoping to find a sword, Maximon probed until he located the man's arm. The soldier held something hard and metallic.

Feeling along its surface, Maximon caught his breath as he recognized one of the stick-like objects used to by the Spaniards to kill people with thunder. *A gun, that's what the conquistadors call them.* Pulling it from the dead man's grasp, Maximon hugged the weapon tightly to his chest.

With his last remaining strength, Maximon climbed to his feet and staggered the rest of the way home. He went first to Bahlam, who slumbered. *Probably cried himself to sleep.* With no food or water to give him, Maximon left his son undisturbed. Instead, he gingerly climbed into bed and tucked the gun under the covers.

***

The noise of someone outside woke Maximon from his sleep. He opened his eyes and discovered the room full of light. He winced. The whole side of his body was soaked with blood. He wouldn't need to pretend much longer. Death would find him soon enough.

The footsteps grew louder, followed by a creaking noise as someone pushed open the front door. Maximon narrowed his eyes to bare slits and tried not to breathe.

A shadow appeared in the doorway. "I've come for my son," said the shadow. Maximon opened his eyes and found Ek Chuaj leaning against the doorframe. In his right hand, Ek Chuaj held one of the double-edged swords worn by the invaders.

"He is not your son," said Maximon, trying to pull himself upright. Instead, he cried out in pain. Fresh crimson seeped through the linens covering his waist.

"He is my blood," said his cousin.

"A cruel joke played by the gods, nothing more," said Maximon. "Lingya and I are the ones who truly love him. Do you even know what that word means, love?"

Anger flashed in Ek Chuaj's eyes. "I loved Lingya more than you ever could! I killed her because she left me no choice," he said. "Now you are the one with a choice. Hand over my son and I will let you live long enough to die on your own terms. Defy me, and I will murder you now. Then I will take my child from your corpse."

"I am already dead," said Maximon, lifting his hand from his wound.

"Then I will get the pleasure of killing you twice," said Ek Chuaj. He brought the sword up to his thigh, pointing it at his cousin.

"Leave now and I will spare your life," said Maximon. "For Bahlam's sake."

Ek Chuaj threw back his head and laughed. "I always knew you were a fool. Tell me, cousin, exactly how do you plan to strike me down when you can't even stand?"

Maximon pulled back the covers, revealing the harquebus he'd discovered the night before. Propping his arm up with his free hand, he pointed the gun at his cousin's chest.

Ek Chuaj froze. "You don't know how to use that," he said, taking a small step forward.

"Come one step closer and we will both find out," said Maximon.

"What about the noise?" asked Maximon. "The thunder will draw the invaders. They will find you and the baby."

"They will also find you, dead on the floor," said Maximon.

"Then who will raise the child?" said Ek Chuaj. "You aren't going to make it."

"You are a cruel man, with no compassion and no soul," said Maximon. "Even the invaders are a better option to raise my son than you."

Ek Chuaj tightened his grip on the sword. Glancing between the gun, the baby, and the look of determination on Maximon's face, he said, "He is my son. I am not leaving here without him!"

"I have already made my peace with death. Have you?"

The two men stood there, staring at one another. Maximon coughed up blood and adjusted his aim. Ek Chuaj stared at the gun and took another step forward.

The sound of thunder shook the tiny room. Bahlam woke screaming. Maximon kept his eyes on Ek Chuaj as a crimson circle spread across his cousin's lower chest.

Shouts rang out. Foreign voices called for someone to investigate the noise. "They'll torture you when they find you," said Maximon. He aimed the gun at Ek Chuaj's head. "Go now and perhaps you can reach the forest before they catch you."

Clutching at his chest, Ek Chuaj staggered from the house. Maximon dropped the gun and pulled Bahlam up to his chin. Setting him on his good side, Maximon stroked the babe. "Don't cry, little one. I may not be around to see it, but your future is safe."

The conquistadors arrived a few minutes later and discovered a young boy in the arms of a dead fisherman.

***

In the half-light of the underbrush, the jungle all looked the same. Giant fronds and rope-like vines dominated the forest floor, throwing up constant obstacles in Hayward's path. With their eyes drawn to every shaft of light, every lesser patch of gray, he and Simpkins navigated using anima, sensing shapes the way bees sense pollen.

Hayward felt more than saw Simpkins raise his hand. By his recollection, they were nearly back to the temple. So why had his partner stopped? Then he felt it. A shadow—the thinnest whisper of movement on the edge of his awareness—winked for the briefest of moments, returning to black almost before his mind could register the change.

"We're being followed," said Simpkins.

"I don't feel anything," said Hayward.

"Neither do I," said Simpkins. "Which is exactly what bothers me."

Indeed, the jungle was quiet. Too quiet. "It must be an animal. Come on, let's keep going. We need to get back and warn the others about the Scarlet Seer."

"No," Simpkins managed to reply. A gust of wind brushed his cheek. Simpkins brought a hand to his neck where three green feathers sprouted from his jugular.

"What the—!" Another burst of air and a whooshing sound. Hayward felt a sting just above his left shoulder, like the bite from a mosquito the size of a hummingbird.

"Son of a mother!" He probed the feathers protruding from his collar bone. With two fingers, he tugged at the barbed dart, feeling a sticky, viscous fluid beneath his fingertips. It smelled of fungus and rotten sap.

"You've got to be kidding me," he growled. The natives had made their presence known. They were easy to detect now. Hayward felt no less than a dozen people nearby; primitives prowling, tucked behind the trees, waiting for whatever ridiculous poison they'd injected him with to take effect. *Boy do they have a surprise waiting for them!* Counteracting poisons was one of the first tricks Hayward had learned as an agent.

Beside him, Simpkins looked as stalwart as ever. These primitives had no idea who they were messing with. The leader of the natives lit a torch and the darkness exploded in amber shades of firelight. Wearing nothing but a loincloth and a pile of beads around his neck, the old man looked more like a drunken hobo than a shaman.

Hayward snickered as six hunters emerged from the shadows, each carrying spears, blowguns, and crude bone-handled knives. "You're joking, right?" he laughed. Savagely yanking the dart from his neck, he tossed it to the ground. "You seriously think you're gonna take us down with a couple of bee stings and some sharpened sticks?"

Two hunters came forth. One had a scar across his cheek: vivid lines gouged by some savage beast long ago. The other had obsidian claws draped around his neck. No longer concealed, their auras radiated with aggression. *Exactly what I need.*

Opening himself to their anima, Hayward reached for their aggression, intending to twist it back upon them and drop them all to their knees. Nothing happened. He tried again, more urgently this time. The hunters remained standing, eyeing him with quizzical stares.

Simpkins lifted a hand to his neck. "The poison—" Votan struck the reed-thin agent hard across the face with the butt of his spear.

Hayward threw up his hands as spears were thrust at him. A searing pain lanced through his abdomen. Something sliced his right heel, severing his Achilles's tendon. With a scream, Hayward dropped onto all fours.

The old man came forth. Lifting his knotted staff, he gestured to the warriors. Instantly, the assault ceased. The shaman's dark eyes glinted in the torch's yellow glow, his expression grim and unforgiving. Next to him, Simpkins twitched twice then lay still.

The shaman retrieved the shiny green dart from the dirt. Brushing the feathery tail, he held it up before Hayward, who blinked at him in dumb confusion.

"La Muerte Verde," said the shaman. Then he lifted the staff high above his head and slammed it down on Hayward's skull.

Splayed out in the thick mud, among wild creatures, crazed natives, and the fetid stench of death, Hayward closed his eyes and knew no more.

CHAPTER THIRTY-THREE

Bobby stretched his arms out wide as he strode out of the packed chamber, heading for the temple's service exit. Now perfectly safe according to Chief, Bobby nonetheless felt the urge to be free of the suffocating stench of cruelty and oppression that clung to the limestone walls, as real as the tremors from the day before.

Outside, dawn had broken bright and sunny without a hint of clouds. Golden light dazzled the treetops, glistening off wet leaves like a million iridescent emeralds. The warm sunlight felt wonderful after a long, wet night spent searching for kids who had fled into the jungle and become lost.

Their search had ended shortly after midnight when Itzamna and his band of grim-faced warriors showed up with half a dozen children in tow. There were at least ten children still missing—children who had spent the night in the jungle just as he and Jinx had done.

Lost in thought, Bobby failed to notice Chief slide up next to him until the old Indian spoke. "We will find them," he said, seemingly reading Bobby's mind.

Bobby turned to look at his mentor's strong, weathered face, cracked with lines of wisdom and weariness. "They've been away from home for so long," said Bobby. "They have families, just like me—people who love them and miss them and have no idea that they're even lost."

Chief's expression was stern, his eyes piercing as if he could penetrate the forest's veil with his naked eyes. "We'll find them," he repeated. "I promise."

"What about the Core?" asked Bobby. "Won't they come as soon as they find out what's happened?"

The deep wrinkles around Chief's eyes softened just a tad. "The Core has no idea their operation has been dismantled—at least not yet. 'The Scarlet Seer' reported in last night and told them all is well. We have at least a day before Sandman or one of the others reaches civilization and reveals the truth, perhaps two more before a team arrives."

"What about the kids still out in the forest?"

"Itzamna and his men are out tracking. The energy around the temple is too congested. Even I cannot find the ones we seek, but Itzamna and his men know the jungle. It should not take long."

"That's assuming the kids don't hide from the big scary men carrying spears and blow darts."

"I have my commandos with them, to speak their language and assure their safety."

"Then I guess there is nothing to do but wait."

"Try to get some rest. The mess hall is fully stocked. My men are preparing meals as we speak. Don't worry. There will be plenty to do in the days to come."

* * *

It took nearly all day to locate the remaining refugees. By the time the last child was found, the shadow of the temple stretched beyond the furthest plateau. During his panic the night before, a young French boy had climbed so high up into an emergent cecropia tree that he was unable to climb back down. Chief and his commandos were brought to the child by Votan, who scaled the tree with a coil of rope slung over his shoulder, fastened the line around the boy's waist, and lowered him down.

Meanwhile, Chief and his men rounded up the remaining mercenaries and Core soldiers. Most put up no resistance, happy to surrender rather than slog through the jungle without food or supplies. No trace was found of Ashley or Willy. Likewise, Sandman appeared to have slipped past them and escaped.

By midday, helicopters began shuttling kids back to civilization. Those who had families would be returned to them. Those without a home would be brought to the Eagle's Nest until something permanent could be arranged.

Bobby's mind was far from all of these things when Itzamna and Chief approached and asked if he would accompany them on a short trip. The old shaman followed a path Bobby now knew by heart. Still, it was quite a shock to emerge from the last of the jungle and gaze upon the natives' village.

In the light of day, without the veil of rain and clouds to hide the horrid truth, the village was a graveyard. All that remained were burnt huts and support beams sticking out of the ground like charred tombstones. The air held the scent of burnt trees and the faint hint of cooked meat; the rotten stench so strong not even the rain had washed it away. The ground was covered with a fine layer of white-gray ash that rustled in the wind and left smears wherever they stepped.

As they broke into the clearing, figures appeared along the outskirts: women and children, young boys and old men too feeble to help with the search. Itzamna made his way to the ring of blackened stones in the center of the village that had served as both cooking hearth and meeting place.

Bobby took a seat beside him as the old shaman crossed his legs and sat down on the northern apex of the circle. Bobby reached into his breast pocket, extracting the idol of Hunhau.

"It's done," said Bobby, gently setting the talisman in Itzamna's palm. "The spirits from the temple have been set free. Your ancestors are at peace."

Itzamna held the idol up before him, soaking in every detail before cradling it in his chest. "Thank you for returning it to me," Chief translated. "This totem belonged to my great ancestor, Bahlam the Wise. It is very precious to me."

Tingles spread through Bobby. "Was he taken by the Conquistadors as a baby?" he asked. "I think I may have seen him in my visions."

Itzamna's eyes grew wide as Chief translated Bobby's question. "Indeed, Bahlam was taken by the invaders as an infant. He was returned to his people years later when rebel Mayans raided the city. He and the rest of my people fled deep into the forest, where we've remained ever since."

The shaman raised his arms and spoke a few words in a solemn voice choked with emotion. Chief disappeared from Bobby's side as villagers began to gather around. From the northeast corner, Tohil and a band of hunters arrived, followed shortly by Votan and another group of warriors.

They drew close, forming a tight knot around the cold fire pit. The last to arrive was an old blind woman, guided by a slender teen boy with wild hair. As she took her place in the circle, Chief materialized at Itzamna's side.

The leader of the commandos had changed out of his camouflage attire. He was dressed similarly to the natives: bare chested with a swaddle of fur wrapped around his waist and a pair of leather moccasins upon his feet.

Fifty people stood around the circle. No one moved or made a sound. Even the infants in their mother's arms lay quiet, their eyes large and expectant.

A dead calm settled over the village. Bobby felt the presence of something powerful, its weight pressing down on them. The villagers stood, watching, waiting.

Then Itzamna began to chant. His reedy voice carried like a clarion bell, delivering his message to the jungle. He set the idol of Hunhau in the middle of the stone ring. He took off one his necklaces, a shiny bundle of black beads, and set it beside the idol. Then he sat back and folded his hands in his lap.

The other natives were moving now. Stepping up to the fire pit one at a time, they lay piles of reeds and sticks atop the idol as well as jewelry, clothes, and other personal possessions. Chief bent over and whispered to Bobby, "They are paying tribute to the souls of their ancestors who were trapped in the temple. They offer sacrifices: what little they have left, to honor their memories."

As he spoke, the dark green reeds began to smoke, then crisp, and turn crimson as orange flames took up the offerings. Bobby caught the heavy fragrance of something light and sweet with a bitter note, like honeysuckle with a hint of lemon.

The Hunhau idol began to glow as it too caught fire. At first pale lavender, the light morphed into a deep purple that paired with the burning reeds to create rosy streaks of fiery violet.

Other voices joined Itzamna. First Tohil and the warriors, then all the villagers. They chanted with the shaman to create an eerie melody in perfect cadence with the fire, the flames leaping and surging in concert with the haunting tune.

Now a blazing inferno, Bobby leaned back as the flames flared, leaping over the blackened ring of stones, singeing his t-shirt and turning his cheeks crimson with heat.

The chanting abruptly ceased and the fire receded, shrinking down to the size of a walnut before winking out of existence with a tiny puff of smoke. When the air cleared, Bobby saw no trace of the fragrant reeds or the obsidian idol.

"May the ancestors be blessed," intoned Itzamna.

"May the ancestors be blessed," droned the tribe.

Bobby rose to his feet and joined Chief as the villagers began a slow procession. Led by Itzamna, they gathered up their meager possessions and struck out into the forest.

"Where will they go?" asked Bobby.

"This place is for the dead now. They will make a new village by the river I saw in Itzamna's mind. They plan to stay close and look after the temple."

Bobby nodded to himself. It felt right. The Core would likely abandon their operation here now that all the mercenaries had fled and the kids had been set free, but others might come in the future. The temple's secrets were not for the outside world.

On a sturdy tree branch high overhead, a black jaguar threw back its head and unleashed a mighty roar. Some of the natives looked nervous. A few of the warriors grabbed their spears.

Bobby just smiled.

Getting back from Guatemala felt almost identical to Bobby's return from the Jade Academy the year before. At first it felt wonderful being home again, but after three weeks of constant attention from his parents, it got a bit much. There were only so many movie marathons and board games he could take. After a month at home, Bobby's parents reluctantly agreed to let Chief pick Bobby up and bring him to the Eagle's Nest.

The bizarre indoor forest looked much different than the last time Bobby had seen it. Dozens of canvas tents dotted the plateau beyond the Nexus. Three more log cabins had been erected around the perimeter, with several more still in construction. Bobby walked alongside Chief, making their way to the middle of the clearing where a group of kids sat meditating.

"Some of the children that originally came here with us have located extended family or asked to be put up for adoption. Those who have no family, and quite a few that do, have asked permission to stay. At first, I was against the idea," said Chief. "This isn't a daycare. But Cassandra and your grandfather convinced me. All of the kids from the academy have tremendous potential, and it's possible that with the right training, we could really do some good."

Bobby froze, hands on his hips. "You want to start up a new academy, here?"

Chief shook his head. "Remember before when I asked you if you wanted to train with me? I operate a team, not just of commandos like the men you met at the temple, but of Exsos: people like you with the innate ability to control anima. Our mission is to counter the forces of other Exsos organizations, like the Core, who seek to alter the course of humanity for their own purposes. Don't forget, Sandman and some of his men are still out there."

"So are Ashley and Willy," said Bobby. "Maybe we can help you find them."

Chief clasped him on the shoulder. "That's the spirit. Come on, let's go meet up with Jinx and the other kids. I'm sure they'll be thrilled to see you."

"What about my grandparents and Cassandra? I thought they were staying here."

"Cassandra took off shortly after we got back. Apparently, she had someplace else she needed to be. From the look of things, that place is as far away from kids as possible. As for your grandparents: they were here for a while but left a few days ago … something about a second honeymoon."

"I thought they couldn't be close to one another?" said Bobby.

The lines of Chief's weathered face cracked into a knowing grin. "They're gonna stay on the move. Besides, after what's happened here, I figure they've got at least a few weeks before anyone comes looking for them."

Chief came to a halt. Roughly a dozen people sat in the middle of the grassy flat, arms and legs folded, deep in meditation. Among them, Bobby spotted his close friends Trevor, Lily, and Jacob. Young Ana also sat among them, her omnipresent raggedy blonde doll resting in her lap. Jinx sat on Ana's left. Bobby thought he saw a slight smile touching the corner of his cousin's lips.

A familiar figure sat at the head of the group. Bobby almost rushed forward, but Chief placed a hand gently on his arm. "I believe they are almost done," he said, gazing up at the sunless domed sky. Sure enough, the group began to stir, first the person in the front, then the students.

Bobby broke from Chief, ran up, and threw his arms around the leader, nearly tackling them both to the ground. "Master Jong! It's so good to see you!"

The tiny monk took a brief moment to straighten his sandy brown robe—the color of the plateau—then dipped his bald head. "It is a great pleasure to see you as well." True delight twinkled in the old master's pale blue eyes.

"I was so scared for you when I found out the Core came and took the kids," said Bobby. "I thought perhaps that they had…that you were dead."

The diminutive monk shrugged. "It would seem the Core had no interest in a bunch of old men. All I know for sure is that we went to sleep in the courtyard with the students and woke alone."

"Still, I'm surprised to find you here," said Bobby. "I would've thought you'd want to rebuild."

"There is nothing left for us there. The Spine of the World collapsed, taking with it the anima that fueled our theological studies."

"So, what did you do after you woke up and found everyone gone?"

The monk sighed and gazed at his students. "Those were dark days, indeed," he said. "We spent several months trying to dig through the rubble, searching for the sacred texts. I must admit I knew in my heart it was no use. The scrolls were buried in the collapse, lost forever. I was searching for a new path when Chief and his team arrived a few weeks ago, looking for clues to the Core's other secret bases. As soon as Chief told me the students had been rescued and were in need of guidance, I knew we had once again found our purpose."

The students who'd been meditating gathered around to welcome Bobby back. Jinx threw his arms around his big cousin. "The gang's all here," said Jinx, staring out over the plateau toward the giant indoor forest.

Lily, Trevor, and Jacob greeted Bobby with a collection of bear hugs, handshakes, and huge smiles. Even Slab was there, with his cherubic grin and massive frame looming over the rest of the group.

274 • R. SCOTT BOYER

Ana got in on the action too, handing her doll to Jinx long enough to squeeze Bobby tight around the waist. "Welcome to our new home," she said.

Jinx snapped his fingers. "I almost forgot! Did Chief tell you about his plan to build a team of Exsos to fight the Core?"

Bobby nodded, and Jinx rushed on. "So, what do you think? You wanna be part of the team? Come on, you gotta, gotta, gotta!"

Bobby ruffled his cousin's hair. "I wouldn't miss it for the world."

To Be Continued in Book Three:
Scions of the Sphinx

ACKNOWLEDGEMENTS

T o...all my friends, fans, and members of the online community that have supported me over the past ten years. In my dark hours, it was your love and encouragement that sustained me.

My mother, for all the times she's helped edit and proofread my books, even after she'd read them half a dozen times.

My father, for his indomitable optimism, and for convincing me that I can always accomplish my goals, no matter what obstacles lie before me.

Shari Stauch, for believing in me and my stories; for her willingness to take a chance and invest not just her time and energy, but her immeasurable talents in pursuit of a common goal.

Angela Bole, Lee Wind, and the entire staff at the Independent Book Publishers Association (IBPA), who have been tremendously friendly and helpful with tools and resources not just for publishing, but writing and marketing as well.

Kathy Murphy and the ladies (and gents!) of the Pulpwood Queens Book Club. I am eternally grateful to all of you for accepting me into your organization with open arms and for sharing your passion for reading, writing, and all things books.

All those who helped pave the way and nurture me along this road: Ron Alexander, Jennifer Niven, Marty Foner, and many others who offered advice and assistance over the years. This book didn't even exist at the time I worked with some of these folks, but their lessons endure. Thanks again for everything you each helped teach me.

R eading The Temple of Eternity in your reading group or book club? Use these questions to enrich your discussions. If you have a question for the author, or would like Scott Boyer to visit your book club, in person or via Skype, please email the author at **ScottBoyerBooks@gmail.com**.

• Melody Ether went to considerable lengths to become the Scarlet Seer. What do you think about her resolve, as well as her willingness to take on that role in order to rescue Bobby? Do the ends justify the means?

• If you could have one eternal moment in your own life, what would it be and why?

• The spirits who inhabit the Mayan temple play a significant role in the story. Do you believe in an afterlife, in spirits or ghosts? If so, do they play a part in the lives of the living? How so?

• Discuss the significance of the various animals that appear in the story: the black panther, giant anaconda, Willy's pet Mercy, etc. Do you think they have any meaning or symbolism? If so, what?

• Explore the relationships of loyalty, family, and love that exist in the ancient Mayan backstory involving Maximon, Lingya, and Ek Chuaj. What lessons, if any, do you think exist? Is this a cautionary tale, a love story, or tragedy?

• Interpret the meaning and purpose of the three trials: (1) riding the anaconda across the piranha-invested river; (2) floating over the electric fence; (3) freeing the spirits trapped within the Well of Eternity. What significance do these trials possess? Were they mental/spiritual lessons, or merely physical tests?

• Bobby's experience inside the Nexus at the start of the book introduces him to the concept of connecting his consciousness with other living creatures. As a source of limitless anima, what other phenomenon would you use the Nexus to explore and why?

• Who is your favorite character and why? With whom do you most identify?

For more about the Bobby Ether Series,
visit www.RScottBoyer.com